GRAY
HERON

JOHN WILDE

Bluewater Publications
Bwpublications.com
Printed in the United States

This work is based on the author's personal perspective and
imagination.

Editor – Sierra Tabor
Developmental Editor – Mickey Lollar
Design Editor – Maria Yasaka Beck
Publisher – Angela Broyles

 Library of Congress Control Number: 2019933510
 ISBN 978-1-949711-00-4

Dedicated to my mother and father,
who opened my eyes to the indescribable strength
of unconditional love.

PROLOGUE

I watched from the balcony of the condo as the waves crashed ashore. The smells and the sounds of the beach had always lifted my spirits and renewed my soul. The young girl I was watching made her way up from the shore-line. Lela was a darling at age thirteen, and she had always been the apple of my eye. Thirteen is such an awkward age for any child. It is a time of turmoil and confrontation, and my Lela was no different. This was her beach trip—a time for her to reconnect with me. Lela had always called me Poppa, but in actuality I was her great-uncle.

Lela stopped at the shower to wash the sand off her feet. She lingered a little longer and did a better job than she had on our previous beach trips. A smile crossed my face. That girl had grown so much, both intellectually and physically. Lela was in that age where all young people must travel—a period of finding one's own identity. It is one of the most challenging times in life, but I reasoned that she would come out the other side having mastered the ageless process of being a teenager. Oh, I did marvel at her constant questions, thought-provoking and probing as they always were. They were difficult to answer, but answer I must. She faced the fact that life was not always fair but with a determination to correct the situation at every opportunity. I noticed that her natural tendency to defend the less fortunate became more pronounced as she grew.

Lately I had been struggling with the feeling that I was losing her. I thought that she was not always truthful with me, and that hurt. It was, I reasoned, a common occurrence that many people experienced, but it still did not help with my anxiety. I worked hard to keep our communications open while also resolving to not be pushy. I had little experience in dealing with any kid going through those difficult times. I tried to draw from my experience with her mother. I felt we had lost communication with Penny when she went through those years, and I was determined not to let that happen with Lela. It was different dealing with Lela compared to her younger brother. I felt comfortable preaching to Rye about my vision of right and wrong. It was all made more difficult by the realization that I had not always been truthful with them.

As she finished with the shower, I saw Lela stand and gaze out at the ocean. I knew what she was doing; I had done the same thing many times in my youth. It hurts to leave a place you love. Lela shrugged and turned toward the condominium, and as she walked past the pool, she dipped her foot into the water. It too was a way to say goodbye.

It wasn't long before the door swung open and Lela bounded in, all excited. "Poppa, I wish I lived at the beach. It's so beautiful here." She came over and hugged me. "When can we come here again? Just the three of us?"

I confronted her quickly. "Lela, this trip was for you. You know I love you more than anything. You have made straight A's in school and you work hard. You earned this trip." I waited for her reaction. I knew she understood where I was going with my statement.

"Sometimes I wonder how different our lives would have been if Rye hadn't been born. He can be such a pain."

I laughed, "Are you still jealous of that little brother of yours?"

She hit me with that smile that had always disarmed me. "You know I love him, but he takes up so much of your time that I sometimes feel left out."

I patted her on the head. "You know you will always be my favorite, but I tell you that in strictest confidence."

Still grinning, she said, "You always have my back and know how to make me feel loved."

I changed the subject. "Did you go through the ritual of saying goodbye to the ocean, the birds, and the sand?"

Lela giggled. It was the reaction I had hoped for. "Yes, Poppa. Just like you taught me to do when I was a little girl."

"You had better go pack up. We are going to have to leave shortly."

Lela kissed me on the head. "Okay, but I still think we should stay another day or two."

I laughed as Lela went inside, and I had to admit I was in no hurry to leave either. The distant sound of the crashing waves lulled me into the past. I could hear the voices and sounds. Smell the scents. I could see everything rushing through my mind like clips of home movies. My past had become tangible once again, like sandcastles from a child's imagination, finding solidity from the abstract. From dreams and hopes and insecurities.

Lela had been five years old when Rye was born, and, as fate would have it, we'd had to race home from a trip to the beach to be there for Rye's birth. It was because of Lela. She couldn't wait to meet her baby brother. It was as though it had occupied her every thought. I laughed as I recalled those moments that had transformed my life, and even though they had been difficult, they had fulfilled my life. There was never a dull moment. My mind drifted back to those times. I could hear those conversations clearly.

CHAPTER 1

It was not your typical day at the beach. Yes, the sun was shining brightly, but the air had a cool crispness to it that you can only experience in April. I made a mental note to myself not to make another beach trip in mid-April. Lela interrupted my thought process as only she could.

As I loaded the car, I heard her voice say, "Poppa, are we ready to go yet? I have to get home."

You might think that a five-year-old would never be in a hurry to leave the beach, but Lela was not your typical child. So smart and so perceptive, I had no doubt she would succeed in life. Flippantly, I asked, "What is your hurry, my girl?"

"I want to be at the hospital when my brother is born."

"I know, baby. We will be on the road in fifteen minutes, and don't worry; we will be home in plenty of time for you to welcome your brother."

I didn't know the reason for her rush, but kids have their own priorities. The only thing I knew was that a seven-hour-long drive faced me, along with Lela repeatedly asking me "Are we there yet?"

My wife and I had always looked at Lela as a gift from heaven, and yes, we spoiled her. Such a sweet and charming child who came into our lives from a niece we also idolized. I had been angry with Penny when I first found out she was pregnant with Lela. I had told my wife in no uncertain terms that I was through with Penny and would not have anything to do with her kid.

Madonna had reacted quickly. "How can you act that way? Get over it!"

Well, sure enough, the first time I held Lela, I melted like a stick of butter on a hot summer highway, and it was on.

"I'm hungry," Lela said from the backseat sometime during our journey home.

I was getting hungry myself. It sure felt like a good time for a burger and fries. A smile flashed across my lips as I thought back to the night we left her dance practice and she was starving after the workout she had just had. As we pulled into her favorite place and went in to get our order, Lela had seen two stray kittens in the parking lot. "Oh, Poppa, those kittens looked starved! Can we feed them?"

I replied, "No, Lela. They probably belong to the house right behind us."

She would have none of it. "If those cats are starving, we are going to feed them, and if they are homeless, we are going to find them a home."

Yes, that is Lela, and I knew the cats were going to be dealt with before we got out of there.

As soon as we got back in the car to leave, Lela said, "Poppa, I want to sit here and eat." I knew what that meant. She never took her eyes off those two cats as they milled around the dumpster nervously as though they were on a hot tin roof. Lela munched on her burger and said calmly, "I'm full. Can I please feed those two starving kittens?"

I knew better, but I reluctantly agreed. They came to her quicker than a duck takes to water, and she was petting them as they ate out of her hand. I had to admit I knew what that was like, as I was as guilty as the two cats.

When she got back in the car, she said, "I have to go to the bathroom and wash my hands." I let her go by herself, because her Aunt Ruby was the manager and I knew she would take care of her.

Shortly, Lela came out. I knew then what she was up to. Lela said, "Oh please, Poppa, please! They are so hungry."

I threw up my hands and said, "Get them in the back of the car, but you are going to be the one to feed them and take care of them." By the time we got home, Lela had named one Sylvester and the other Sly.

As I approached retirement, I was not exactly thrilled with the prospect of a second kid in my life. I had Lela to contend with, and the joy that brought me also required a lot of my time. I was such a pushover for anything she wanted to do, and Lela had realized by the tender age of three that she had me wrapped around her little finger. At five it was dance lessons. It was crazy—usually a bunch of moms and grandmothers sitting around gabbing while the kids ran through their paces. I stuck out like a sore thumb, an old white-headed guy that must have looked like some nut. My Lela didn't care. She just wanted to dance, and that was fine with me.

I was jarred out of that memory by Lela reminding me she was still hungry. After stopping for some breakfast, we hit the road again. We had barely gotten out of town before Madonna looked over at me and said, "I think I'll take a little nap. You watch your driving and don't get another speeding ticket."

I laughed, "Oh, don't worry. I have precious cargo in the backseat."

It wasn't long until both of my copilots were asleep, and I was left alone to my thoughts. Driving had always given me time to think deeply. As Madonna and Lela slept peacefully, it was as though I was trapped within a prism of time.

Lela's mom had spent so much time with us when she was growing up, and we had showered her with our undivided attention. When Lela came along, I was prepared to do the same for her. Over the years, for Madonna and me, it had always been about the kids. It didn't matter whose kids—it could have been any of them. When Lela was born, I realized that we both regretted not having kids of our own.

Tomorrow was always a new adventure, even with all the problems that came with the rising sun. Time was never my friend; it was too fickle and had too much control. It always seemed that spring would never arrive, but then summer was just a memory. My life was flashing before my eyes, and I was powerless to slow it down. I was losing way too many friends to death from all manner of causes.

It was as if each day brought a new crisis for someone I knew. We fight our own battles. We are always in the throes of death with seemingly no escape, and for what? What is life's purpose? I had to slow down; I had to have enough time to absorb what was going on around me. I looked at Madonna and realized that as sure as we got up the next morning, we would be confronted with a different challenge around us. It seemed that every conceivable thing life could throw, we experienced. Car accidents, surgeries, divorce, killings, suicides. And as the list continued to grow, so did the challenge of becoming old.

If all of this was not bad enough, it seemed that our very own country was entering a stage of unrest that bordered on anarchy. It appeared that protest was more and more the norm and increasingly violent. I always felt somewhat untouched by all the upheaval that was going on in America as I sat on the back deck each morning, read the paper, sipped coffee, and observed my old friend the Gray Heron. We, as Americans, mostly all knew for a fact that what was happening was that the bill was coming due for decades and decades of overspending, lack of responsibility for our own actions, and the pain that was soon to follow. I dreaded the future for my country, and every time I looked at Lela, I feared for the world that was about to be hers.

Perhaps it was something that I would never know the origin of, but my spirit, my inner self, would not let me be defeated. I remained upbeat, I stayed positive, and yes, I

remained defiant. Defiance is probably the sole charac-
teristic that one needs to possess in this world to cope, to
succeed, and to enjoy life. It had become to me a sense of
challenge to not let depression and old age defeat me, yet
instead to go out like my mother said I came in—smiling.

I was struggling with how fast it had slipped away. I
realized that Madonna and I had been so busy with life
and enjoying the moment that we had never had children.
We had both just woken up one morning and realized we
were too old to become parents. We both loved kids, and
our nieces and nephews were always around. We spoiled
them every chance we got, but we never slowed down long
enough to have our own. I figured it was mostly my fault.
All the travel, all the good times. Yes, I never took life very
seriously.

Oh, we had a good life. We loved and we played. We
traveled, and, like most married couples, we had our ups
and downs. Over the years we had grown closer; I could
not imagine a life without Madonna. It was that thought
that always gave me concern. Although we had been lucky,
health-wise, we were aging. I wondered how long we could
keep up a pace that seemed to push faster and faster.

Madonna and I lived on a lake. It was a quaint little
place that had a body of water flowing behind it about
two hundred yards wide. We had a nice long pier, and
my pontoon boat was always ready to ride. It was an area
that had long ago been named Bluff Creek, because right
across there rose a majestic bluff that had been hewn out
of limestone rock over the ages. The neighborhood was a

tiny, tight-knit group. Wildlife and dogs roamed freely, and we couldn't help but accept the raw beauty and freedom of that place. It had been an excellent place for Penny, Lela, and Rye to enjoy the beauty of the outdoors, to explore, and to swim in the cold water of a flowing, gentle creek.

Bluff Creek was one of the few places that remained where neighbors left their keys in their cars. You could sleep with your doors unlocked, although Madonna always insisted our doors were to be locked at night. Occasionally I would forget and leave the key in the boat, the car, or some valuable fishing equipment lying on the pier, but never once did we have anything come up missing. It was indeed a safe place, and the beauty had hooked me the first time I saw the site.

It was my life-long friend, Tony, who had given our home the nickname the "Southern Whitehouse." I had laughed when, at a cook-out, he told some of our friends, "You all should know that Leroy doesn't have to work. He only does because Madonna wants him out from under her feet. Why, if I were in Leroy's shoes, I would never leave the Southern Whitehouse." The group all laughed, and Madonna gave him that look that, I must admit, I had seen a few times. Tony was no rookie, as we had raised the ire of Madonna on more than one occasion. Tony picked up on it quickly. "Madonna, you know I'm just kidding. Leroy worships the ground you walk on."

I quickly glanced at her, and she laughed, "Tony, you want me to share some of the things you and my beloved Leroy have gotten into over the years?"

The prism I was looking through was glowing red hot, and the picture started to blur. The mental movie continued to play and I was no longer mentally, emotionally, driving home from the coast. I was trying to put into place all the events that had gotten me to this point. It was useless to dwell on the fact that Lela was now five, but I tried to piece together how it all fit and how I could make things better. I was a firm believer that for every action there is a reaction, and as my mind wandered, I recalled some of the people and places that had affected my life.

CHAPTER 2

Forty years of work and travel had not prepared me for all these kids. I had sold agricultural equipment all over the world, but there was a darker side to my work. When my work took me out of the States, I usually had another mission. I kept my eyes and ears open to the situation on the ground in whatever country I was visiting. I would report back to Washington on anything I detected out of the ordinary. I was a mole for the country. I had no qualms about what I did; it was my way of serving my nation. A two-year stint in the military had made me realize that this great country had many enemies who would love to destroy us. I had one great ability, and that was getting people to tell me what I wanted to know without arousing suspicion.

My involvement was limited, and it was something we kept very close to our vest. Madonna knew exactly what I did on some of these trips, and although she didn't exactly approve, she tolerated the situation. I was, perhaps, not the most comfortable person to live with, or to love for that matter. I knew that I had a loving wife, and I honestly loved her, but my restless spirit, my stubborn streak, and my inability to compromise made me a pain in the rear. I often tried to make up for my faults, but in truth, it was Madonna that was the rock, the sole source of our love, and I was truly blessed.

Friends were a blessing too.

The ruminations in my mind shifted from my domestic comfort to past uncertainty in foreign fields. Before the trip to the beach, I had gotten a call from an old Army buddy out of the blue. I was driving then too. I could still recall that conversation vividly, word for word, as I knew the resulting ripples would eventually travel into every aspect of my life if left unchecked.

My surprise caller, Manny Diaz, had moved back to his native country of Nicaragua after retirement.

"Laroy, I hope you are well."

I laughed. With Manny, my name always sounded like "Laroy." I replied, "I'm fine, Manny. I just left the doctor's office; I had to get the old ticker checked out." I laughed again, but Manny had always been a bit more serious.

"Laroy, I won't keep you, but, when you have some time, give me a call. I need to run something by you."

I knew something was wrong; something was cooking. It troubled me. I could hear it in Manny's voice. I said, "Go ahead. I'm driving, but I'm alone, and I can tell you got something on your mind. Shoot it at me."

Manny was one heck of a guy, and I had always respected him. Being a naturalized citizen and having spent his youth in Nicaragua, he was a gung-ho American. Manny and his parents had immigrated to the U.S. when he was fourteen, and at twenty, Manny was sworn into the U.S. Army. We attended boot camp together. I was only a two-year guy, but Manny made it clear he was going to make his career in the Army. During those two years we spent together, we became good friends. I was convinced this guy was the real deal and would make America proud. Manny had a vision of what he wanted to accomplish in life, and it was admirable.

Manny had often said, "I want to serve this country for twenty or thirty years, and after that I want to be able to go back to Nicaragua and give back to my people in whatever way I can." Manny served twenty years in the Army and then took a job in security with NASA, where he continued his career for ten years. Manny knew what I did on several of my trips outside of the country. In fact, I had even worked with Manny on a couple of those missions. After thirty years, Manny retired and moved back to his birthplace, the little town of Rivas, Nicaragua. We had developed a bond between us that you spend a lifetime searching for. Not much had to be said. Our friendship was built on understanding and trust.

Manny's voice continued in its serious tone. "My country has taken a turn for the worse. We have some thugs down here who are stirring up trouble, and I think I may have to come out of retirement. I was wondering if you could come down to Nicaragua for a few days and put your eyes on the landscape and tell me what you think."

I was stunned. This *was* serious. "Let me see, Manny. I'll have to clear out a few things. Let me call you back in a couple of days."

Manny and I parted ways once again, with the uneasiness found in loose ends and empathy.

Oh Lord, how was I going to break this to Madonna? She would never understand why I would willingly go traipsing off to Nicaragua and involve myself in Lord knows what for a friend I had not seen in over fifteen years. Although it wouldn't be the first time I had done something that didn't make sense to anybody.

It suddenly hit me like a ton of bricks to call my old buddy, Bill Parker. Bill had a long career at the IMF and had traveled all over the world. He knew every nook and cranny on the planet. When Bill retired, he came back home and entered the zany world of politics. He had also somehow managed to get me up off the couch to work nonstop for him for four years to get him elected to office. Not many people I would do that for, but Bill was a different kind of cat. After we got him elected, packed up, and off to Washington, I wondered why in the world a person would want to put himself through all that just to get elected.

Then I remembered what Bill had told me. "Leroy, when you have traveled the world as I have, when you have seen the human misery that I have seen, when you understand that people can go crazy with power and lose all sense of humanity, then you come home to run for office to make sure it never happens to the people you know and love." I never questioned Bill's intentions about anything again.

I kept thinking about Manny. I knew that I had to tell Madonna that I was planning to go to Nicaragua. I wondered what her reaction would be, and I did not doubt that her Cherokee blood would let her tell me exactly what she thought.

Before I called Bill Parker, I told Madonna about my conversation with Manny. I could see by the reaction on her face that she was not too happy about it.

"When are you thinking about going?" she asked.

I studied her eyes intently as I replied. "It will take me a couple of weeks to get everything in order, and hopefully I should only be down there for a week or two."

"Well, let's talk about this some more," Madonna said. "I think you need to think this thing through. You know you almost got killed when you went to Canada on one of your trips."

I had forgotten about that incident. It was not as dramatic as it sounded, but I almost got shot while nosing around in that country. The life lesson I learned during that little escapade was that if you are trying to obtain information on the ground, you better learn to blend in.

I took Madonna's advice to think it through and decided to sleep on it. I got up early the next morning and looked across Bluff Creek at the small waterfall that trickled into the creek. There stood my old, trusty companion, the Gray Heron, looking for breakfast as usual. I wasn't sure that it was the same one I had seen every morning all these years, but it still looked the same. I realized I should find out what the life expectancy of a Gray Heron was; surely it was not twenty years. I fumbled for my phone and pulled out a crumpled piece of paper with Bill's number on it.

The phone rang several more times than I expected. Maybe they weren't in the office yet. I was about ready to hang up when a pleasant voice said, "Congressman Parker's office. How may I help you?"

I knew before I asked that I was going to get the standard reply. "Is the congressman in?"

The receptionist responded, "No, he is not. May I take a message?"

I had no patience and always had to bite my tongue when it came to responding to people on the telephone. "Yes. Will you tell him that Leroy called for Wango? The congressman has my number."

Stunned silence. The young lady must have been new, as it appeared she didn't know what to say. Finally, I got the response I expected.

"I will give him your message."

"Thank you," I said. I hung up and returned to my coffee. I wondered about the coffee they grew in Nicaragua. I thought I might ask Manny if he knew Juan Valdez and if he could get me some of his private stock, but then I remembered Juan Valdez was from Colombia.

Madonna was not exactly an early riser, and she preferred her day to be one of leisure with no set schedule. It drove me nuts sometimes as I wondered how she ever got anything done, but I didn't lose a lot of sleep over it. I wanted her to spend her day precisely how she pleased, as long as I wasn't required to go on one of her almost daily shopping trips. It seemed to me that God intended for women to have the patience to go into stores and look at each garment, rag, purse, or whatever till a man's blood pressure soared to impossible heights. It's probably why men have a higher risk of heart disease.

As I sat down to a breakfast of eggs, bacon, and toast, my phone rang. I looked at the area code and saw "202." I answered, "Wango, my old buddy, how are things in the asphalt zoo?"

He laughed, "Leroy, you will never change. As you might guess, it's nuttier than one of Aunt Hazel's fruitcakes. You know I was thinking about you the other day, and how you lay up on the creek and soak up the sun. You are one lucky devil. I told some folks that if they ever get down that way, they should look you up and you would take them out on the boat and show them all the beautiful water and places we have in our fair state."

I replied, "Still having to go to them fundraisers, I see. Is that guy you were talking about before a big potential donor or is he a real American?"

Wango laughed and said, "How is Madonna?"

I often got the impression that some people were more concerned about Madonna than me. I smiled and said, "She's sitting on the couch and looking at me like, 'Okay, what you are two up to now?'" I picked up my coffee cup and stepped out onto the screened porch. "I need to know if you have ever spent any time in Nicaragua."

"Oh, you bet. Off and on I probably spent over a year down there when I was with the IMF. There's a lot of stuff that goes on down there, and it gets pretty interesting pretty fast."

Bingo, I had found the source of information I was looking for. I asked Wango where he stayed in Nicaragua and what he could tell me about what was going on down there, and if he still had any contacts.

"Nicaragua is one of the best-kept secrets on the planet. The people are warm and friendly, the climate is great, and oh the water. They have some of the most beautiful places that you will ever see."

"What's the downside?"

His mood took on a more serious tone. "They have their problems, and from what I hear there is a group that has the potential to stir up some big trouble. Oh, but before I get into that, I always tried to stay at a little hotel called San Lupe. The food is great, the rooms are comfortable, and you will usually find quite a few Americans staying there. It's in a little town called Rivas."

Rivas. My mind was spinning. I interrupted, "In your time in Rivas, did you ever run across a guy named Manny Diaz?"

"I sure did. How in the world do you know Manny Diaz?"

"We served in the Army together and have been friends for years."

"Manny is one of the good guys in Nicaragua, and he is doing his part to help hold that country together. You're not fixing to get involved in something down that way, are you?"

I told him about my conversation with Manny and that I was getting ready to leave and help my friend if I could.

Wango got excited. "I'll call an employee down at our embassy in Nicaragua. She's a good friend of mine. I'll alert her about your expected arrival and see if she can update me on anything imminent that you should know. Also, if you stay at the San Lupe, there is a guy who works there named Castillo. He knows all the players, so be sure and look him up."

I felt a lot better already. I knew Wango had the sources I needed. It would help me finagle my way through all the clutter and get a clearer picture of what was happening in that place.

"I have to go to a hearing, Leroy, but before I go, I never did get the story on why you nicknamed me Wango."

I laughed; it was the right time to tell him. "My nephew's name is Terry Wayne. He was the quarterback on his high school football team, and a darn good one. One day at practice, one of the linemen was supposed to pull and come around the end to block the linebacker, who was as big and tough as they get. The linebacker knocked the stubby lineman on his can, but when Terry turned it upfield he could fly, and on that play, he ran it all the way to the house. The coach started yelling at the lineman for his miserable block on the linebacker, and the lineman said, 'Coach, did you not see Wayne go.' The coach laughed and said, 'Okay, guys, line up and rerun it. From now on that play will be called Wango.' Bill, it came to me that when I was burning up all that shoe leather trying to get you elected, that I was like that stubby lineman. I knew if I could get you around the corner, you would Wango."

The hearty laugh on the other end of the phone told me Bill got it.

CHAPTER 3

Pulling into the driveway meant we had had another safe trip. As we began unloading the car, I wondered if Penny was in the hospital yet. I knew they would call if she'd had the baby already. I thought about what it was going to be like having to contend with both a boy and Lela. I knew it would be wild.

I was delighted that Penny and Jon were married and that they had turned out to be good parents. I had so wanted Penny to go to college, but love has a way of changing lives. When she gave birth to Lela, I knew college was not in her future. Penny had spent a lot of time with Madonna and me while growing up. I loved her as much as I loved Lela. I had slowly come to grips with the situation, and if Penny was happy, I was as well.

I glanced at Lela as she helped take items into the house. "Lela, you got just about the right amount of sun. You look beautiful."

That round pie face lit up, and Lela said, "Poppa, you always say I look beautiful."

Well, she was right. Her smile, her whole persona, said one word to me: beauty.

After we finished unpacking, I could not wait to get on the porch and soak up the scenery that surrounded our home. It was a place of rest, a place to recharge, and if I do say so, it had a strange beauty second to none. I thought of how my dear mother had described it when she first came to visit: "Leroy, you got your own little piece of heaven."

Yep, Mother was right, and over the years I had gotten quite comfortable at the Southern Whitehouse.

The door blew open and out bounded Lela. "We got to go! Momma just called, and she is on the way to the hospital. I want to be there when my brother is born. Hurry, Poppa! We have got to go!"

Oh, I just laughed and said, "Child, there is no rest for the wicked." And back in the car we went for the thirty-minute ride to the hospital.

Lela was so excited and nervous. "Poppa, do you think everything will be all right? What if something goes wrong? I knew I should not have left Momma and went to the beach. Please hurry!"

We had just gotten in the car when my cell phone rang.

"Poppa, don't answer it. You always drive slow when you talk on the phone," Lela said.

I laughed and assured her it was okay. It was Manny. I answered and detected a sense of urgency in his voice when he replied. "Laroy, have you figured out when you are coming?"

"We're on the way to the hospital, Manny. Can I call you back?"

The dejection was obvious, but Manny responded, "I hope it is nothing serious."

"No, just the birth of a great-nephew, and I have a great-niece who expects me to drive like I am on a race track."

Manny replied, "I seem to remember that you always drove like you were on a race track. You guys be safe."

Madonna quickly figured out what the phone call meant. "You can't be going down there right now with all we have going on."

That was all it took to get Lela started. "What's Nonna talking about?"

I wanted to delay the questioning, but I knew it would be of no use. "I have to go and help a friend, Lela."

"Why?"

The battle was beginning, but now was not the time. This was one time when Lela was not going to get her way. I gave her a look that over the last five years she had only seen on a couple of occasions. "Lela, this is not the time or the place to ask me questions. We are on the way to the hospital for the birth of your brother, and we will talk about this later. Do you understand?"

She slumped down in the seat, and the hurt look on her face gave me chills. I was such a cupcake when it came to Lela. I laughed and said, "It's going to be fine. You'll see."

When we walked into the hospital room, Penny was laying on the bed, looking like the picture of contentment. I could tell she was glad to see her baby girl, but how could she be so relaxed and so at peace with everything going on around her? Jon couldn't get the camera working to take pictures, and Penny calmly said to him, "Let me do that." Her fingers worked the buttons as she fixed the settings and handed it back to him. I laughed at how calm she was. The door opened. It was the nurse to take her to delivery. In a short period of time, we would have a boy named Rye. My whole world, my entire life, was soon to be upended, and I did not have a clue.

The nurse wheeled Penny out of the room. I breathed deeply, then I laughed. I was more nervous than anyone in the room. As I paced the floor, it suddenly dawned on me that I needed some fresh air. Lela was watching cartoons, Jon was reading the paper, and my wife was doing what she always does: cleaning and straightening things in the room.

Lela looked up at me during a commercial and said, "Poppa, it's going to be all right. You don't need to worry, but I do wish they would bring Momma and the baby in so I can hold him and kiss him."

I figured that was unlikely to happen anytime soon, but no way was I going to tell Lela. I excused myself and went outside; I had to call Manny. As I went out the door, I was relieved that neither Lela nor Madonna questioned what I was doing.

Manny answered on the first ring. "Thanks for calling me back so quickly. Has the baby arrived?"

I laughed, "Not yet."

Manny got right to the point. "Laroy, I may have jumped the gun in getting you to come down here. I think I need some more time to put all the pieces together."

I was puzzled. Manny had been so anxious to me down there, and now he was backing up. "Are you sure? I was about ready to pull the trigger and head your way."

There was a moment of silence. I knew Manny was measuring his words. "I'm working on some stuff. I think we may need some more time. I believe I still may need you to come, but now is not the right time."

I exhaled. It was good for me. I had a lot on my plate, and with Rye set to arrive any minute, I was glad for the extension.

"Laroy, what I am planning to ask you to do is dangerous. There is a mountain very close to my house that has been overtaken by a group of rebels. I believe they are planning to try and overthrow the government. I have concluded they are up in the mountain, planning and arming themselves to capture the town of Rivas and establish it as a base to assault Managua. If they are successful in capturing Rivas, they will be able to attract the more extreme elements from other parts of the country. I fear that this is being done under the nose of authorities. I have tried to alert them, but they are either unconcerned or stupid."

I had no conception of all that Manny was trying to tell me. I only knew that we were expecting a boy at any minute. I mumbled, "Whatever I need to do, you know I will be there. If you see that I should come tomorrow, I will."

"You don't need to worry. After all we've been through, we can move mountains. I will let you get off the phone. I know you are right in the middle of something very important." He paused. "You know, sometimes I wish I had been blessed with a houseful of kids."

It struck me as odd. I had never thought about it, but Manny and his wife were childless.

Before hanging up, I cautioned Manny, "Don't get on your warhorse and do something stupid. At least let me in on a part of the fun."

He chuckled, "That is what worries me. We are getting too old to have any fun. I will talk to you in a few days. Let me nose around some more. I want to know for sure what we are facing before you get here." As we hung up, I had a sinking feeling that at some point I was going to Nicaragua and climb a mountain.

As I made my way back up to Penny's room, my thoughts were all jumbled. The conversation with Manny and the thoughts of greeting a baby boy. What did it all mean? How did I find myself being pulled in so many directions? I was at the age and point in life where I needed to make some changes, but I had so much left to do and so much left to give.

After only about forty more minutes, they wheeled Penny into the room, looking as bright and radiant as she always did. The thought ran through my mind, *Did she give birth to a child? How can this be possible?* I reasoned that what I was seeing had a lot to do with pain medication. I knew nothing about childbirth, but based on this experience it must be some magical occurrence that only God can make happen.

The nurse looked at Lela and said, "You ready to meet your new brother?" Lela lit up like a Christmas tree as only she can do. The nurse responded by saying, "I am going to bring him in here in about thirty minutes, and maybe your mom will let you hold him." I almost passed out. This was moving way too fast for me to comprehend.

The next thirty minutes seemed like an eternity as we waited for Rye. Lela was fidgeting with the remote and singing softly to herself. My wife was babying Penny like she always does, pouring her ice water she did not want, fixing her pillow, and just otherwise trying to make her comfortable.

I googled Manny's address in Rivas, Nicaragua to get a lay of the land. As I zoomed in on Manny's house, I began to realize he lived in the boonies. I scanned the area around him and saw an unbelievable mountain and what appeared to be a beautiful lake. I was impressed. It was typical Manny. I could see him living in such a place. I wanted to know more, but even with today's technology, it was not like being there in person. I worried that Manny had landed in a bad place. I knew he was worried, but Manny always worried. I laughed to myself. He was a bit like Madonna. I scanned the internet for articles on Nicaragua, and the hits were pretty much negative. It seemed that there were the makings of civil war in the background. Some areas of the country were obviously being controlled by rebels. I had seen enough in my travels to know when you have a breakdown in law and order, anarchy soon follows.

I made a promise to myself that as soon as this boy was safely at home with Penny and Jon, I would call Manny and push him to tell me what was going on at that mountain. I was torn. It was uncomfortable for me. I was sitting in a hospital room waiting for a baby, and I knew my friend needed my help. So I did what I always do in those situations: I relaxed.

It was a gift I had been born with. I didn't know where it came from, but I wasn't going to let it slip away. It had saved me many times, and I believed that the solution in times of stress is to act naturally. I laughed to myself and mumbled, "Easier said than done."

Lela picked up on it. "What's so funny?"

I flinched. "Why nothing, my girl. I was just wondering if you were going to change your brother's dirty diapers."

Lela busted out laughing "Don't you know that's what moms are for?"

I couldn't help but laugh. Lela was as quick as she is smart.

Jon and I made small talk as if we knew what the other was saying. Every time Lela heard somebody walking down the hall, she would stare at the door as if she was trying to be the first one to see the kid.

Finally the door slowly swung open and in came the nurse holding a bundled up blue blanket with a blue toboggan on top. The nurse placed Rye in his momma's arms, and she pulled that blanket back to reveal a wide-eyed boy who was born ready. Lela was immediately in his face and kissed him with one of her big, wet kisses. I thought my wife was going to faint. I finally got close enough to the baby, who didn't seem at all scared about anything.

It was only a matter of moments until Lela was up in the bed with Penny and holding her brother for the first time. I marveled at that scene and realized that Lela was thrilled and that Rye couldn't seem to take his eyes off Lela. This lovefest lasted for about twenty minutes with Lela soaking up the fact that she indeed had a baby brother. It ended with Rye going to sleep in Lela's arms with a look of pure contentment.

I had no clue what these two would achieve in their lives, but I knew Lela had a personality that said "Look out, world! Here I come!" and as I looked at the sleeping baby, I saw something that said "I have no fear."

Lela insisted on spending the night with her mother that night to make sure everything was okay. Nobody argued, because we all knew that Lela would not be denied.

On the drive home, Madonna and I savored the excitement of the day. As we pulled into our driveway, it was as though I had Rye with me. That boy was on a mission. A cold shiver ran down my spine as I realized that whatever that mission was, whatever it involved, it was going to be a wild ride. So much for a calm and laidback retirement. It was beginning to look to me like life was running at full speed ahead.

CHAPTER 4

Up early and well rested the next morning, I made coffee and found my way out to the back deck. I glanced across the creek to see if the old Gray Heron was already searching for his morning breakfast. He was not. As the first rays of daybreak began to rise above the bluff, I heard the bird squawking noisily as he came down the creek. He landed at the base of the waterfall, not very gracefully, and was soon on patrol for his morning food.

The old bird was my sounding board. I had run many a difficult decision by him, and he always listened patiently and never once contradicted me. The only time he ever replied was when he squawked as if he had missed his breakfast. Today was not that different, but I had much to run by my old friend.

I assumed that in a few days Penny would be taking Rye home from the hospital. It would begin a new world for all of us. As the heat from the morning sun started to pierce the coolness of the morning air, I knew the first call I would make would be to Manny. There was something very troubling about what was going on in Manny's world, and I wanted to get to the bottom of it. I went back inside to refill my coffee. As I came back outside to the deck, the old Gray Heron let out a squawk and took flight. I had never figured out where the old bird spent the bulk of his day.

I couldn't stand it any longer. I picked up the phone and called Manny.

"How are you doing, my friend?" Manny was wide awake. Like me, he was an early riser.

We exchanged pleasantries, and then I got to the heart of the matter. "What has changed on the ground in your situation?"

Manny replied, "Whoever was on that mountain has left. I never could get an accurate count, and they seem to have vanished. I am sure they were laying the groundwork for an attack on Rivas. I fully expect them to return. I just don't know when."

"I am committed, Manny. So whatever it is you need me to do, let me know."

I heard a sigh. "I hope it doesn't come to that, but I know I can count on you."

I felt a sense of foreboding in Manny's voice. It was not a matter of if but when. As we hung up, I said to Manny, "Stay in touch and let me know."

I knew that at breakfast I was going to make my intentions known to Madonna. If Manny called, I was going to

Rivas to help him. I expected an argument and I was prepared for one. I would not be disappointed. As I kissed her before I sat down to breakfast, she looked at me and said, "Do you have something on your mind?"

I plunged right in, "Madonna, at some point I may go to Nicaragua and help Manny. I don't know when. It could be soon or maybe even months from now."

Her shoulders sagged. "Leroy, do you know how old you are getting? Don't you think it's time you let somebody else take up the crusade? You have been doing this crazy stuff for longer than I care to remember, and I want it stopped." The strength of her convictions poured out of her soul like water from a bursting dam.

I simply nodded my head. "My dear, I promise this will be the last time. If Manny calls, I am going."

She looked away and said, "I take you at your word."

I studied Madonna's face intently as she ate her breakfast in silence. I observed the high cheekbones, the dark piercing eyes, and I realized my Indian Princess had spoken her piece. It was to be my last time to run with the big dogs. If Manny called and I went to help, when I returned I would be home to stay on the porch, Madonna's porch, with the pups. Something was happening down in Nicaragua, and my restless spirit would require that I find myself in the crosshairs.

Later that day, I called Penny to check on her and the children.

"We will be going home this afternoon."

"What? I figured you would be there at least a couple of days?"

Penny laughed, "I had a baby, not a heart transplant."

I still couldn't accept the fact that the boy was only twenty-four hours old and they were sending him home. "Penny, I don't want you to overdo it. If Madonna and I need to come out there and help you, we will."

"That won't be necessary. Lela is a fantastic nurse, and she has volunteered to work for free."

As I hung up the phone, I could see those two kids, and in my mind I was convinced they would fight and fuss like normal kids, but they would always have each other's back.

By the ripe old age of fifteen months, Rye had spent the night several times. Madonna and I had him over primarily to give Penny and Jon some time to themselves. Lela was good with Rye. To watch them play and react with each other was a lot of fun. It was about this time that I started to notice some differences in Rye when compared to Lela. Lela was always concerned about everybody and their feelings. Lela was continually mothering and protective of everybody. Rye, on the other hand, had his own tendencies. It started playfully enough when Lela would come sit on my lap when I was holding Rye, and she would hug me or push Rye's hand away and say to him, "My Poppa." It would get to him, and his reaction would be to shove her hand away and grunt his displeasure. We all laughed when he did it, but with Rye, you could see his intensity.

There had been no news from Manny. I scanned the news daily for anything connected to Nicaragua. Nothing, zero, nada! It was as though the country was in a peaceful state of existence. I didn't trust the silence. I trusted Manny's take on the situation, and I reverted back to an old adage, "There is always silence before the storm." My concerns were never far from my heart, but deep down inside, I hoped that Manny was wrong.

It was one mess after another. I never knew a one-year-old and a six-year-old could spill so much, break so much, and dirty up so many clothes. I gained a whole new perspective on what parenting was all about, even though we only had those two a couple of days a week. Lela was getting into school big time, and she was a perfectionist. Perfect grades became her goal at school, as with many her age. It became her life. The teachers bragged about her and how she was very thoughtful and helpful to others. That did not surprise me at all. It was who she was. I had seen it firsthand for several years. Rye, on the other hand, was beginning to walk and talk and that was also something to behold.

I wondered how Rye came up with his particular name for me. One day he just started calling me "Dee." I did not pay too much attention to it at first, as with most kids, the babble can change often. But Dee stuck. Those little legs would follow me through the house, and it almost seemed like a constant mumble. "Dee." It wasn't long before Rye started grabbing me by the finger and pulling me to the door, pointing outside. I knew exactly what that meant. He was an outside kid who wanted to be out there exploring. Well, I guess it was partly my fault, since every time he came I would take him outside and talk to him as if he was about ten years old. I would walk up to a tree, pat it, and say "tree," and Rye would laugh. I would pick up some leaves off the ground and say "leaves," and Rye would laugh. I would pick him up and start towards the house as if to go inside, and he would mumble, "No, Dee."

I was shopping one day, and I happened to see a bright orange toy cap pistol. I knew it was not the proper procedure to buy a one-year-old a toy cap pistol. Rye was different, or at least that was what I kept telling myself.

I had been raised with guns and hunting, and my father had always taught me gun safety. If Rye was to be an outdoorsman, then I was committed to pounding safety into him, as well as teaching him to respect nature and all its beauty. I decided to get the toy pistol and enough caps to last about six months. My reasoning was that I could always put it up till he was a bit older, and the caps would be okay as long as I kept them dry.

A few days later, Rye came in with my wife who had gone to pick him up. I took Rye into the living room and pulled out the toy pistol. He looked at me, looked at the pistol, and just grinned. He acted as if he knew exactly what that was. I finally was able to get the thing out of the box. The plastic ties they use on these toys nowadays are excellent. Rye watched intently as I loaded the toy pistol with the caps. I sometimes had the feeling this kid knows, and it was almost like he had done this before and wanted to make sure I was doing it correctly. I studied his face as I fired the first cap, and he showed no surprise at the sound, only joy. He laughed in delight. It was a genuine laugh, as if to say "Dee, you got it right." Rye reached over and grabbed the toy pistol and pulled the trigger. As the cap blew, he laughed again.

The next morning was a beautiful summer day. It was just perfect for me to take Rye on his first boat ride. I packed up the cooler with his favorite drinks, got the unending supply of snacks, and we were about ready to set sail. I broke out his new life jacket and said, "You have to wear this because the water is too deep, and if you fall in, Dee might not be able to save you."

I knew I was more scared than he was as he gave me that quizzical look that said "Why are you worried?" It was difficult to explain things to a one-year-old, but it was just my nature to try. Madonna would laugh at the one-sided conversations I had with Rye, but deep down I felt there was a level of understanding that encouraged me to continue.

As we got onboard the boat, Rye's eyes told me that he got it, that he knew this was a new adventure. He was very quiet as I started the engine and maneuvered the boat to head up the creek towards an area that was called Goose Bottoms. I saw a small grin come over his face, and those eyes were eagerly scanning the banks as if he could not soak it in fast enough. I knew I had me a boat captain and a young man that would love the water as if it was his second home.

When we approached Goose Bottoms, I slowed down to a crawl, and Rye sat up to investigate. Goose Bottoms is an area that turns into a gravel bar, and a lot of boaters pull up to that area and anchor out to swim and relax. The water is very shallow, very clean, frigid, and just a great place for young and old to enjoy. In the hot summertime, boaters are always looking for more refreshing water to swim in, and this place was spring-fed, which kept the water a lot cooler than the main lake. No one was around because it was in the middle of the week and mid-day. If it had been the weekend, I would not have taken Rye up there, because I wanted him to experience the place for the first time by himself.

When I threw the anchor in, the inevitable splash got Rye's attention. He seemed to sense something was up as I placed the ladder down the side of the boat. I swooped him up in my arms and descended into the cold water that awaited us. I had forgotten how cold that water was in the summer. It almost took my breath. I began to walk away from the boat, and I glanced at Rye to see his reaction. His eyes were glued to the water beneath him.

As I waded farther away from the boat, it got shallower, and it was eventually just below my knees. The sun danced off the water and gave the rocks on the bottom a shimmering and inviting look. I slowly took Rye from my arms and gently placed his feet in the water. No moan, no sound, no reaction at all from Rye as his eyes stayed fixated on the rocks below the surface. I picked him up, and he started to squirm as if he wanted back down. As I let him back down, it dawned on me what the sense of urgency was. He wanted to feel the bottom.

I carefully let him place his hand in the water, and it plunged to the bottom and secured a handful of creek gravel. A big smile and a laugh ensued. It was as though he was saying to me "Dee, I got some." I laughed, he laughed, and the more I laughed, the more he laughed as he clutched his handful of gravel. It was not to be his last trip to this place, as he had found a sweet spot. I suddenly realized we had spent much longer at Goose Bottoms than I thought we would. The sun was slowly sinking in the west, and I knew we needed to start home. Ah, time to break out a Dr. Pepper and those snack crackers that Rye liked. The ride home was smooth and uneventful. Rye sipped on that Dr. Pepper from his sippy cup and never took his eyes off this whole new world that he had just been exposed too.

As summer came and went, Rye became much more of a conversationalist. I was amazed at how his vocabulary was growing by leaps and bounds.

On a particularly hot day, Rye wanted to go on a boat ride. I ask him which way he wanted to go, and he pointed towards Goose Bottoms. We headed that way, and he seemed pleased. It was at this point he tried to drive. As he slid behind the steering wheel, I offered no resistance. There was no traffic on the water as it was fairly early on a Saturday morning.

As we rounded the bend in the creek, I asked Rye, "Where do you think we are going?"

As he turned the wheel to make the curve, he never looked up but said in that clear, loud voice, "Monkey bars."

I never knew where "monkey bars" came from. I just assumed it was from Rye's imagination. From that time forward, as we loaded up the boat, it was understood that we were going to the monkey bars. It was such a quick but fun summer. Lela and Rye both loved the water and always played until dark whenever they were at the house.

CHAPTER 5

It was late summer a couple of years later, and Lela was already back in school. Rye was at the house, and after breakfast we went out to play. When we started out the door, he grabbed his toy pistol and another roll of caps. I assumed from the look on his face that he had something in mind. As we walked toward our detached garage, a squirrel darted across the ground in front of us. As quick as a flash, Rye pointed his toy pistol at the squirrel and fired repeatedly. I was shocked. His reaction was so natural, clean, and swift that I just shook my head.

He looked up at me and grinned. "I got him."

It was at that point that I knew he had something I had never seen before.

Then Rye said, "Dee, let's ride the golf cart."

I had always kept a golf cart, since the creek was about three hundred feet from the house. I liked the fact that our house was set back off the water, because during the summertime we would come up from the water and get a more residential feeling.

The more Rye drove the golf cart, the more he liked it. Yes, at the tender age of three, he would drive the wheels off that golf cart. He was so small that he had to stand up to reach the gas, but it did not bother him. He was just a natural.

I wasn't sure who introduced Rye to the Lone Ranger—maybe it was Jon—but I became known to Rye as "Tonto." Rye was always after the bad guys, and we pursued them till the end of time, which usually meant bedtime. Rye decided that if he was going to be the masked man, he had to have a mask and a cowboy hat. Lela had an old cowboy hat, so that was commandeered, and the mask turned out to be a purple Ninja Turtle mask. Rye was a sight in his get up with that toy pistol strapped onto his side, the old cowboy hat, and the mask. It made Tonto proud to be the partner of such a noble crime fighter. We found some old movies and watched them over and over to make sure that we were carrying out our missions, just like the real Lone Ranger and Tonto.

In one episode, the Lone Ranger had to fight Red Hawk to gain the release of a small child the Indians had taken during a raid on a white settlement. When the Lone Ranger needed to practice for the upcoming fight against Red Hawk, I, as Tonto, would be the substitute. It seemed the Lone Ranger would take it very personally if Red Hawk got too rough, but Red Hawk thought it was funny.

Sometimes the practice sessions would evolve into a full-fledged pillow fight. At some point, the Lone Wolf, who was the Lone Ranger's grandmother, would intervene, break up the pillow fight, and otherwise restore order. It was becoming quite clear to me that I was a supporting actor in this young boy's romp through life. It did not bother me at all. Being a kid was always Rye's top priority.

At some point I started trying to read stories to Rye at bedtime. He was very attentive, but one night I made up this long story about Jelly Belly. That was all it took. After that, every bedtime he would plead with me to tell him Jelly Belly stories. I began to expand on those, and it became apparent that teaching him through my own made-up stories was more useful than reading something from a book. Rye began to co-opt my storytelling by injecting titles that he wanted to hear.

He would say, "Tell me about the time that Jelly Belly went hunting, climbed the big mountain, and ate all the ice cream."

I put in a kid named Sambo, who was Jelly's best friend. When Rye particularly liked a story, he would ask me to tell it again, even to the point that sometimes I would have to tell it three or four times. It dawned on me that I had to be careful to tell the story correctly each time or Rye would correct me. When that boy was focused, he had a mind like a steel trap.

Lela, on the other hand, was quite the opposite of Rye. When she was that age, she would go and get a stack of books big enough to challenge a speed reader and would listen as I read each one. When it appeared to me that Lela was sleeping, I would stop and invariably she would say, "Don't stop, Poppa. Read me some more."

On more than one occasion I read myself to sleep.

As the years went by, Lela stopped going to her dance lessons. Now it was softball. She was growing, and her feet couldn't keep up with her body, but she did show a lot of promise. Penny and Jon fell into the softball mom and dad routine and worked with Lela to see that she got every opportunity. It was good to see them grow as a family unit, and the effort they put into softball was great to watch. I will admit that I did not miss taking Lela to dance, and I certainly did not miss sticking out like a sore thumb.

The excitement began to build during that last summer before Rye began kindergarten. Lela was preparing for a beach trip to go play in the Little League Softball World Series. I marveled at her progress and how she truly was becoming a student of the game. When she was involved, she was committed 100%. As we planned the trip to the beach, it became apparent that Madonna was not going to be able to go because of some health problems. Rye let it be known he was riding with Dee. I thought, *Lord have mercy.* I could not imagine what that trip would be like with Rye riding shotgun.

It wasn't long until it was decided that Honey would be going with us. Honey was Rye and Lela's grandmother, who had lived through a horrible accident and was paralyzed from the waist down. It was a result of the accident that Penny had spent so much time with us while growing up. I wasn't sure if Honey understood what taking a trip with me and Rye would involve. Lela, however, was planning, packing, and focused. I had my doubts about how the team would play, but I knew the effort would be there.

The trip was a nightmare; we hit every conceivable traffic delay possible. We set a schedule for Rye; he got to ask every fifteen minutes how much longer it is till we get there. That young man would watch the clock to make sure he was on time for his question. After about the third thirty-minute traffic delay, I thought I detected Rye was getting a little bit sleepy. "Rye," I said, "you want me to tell you some Jelly Belly stories?"

"Yeah, Dee. Let me hear the one about the time Jelly Belly and Sambo drank all of Jelly's mom's lemonade."

I had almost forgotten that one since it was about six months ago that I had told Rye that story. Luckily it came back to me, and Rye needed a nap, so I was game. I felt sure that Honey would probably never drink a glass of lemonade again, but at that point if Rye had drifted off to sleep she would have been good with it.

All of a sudden those little eyes were no longer sleepy, and that burst of energy and enthusiasm came busting out. "Look, Dee! It's a gold Corvette, just like the one I want."

Yep, that boy sure knew his cars. He could spot a Corvette a mile away, and when he did the inevitable question would follow.

"Dee, you think a Mustang can beat a Corvette? Will it go 140 or 160?"

I had to answer, and I had to get it right.

The opening ceremony at the Little League Softball World Series was a culture shock for me, as I'd had no clue it was that big of a deal. There must have been six or seven thousand people in the stands and at least eight hundred eight to twelve-year-old girls that were the toast of the event. The parents and kids took this very seriously, but I was even more impressed by how friendly and courteous all these people were. It was a joy to see.

After the ceremony was the parade. Rye was taking it all in and had no trouble getting a record number of beads and one heck of a pile of candy. All he did was stand there with his arms outstretched and they covered him with beads. It was a hoot. We had the next day for beach play before the games began, and it was nonstop. Lela had brought a teammate who got to stay at the condo with her, so they were all over the place with Rye right behind. Pool, beach, pool, beach, pool, beach. Everyone slept like babies that night, myself included.

Early the next morning, I decided to call Manny. The situation in Nicaragua was seemingly very stable. A lot of time had passed and Manny had obviously been wrong about whatever it was that was going on upon that mountain in Rivas. I figured I would rib him a little about being such a worry-wart.

"Good to hear from you, Laroy."

"Manny, I just had to call and see if you had personally gone up on that mountain and taken care of business. From what I hear and read, things are pretty quiet down your way."

Manny laughed, "I don't think you know, but I could not climb that mountain if I wanted to. I have a bum knee."

"I told you years ago that jumping out of those airplanes wasn't healthy."

Manny laughed again, and then his voice took on a more somber tone. "You don't understand. These rebels, these scum, are the most patient people on the face of the earth. I wish I could say that they have vanished forever, but I know better. They care about only one thing, and that is power. It is what sustains them, what drives them, and they will continue the struggle as long as they breathe."

"Have you seen any activity on the mountain?"

"That is what is crazy about this situation. Like a couple of weeks ago, I was awakened by a noise off in the distance. From what I could tell, it sounded like several motorbikes. I thought it was strange, but I dismissed it, and then for the next few days, on a couple of occasions, I observed some smoke on the mountain. I knew they were back, but I kept my eye on the place and saw no comings or goings. I don't know what to think. After a few days, I saw no more smoke, no signs, nothing. It was like everything was normal. I have about decided, whatever it is they are doing is preparation for something that is not good."

"I don't know if I ever told you this, Manny, but I thought I was married to the biggest worry-wart in the world. However, maybe you could give her a run for her money."

"Perhaps you are right," Manny said, lightening up again. "Speaking of the Indian Princess, how is she?"

"Let's just say she still throws a mean tomahawk."

Our conversation shifted to more pleasant things. We talked about our wives and how lucky we were to have two good ones. Then he asked me what I was up to that morning.

"Manny, you wouldn't believe me if I told you. I am at the beach, getting ready to go watch my great-niece play in a softball world series. The anticipation is at a fever pitch for these kids, the atmosphere is as charged as if it was the seventh and deciding game between the Yankees and the Dodgers."

Manny laughed. "You are living the dream. I bet you are as charged up as the kids."

"You guys are going to have to come and visit. You have got to meet these kids. They're growing like well-fertilized weeds." We both chuckled before I continued, "I've got to go. I see Rye in the kitchen, and that boy will be wanting breakfast. He is something else. Strong as a bull and full of energy. Lela will be up shortly. I bet she didn't sleep much last night, worried about how she will play. I hate to admit it, but they are both a lot smarter than I ever was."

"We have talked about coming back to the States one of these days to see you all. I don't know… we are not getting younger, but who knows? Maybe before long."

"Let me let you go. I'm on the balcony, and I can hear Rye's stomach growling from inside the kitchen."

"You had better get inside and cook that boy some breakfast. I will stay in touch. Let's talk again soon."

I looked out at the ocean as I got up to go inside. I could

feel the pull of the waves and the warmth of the morning sun. It was going to be a good day.

It was time for the early morning game, and Lela was so nervous. "Poppa, what if I don't do well? What if I stink the place up?"

I laughed and said, "Lela, you will do just fine. All you got to do is play." Nobody likes to see their kid fail, but somebody wins and somebody loses. I knew one thing about Lela; she did not like to lose.

They were just fixing to start when Rye found the playground. "Dee, let's go to the playground." I was very torn between wanting to see Lela play yet knowing Rye would be miserable. Every time Lela would come up to bat I would race back from the playground to see her hit, then run back to the playground to check on Rye.

A retired grandmother from Louisiana saw what I was doing and said, "You got a granddaughter playing, don't you?"

"Yes, ma'am. I do."

She replied, "Well you go and watch. I'll keep an eye on the boy for you since I am here with my granddaughter."

I thought it was really nice for her to offer, and that was how it was for the rest of the week. People were helping people.

Lela and her team were behind by one run with two outs and runners at first and third. It was Lela's turn to bat, and I admit that I had butterflies. The very first pitch, she lined a shot between the centerfielder and the right fielder that rolled all the way to the wall. Her teammates mobbed her as they won their first game by 7 to 6. I wasn't sure if I really believed what I had just witnessed, but you could bet a doughnut I was one proud Poppa.

I had always heard so much about how parents put too much pressure on their kids and how sometimes their actions at a ballgame are just horrible examples for their children, but I saw nothing of that sort all week at that World Series. I saw encouragement; I saw display after display of sportsmanship, and it was just like one big happy family. Lela and her team did not win the World Series. They came in a very respectable third place. The team from Arkansas that put them out of the tournament won in the final game.

I did see one other thing while at the tournament, and yes, it involved Rye. I had gone to get Rye a drink at the concession stand, and as I was walking back, I saw a mom holding a young man by the arm who appeared to be crying, and she was talking to Rye. This young man appeared to be about nine and was much bigger than the other kids that were playing with Rye.

I picked up the pace to get there quick and asked the lady, "Is something wrong?"

She answered by saying, "It's nothing. I got the story from these other kids. My boy was showing out and was pushing them down, and this little man here came running up and must have put one more tackle on him. He hit the ground pretty hard, but he'll be alright."

I turned to Rye, and I said, "Tell him you're sorry."

"Dee, he was pushing all the little kids down, and he would have pushed me down, but he couldn't catch me.

When he pushed that little boy down over there, it made him cry, so I tackled him and told him not to do it no more, and he started crying."

The mother grabbed her kid by the ear and dragged him away, and I didn't know what to say. That was just Rye.

Summer was fleeing too fast. I held on and complained, but it did not stop the steady trickle of leaves falling into the yard which soon became a full-blown rain from the sky. It meant the end of summer and the time I treasured the most.

It would not be long before there would be no more Jet Ski rides with Rye and Lela. It meant no more barbecues on the back deck with those mounds of ribs piled high with that special sauce that made them lick their lips. Fall was always a depressing time for me. To me it signaled death. I knew people loved the beautiful colors of the leaves, the cooler temperatures, and even the coolness at night that sometimes required a jacket. Not me. For me it meant a long and desolate winter was about to ensue.

CHAPTER 6

Rye was officially in school, and Lela was in the fourth grade. I couldn't imagine what Rye would say to his teacher about all of our great exploits. It gave me cold shivers to think what would happen if he started talking about how we had tracked Yellow Eagle through the mud and bushes for two days before finally capturing him at a place called "The End of the World." I sure hoped his teacher would realize what an imagination this boy had and encourage him. I felt I had done my part. There had been so many adventures, and Rye could talk endlessly about each one.

I just hoped he wouldn't tell her about the time we were chasing Red Eagle and I tripped and fell in a hole and sprained my ankle, at which point Rye had said, "Oh, Dee, quit faking. You just don't want to play this anymore."

Rye will never know, but nothing could have been further from the truth.

I was no longer Tonto, and I am not quite sure when he grew out of the Lone Ranger, but he had, and we graduated towards more outside excursions and more hunts in what Rye called "the big woods." Uncle Tony had sent Rye a pellet gun which would kill a rabbit, squirrel, or bird— that is, if you could possibly hit it. The gun was too big for him, but he toted it with much pleasure and got to where he could shoot pretty efficiently with it as long as he had something to prop up the gun.

One day we took the golf cart with everything we possessed hunting wise up to a hunting place that I had promised Rye I would take him one day. It was a bluff, and it went straight up. I did not know for sure that we could even climb it, but we were fixing to find out. If Penny or Madonna had known I was taking this boy on that kind of adventure, they would have shot me.

The road that we could travel on the golf cart got us within about a quarter mile of the bluff. We started unloading, and Rye had to go through his mental checklist to make sure we had everything. The backpack took the longest, as it was stuffed with all kind of goodies. There was his knife, my knife, cookies, chips, his Dr. Pepper, my Diet Coke, extra bb's, pellets, marking tape, compass, and numerous other items.

As we approached the base, I asked Rye, "How tall do you think this bluff is?"

He studied it intently and finally said, "I believe that it is about two thousand feet high."

I smiled and told him, "You're probably off a little bit. My guess is it's about five hundred feet high."

He just smiled and said, "Let's get to climbing, Dede."

Just as I was no longer Tonto, I was also no longer just Dee. I wasn't sure when that occurred, but I had just begun to get comfortable with the name Dee and now it was Dede. The climb became very hard very fast, and Rye was struggling. I was struggling too, because I had to make sure he didn't fall, and it would have been easy to slip. I pushed, I pulled, I hung on for dear life, and Rye was doing the same. As I became a bit winded, I began to think about taking a break and could even hear Rye grunt as he struggled with the bluff. About fifty feet above was a massive rock that jutted out of the bluff, and it looked like the perfect place for us. I could feel the cold drinks in the backpack.

"Rye, let's take a break on that big rock."

His simple response was, "If we can ever get there."

I got us both seated on that big, beautiful rock, and we attacked our drinks and a pack of those snack crackers as if we were a pack of hungry wolves.

As we continued the climb, I looked at Rye, and I thought, *You have got to be crazy putting this boy through this kind of challenge.* The slope was more vertical now and became more difficult. I tried to keep Rye in front of me so I could catch him if he started sliding. Oops, it was too late. He somehow slipped by me, and I watched in horror as he slid helplessly about twenty feet down before he was able to grab a small tree and stop his slide. I thought, *This is it; this is far enough.*

He looked up at me with that big grin on his face and said, "Dede, this is fun."

He struggled to get back up to me, and we continued the climb as I began to realize this was making me extremely tired. We were about three quarters of the way to the top, and I had to sit.

Rye did not complain when I said, "This is the perfect hunting spot. Let's sit here and watch for a deer."

We sat for about fifteen minutes, and Rye was soaking it all in. The view from up there was breathtaking. He asked for his backpack, and I handed it to him. It slipped from his grasp and started a slow-motion roll that went all the way to the bottom. 380 feet it tumbled, and it picked its way by every tree and every brush pile till it made it to the bottom.

I looked at Rye, and he looked at me and smiled. "I'm not going to get it. I guess we will just do without it."

Finally, we got to descend that bluff, and we did so very carefully. On the way home, Rye asked me, "Did you know that we didn't need that compass?"

"Why do you say that, boy?"

"When we got up that bluff, I could see our house, so it was no way we could have gotten lost."

Yes, my boy was learning.

Lela got her first report card, and true to form it was 99s straight across the board, and she was in the advanced classes. I was so proud of her. She was growing into a beautiful young lady. It was about that time in her life that I knew that Lela's real passion was softball. She seemed intent on being the best she could be in that sport. As softball moms know, it is an endless regime of practice, practice, and more practice. I was beginning to worry that she did not have enough balance in her life and that other areas of development were being neglected. I talked to Penny about that, and I came away feeling that she had that part under control.

I had never been to a mini-midget football game, but Rye started playing for the Wildcats that year, so many of my Saturdays became football focused. The first time I went I laughed so hard. It looked like a bunch of shoes with a helmet on top, running around willy-nilly. It was so neat and so much fun to see those kids at play. The size difference was pretty big. The age group was four to six years old, and the parents there seemed so much more aggressive than the softball parents. It was apparent rather quickly that Rye was comfortable in this environment.

The first thing I noticed was that Rye was not afraid to tackle the bigger boys, and he almost seemed to hit them with a little extra pop. That boy was not afraid of anything. The rougher the better. It was going to be fun watching him develop, and I had no doubt that he was going to be good at it and that his potential was unlimited. Lela enjoyed watching Rye play as much as the rest of us, and she was his biggest cheerleader.

One day around that time, my phone went off, and I looked down to see a text from Rye. "Dee, I am coming this weekend."

That boy. He was always short and to the point. Penny was teaching him how to text. I texted him back, "Bring it on."

It was approaching the weekend, and I was looking forward to spending some time with Lela and Rye. I didn't get much rest when those two were around, but that was the least of my worries. I didn't know what they would think when I told them I was going to be gone for a few weeks. Lela would insist that she should go with me. That I might need her help. I knew that's what Lela would say, but with Rye, I didn't have a clue what his reaction would be.

As I sat on the back deck on a partly cloudy Friday morning, the Gray Heron arrived for his daily search for breakfast. I was a bit lazy that morning, but I was looking forward to picking up Lela and Rye at school that afternoon. I glanced across the creek. The old Heron seemed somewhat lazy this morning as well. I laughed as the thought crossed my mind, *Maybe we have a lot in common.*

I got up to go and refill my cup. The TV was on. I usually turned it on in the morning. I seldom watched it, rather I preferred to just hear it. As I made my way to the coffeepot, I heard, "Breaking News." I laughed. Everything is always breaking news. As I filled my cup, I listened.

The reporter said, "We have breaking news from Nicaragua. It is being reported that a group of rebels attacked a police station in the small town of Rivas, Nicaragua. According to government sources, five police officers were killed in the attack. The government is still investigating and believe it to be an isolated incident. We will bring you further news as updates become available."

I returned to the back porch. My mind was racing with all kinds of thoughts. Why had I not heard from Manny? I quickly picked up the phone and called but got no answer. I wondered if Manny was okay. Was he somehow involved in the attack? Surely he would call me any minute. As I waited, I scoured the internet looking for information.

As I pulled up some pictures, I thought, *Wow, this place is beautiful*, and I started to understand why Manny wanted to go back to his country of birth. I started to dig in and tried to understand more about Nicaragua, and it was becoming rather clear that my own country had played a significant role in shaping the history and politics of the place. All this stuff you read is great, but unless you have been there or you know somebody that has been there, you never trust the warm and fuzzy feelings of what you read.

I tried to call Manny again, but still no answer, I was worried. It was evident I was going to have to bone up on my history of the place and get up to speed on what had been happening down there that had Manny so upset. I had assumed it was just a group of thugs who were trying to create doubt and fear in the hearts of the local people. Probably drug related. I laughed at myself. *There you go, jumping to conclusions again.*

As I began to uncover what the press had been reporting, I began to realize this violence was more than any drug war. It was a battle for the heart and soul of the country. The attack on the police station had occurred in Rivas, Manny's hometown. It was a war in which, like most wars, the innocent men, women, and children who were just trying to live their lives in peace would be the ones to suffer the most.

I had often heard Manny speak of how beautiful the country of Nicaragua was and that it had some of the rawest beauty in the world. As I began to get a feel for the place, the first thing that jumped out at me was that Honduras lay to the north and Costa Rica to the south, and sandwiched in between was Nicaragua with a huge lake and tributaries everywhere.

Later that afternoon, I was on the way to pick up Rye and Lela at school. Penny called to tell me that Lela was not going to be able to come to the house because she had a softball tournament over in Xavier that started at 11:00 AM on Saturday. I couldn't hide my disappointment, and Penny went on to say, "Lela wants you to come to her game tomorrow."

"Of course, I will," I replied. "Send me the address so I can find the place. I don't know if Madonna will come, but Rye and I will be there."

I had no sooner hung up with Penny when my cell phone rang again. It was Manny. I instantly recognized that he was very upset. "Laroy, they have attacked Rivas, and they have succeeded. They hit the police station and killed all of them but one. The bastards got my best friend, Stephan. I just came from the funeral. It is horrible what that bunch of scum has done to this little town."

"Slow down, Manny. I heard this morning that there had been an attack. Back up and fill me in on the details."

"It happened early yesterday morning. They caught the police by surprise. It has been terrible. The town is in shock. Everybody is scared out of their wits. We have no police protection, and the government in Managua is saying they are stretched too thin to help us. I don't know what is going on in Managua, but I think they truly don't care. The fear in Rivas is that the rebels will return and take over. I knew I should have tried to intervene. I should have went up in that mountain and confronted them."

"That is the last thing you need to do. Do you think the rebels returned to the mountain? Are they still there?"

"I am certain of it. This morning before I went to Stephan's funeral, I hid in the woods close to the mountain, and I saw several people come and go. They are not afraid. They know they have dealt a blow to the police. They have nothing to fear."

"I should have recognized the seriousness of what you have been trying to tell me a long time ago. I want you to do one thing; you and Melinda stay close to home and be safe. I will make arrangements to come in a couple of days. Listen to me, Manny, two heads are better than one. I can't live with the thought of you trying to fight this battle by yourself, you get me?"

"I am afraid it is no use. Without some help from the government, they will overtake Rivas."

"You aren't alone. We must find a way to get you some help. I'm asking you as a friend, let me help. I want you to keep an eye on that mountain, and I stress, I want you to be extremely careful. I will be there in a few days. I want you to give me your word."

There was silence. Finally Manny said, "You got it, Laroy."

"I'll see you in a couple of days." As I hung up, I realized that I would soon confront that mountain in Rivas. In life you sometimes just grasp the fate that awaits you.

I called Madonna. "Young lady, I just got a call from Manny. I need you to do a couple of things. Dig out my passport and make me some flight reservations to Managua, Nicaragua for Monday. I don't need any discussion. I need your help."

Madonna was silent for a few seconds. "Leroy, you know what I have told you about this, but I will get it done. I will get your suitcase out and have it prepared by the time you get home. I sometimes wish I didn't love you, but I do."

I laughed, "Girl, in case you never noticed, I am crazy about you." I knew she was seething inside, and that Indian ancestry was encouraging her to let me have it.

Madonna's response was simply, "You be careful driving Rye home from school. I'm going to fix dinner for you two. Spaghetti and salad. Your favorite. I love you."

I heard a click, and Madonna was gone. As I pulled up to the door where I picked Rye up, he was sitting on a bench with his best buddy, Bryson. I just looked at him in amazement as he swung his leg back and forth as if he had no cares in the world. You could see it in his mannerisms that he knew he had the world by the tail. That mouth never stopped moving as he rattled on and on in Bryson's ear. When he saw my car pull up, he jumped up and grabbed his backpack and made a beeline for my car. As he blew past his teacher, he smiled at her and said, "Goodbye!" He had her wrapped around his finger too.

Once in the car, he asked, "Dede, can we put the Jet Ski in when we get home?" The boy had a passion for speed, and the more waves we could jump the better he liked it.

I said, "I don't know why not. It just looks like the perfect day to jump some waves." He looked at me and smiled. Life was good.

The next morning after Rye got up and we started eating breakfast, he asked, "Are we going to see Lela play today?"

I didn't think he would want to go, as he usually preferred to be on the water or exploring. I answered, "Boy, that it is an excellent idea. Do you think they will win?"

"You just don't know how good they are. Lela has been practicing, and she is getting really good. The whole team is good."

After breakfast we started loading up to get ready to go, and Rye decided that we needed to take his football.

I said, "Boy, we are going to a softball game. Why do you want to take a football?"

"There will be some of the bigger boys at the game, and they may want to play football with me. I'm good at football, Dede, didn't you know that?"

There was that name again. I was beginning to pick up on the fact that when Rye referred to me as "Dee," it was serious, and when he said "Dede," it was a playful signal.

We made the hour and a half drive without incident and found the ballfield without any trouble. That old GPS I had still worked like a charm. Rye would always laugh because every time it told me to turn, I would say, "Thank you, Hazel."

"Dede, why do you call that thing Hazel?"

"Because that's her name."

That particular morning we were getting close to the site, and Rye was screaming he needed to go to the bathroom, and I kept telling him to just hold on because we were almost there.

We drove about a mile in silence, and then Rye blurted out, "Talk to me, Hazel, talk to me!"

I just busted out laughing, which did nothing but compound the problem for Rye. Luckily, we arrived just in the nick of time. Lela and her team were already out on the field when we got there, and she spied me right away. There was that warm grin of hers and a big wave.

She jogged over to the fence and said, "Poppa, I'm pitching today."

"Girl, you go get them. It's just like practicing in the backyard. You will do fine. They can't hit what they can't see."

"Poppa, you're so funny." And with that, she turned and ran back to her teammates. What a kid. She was growing way too fast for me, but she had a quiet confidence that said she would do just fine with anything she attempted.

As game time approached, we all sat down, and I noticed that Penny seemed preoccupied with something.

I asked, "Is something wrong?"

"No, it's just that Lela is worried that she will not pitch well."

I reminded her, "Kids will be kids, and if she doesn't do well, it'll be a growing experience." Well, ten strikeouts later, all the worry was gone. I was right, they can't hit what they can't see.

Rye was the typical proud brother. At every strikeout he would stand up and say, "You got this, Lela, you got this."

I thought to myself, *What am I worried about? These two kids, they got it together better than most adults.* I sat back and enjoyed the game.

On the way home, I told them about my upcoming trip to Nicaragua and that I would be gone about two weeks. Lela asked me about two hundred probing questions, and I told her she should be a lawyer.

It was Rye who pitched the biggest fit. "Dee, you know good and well that I can't come out to your house and help you fight the bad guys if you are gone running around in some country that I don't even know where it is. When we get home, you are going to show me on a map where this place is. Is there a lot of bad guys over there? And are you going to have to fight them?"

"I don't know for sure what is going on over there. I think that's why I'm going. My friend Manny wants me to help him figure out what is going down."

"You mean you are going and you don't even know why you are going? That don't sound too smart to me."

Lela laughed, and I couldn't help but laugh too. Soon we were all laughing. Once we started laughing, we just couldn't stop, and Rye piled in, right on cue, "Dee, you don't even know why you are going!"

I felt a tinge of sadness as I hugged Penny and the kids goodbye. I held those hugs a few seconds longer than normal, and I got a deep stare from Penny as if to say "What is this all about?"

As I was driving home, I suddenly became forlorn. I felt like a youth in the jungle with no weapon with which to defend myself and a bloodthirsty predator circling me, ready to pounce. I felt that all-encompassing dark cloud that shuts out the light and deprives one of hope, of any belief of anything good in the world.

CHAPTER 7

I knew when I got home I would face Madonna and the joys of packing that big old suitcase. I could see that suitcase in my mind, and I laughed. Why did I even buy that big thing? It was one of those spur-of-the-moment deals that I thought would carry everything I ever needed. It sure would, but it also turned out to be too big and bulky. I had never filled it to capacity.

When I walked into the house, Madonna said, "Were the kids okay with you going? How did they take it?"

"They were fine. Rye cracked a joke and thought it was funny that I didn't even know for sure why I was going, and that got Lela laughing, so we were all okay."

I walked into the bedroom. There in the floor was that monster of a suitcase. Madonna, the perfect wife, had already gotten it out of the closet and checked it several times for spiders. It was one of those things she would do that always made me laugh and was probably one of the reasons why I loved her so much. I knew there was a decent chance that I would never die from a spider bite.

I was almost packed and ready to go when Madonna said, "Are you going to call Manny?"

"I will probably call him on the way to the airport."

"I know you. You're just going to show up and take a chance that he is home. You beat anything I have ever seen."

It was my way. My trademark. All my life I had never been one to make meticulous plans. It was just not my M.O. I had always believed that one should approach most life situations with the greatest degree of flexibility and surprise that one can muster. You must be able to adapt, adjust on the fly, and do it with precision. I had been relatively good at that; I felt that if God had granted me one talent, it was the ability to scramble and respond to almost any situation without thinking it completely through.

I knew I wasn't going to call Manny. At this point, I did not want to alert anybody to my travel plans, and, hopefully, I would just show up in Nicaragua as a tourist. I planned to wander the streets and check out the local cuisine. It would be nice to be able to meet a few of the locals and get a feel for what they were like. The best way to do that was to act as a lost tourist.

My cell phone rang. It was Wango. "Leroy, I called to tell you that you may have stepped in a hornet's nest. I checked with the State Department, and I also got a call from the CIA. They see the potential for big trouble. The

State Department is going to alert the Nicaraguan government and ask them to give you their full support. I've known for some time about your service to our government, Leroy, and I want you to be careful. I don't like the smell of this."

I laughed, "This will be easier than getting you elected, Wango."

He replied, "I'm concerned that we may not be able to help you if you get in too deep. You can depend on Leanna and Castillo. I hate to say it, but you will be alone on this deal."

It was almost time to head to the airport, and I checked my luggage a couple of times to make sure I hadn't forgotten anything. There was the usual small stuff, so I thought, *Hey, you did pretty well. Now if you just don't forget that huge suitcase, you will be doing great.* As I kissed Madonna goodbye, I held her tight and thought of all the years and how quickly they had passed. I thought of all the times we had argued and fought. I thought of all the good times and laughs we had shared. And as I had gotten older, I honestly hoped that one day we could just relax and spend more time together.

As I drove to the airport, I thought about Manny and Nicaragua. Pretty much all I knew was that Rivas was a short drive from Managua. I was flying into Managua and just assumed I would rent a car to make the short trip to Rivas and see about checking in at the San Lupe. I hoped this trip was not going to become one of the more stupid things I had ever done, but I could sense that there was a slightly more substantial element of danger than what I usually encountered. That gave me pause, but not for long, as I never seemed to dwell on what might be.

I arrived at the airport and checked in, boarded, and departed without mishap. As the plane approached Managua, I snapped out of my thoughts and glanced out the window to get my first visual of Nicaragua. It was more mountainous than I had imagined, but I could tell it was beautiful. The water surrounding this country reminded me of the Caribbean, and I loved the Caribbean. As we banked and slowly made our approach, I thought, *These guys do a heck of a job landing these aircraft on these short runways. Man, what would they give to have some of those big long runways as we have in the States?* I knew when we hit this was not your typical landing, as they had overshot by a good bit. We hit so hard that the oxygen masks popped down from overhead. There were a few screams. When we stopped, we were about twenty yards past the runway in a short field, and we only had about thirty more yards to the ocean.

The pilot jockeyed the plane around and got us on the runway. He came over the speaker and said, "Ladies and Gentlemen, we do not usually make a practice of landing that way. If you all have the time, we will take it back up and do it right." There was nervous laughter among the passengers. The pilot calmly said, "Sorry, I see we have no takers. Thanks for flying with us today, and welcome to Managua."

After exiting the plane and clearing customs, I entered the main concourse. There were not too many people, but a few were milling around. Some waiting and some going.

I glanced to my right and caught sight of a beautiful young woman with long, black flowing hair, dark skin, and beautiful dark eyes. I was thinking to myself, *If I were only twenty years younger.* I was almost past her when I saw that she was holding a sign. To my amazement, it had my name on it. I stumbled a little bit, as the big suitcase I was pulling almost ran over me. As I approached her, she looked at me with a fair amount of caution, but I saw no sign of nervousness.

"Uh, my name is Leroy Overstreet, but I may not be the right Leroy."

She broke into a grin and said, "Mr. Overstreet, it is so nice to meet you. Congressman Parker had emailed and asked me to assist you in any way I can. My name is Leanna Futrillo, and I am with the U.S. Embassy here in Managua."

I replied, "I knew old Wango would take care of me." She looked puzzled. "Just a nickname I have for the congressman."

"Mr. Overstreet, I have a car waiting to take us to the embassy. We will get some lunch and give you some background and try to answer any questions you have for us."

"Please. Call me Leroy." What came out of her mouth was "Laroy," and it sounded so much more beautiful than when Manny said it.

"Laroy, I will be able to assist you in getting you a rental car for your drive over to Rivas."

How much did Wango tell her? I just nodded my head. I had to do a better job. I knew I must have been staring at Leanna.

Once at the embassy, I realized why all those people wanted to work there. It had to be a good gig if you could get it. I hoped I wouldn't have to have lunch with anybody important, as the fewer people I met, the better it would be for me and my buddy Manny.

Leanna must have seen the wheels turning in my head. "I have taken the liberty of reserving you a room at the San Lupe in Rivas. I hope you don't mind. Bill had said that he thought you would want to stay there." I nodded my head approvingly.

"I have our lunch set up in my office so we can talk. I did not set up an appointment with the ambassador, but I will if you want me too." It was evident at that point that Wango had me covered.

"Leanna, you have everything covered just right, and our country should be proud to have someone as talented as you representing them." That smile told me she was way ahead of me, and that although she did not understand, she knew that it would turn out all right. I just could not believe that this was going so smoothly, and it unnerved me a little bit.

Once in Leanna's office, I looked around to see a sparse looking room but with a touch of elegance. It fit Leanna to a T. She picked up the phone and asked someone if they would bring lunch to her office. "Laroy, as you probably know, we have some people who are determined to cause trouble for our government, and I would say you need to be very careful about where you go and with whom you associate. It would be my advice to avoid certain cafés and the bars in the town of Rivas. I will give you a list of those people in Rivas that may be able to help you and give you an assessment of the lay of the land."

A sudden knock on the door and Leanna said, "Come in." A young woman walked in pushing one of those carts that were topped by the usual silver trays. Leanna thanked her, and the young lady smiled and left. Then she looked at me and said, "I hope you are hungry."

The food was delicious, and it has always been a habit of mine to consume whatever is in front of me without asking too many questions. The fish had a Caribbean flavor to it and a somewhat smoky flavor that I couldn't identify, but it was good. The salad was different than I was accustomed to. It was fruitier than I liked, but I managed to eat every bite by telling myself it was healthy and good for me.

As I looked at Leanna, I wondered what her background was and how she wound up working for the embassy. I also wondered if she was married, had kids, or if she was one of those souls committed to a cause and never had time for a life. I knew that Lela would have loved Leanna and would've quickly bonded with her. The only pictures in her office was of a couple of dogs and one picture of a kitten. Yep, Leanna and Lela would have hit it off.

After our lunch was finished, I asked Leanna, "You say you have people in your country who want to cause trouble. What is their purpose?"

"The history of this country has been a constant battle of people who want to take away freedom and enslave the populace."

"Leanna," I countered, "That is what I have seen all over the world in my lifetime. I hold a simplistic view that good will triumph over evil in the long run. What are your thoughts?"

Leanna appeared to be nervous, and I wasn't quite sure why. Then she emptied out her soul about the struggles of her parents, her grandparents, and all the many people who had paid a tremendous price for their freedom. It was emotional, but delivered with a calmness that belied the inner strength of this beautiful woman. I knew I had someone I could count on if this deal with Manny got very involved, and something told me that was just about to happen.

As much as I hated to leave Leanna's company, I said to her, "I so much appreciate your hospitality and your counsel, but I am sure you have more important things to do. I want you to know that my first impression of your country is that if it is as beautiful and talented as you, then this place has to be blessed."

She blushed and said, "Bill said you are a charmer. Before you leave for Rivas, let me give you this list, and I will call and have them bring the rental car." Leanna was a first-class lady who did a first-class job and with very minimal effort.

Once in the car and heading north, I missed the warmth and comfort of Leanna's office and that reassuring confidence she exuded. It was beginning to rain, and I told myself that this was something I had better get used to, as it was indeed their rainy season. I couldn't help but think about Madonna. Back at home, I was sure it was quite hot and dry. I made a mental note to call her as soon as I got settled at the San Lupe. I was beginning to think about calling Manny, but I decided against that and knew I would get up in the morning and venture out and find his house. I knew I should get there early, because if I didn't I might miss him, and he would be up and gone.

There were very few cars on the road, and the rain was beginning to pour down in buckets. Visibility was bad, and I had to keep my eyes glued to the road. My fingers gripped the steering wheel hard as I contemplated each turn and dodged each pothole. The roads looked like they could spend a few taxpayer dollars to upgrade, but then I thought about some around my house and concluded that there was not much difference.

There was a sign that read "Rivas 19 KM." I was making progress and beginning to hope it would quit raining, but that was something I was going to wish many times on this trip.

CHAPTER 8

As I approached Rivas, I began to realize how poor the country was, and amid all the beauty was a lot of despair. The town of Rivas was pretty much as I had started to suspect. One main street in town, and the roads were narrow and poorly paved. I had no trouble finding the San Lupe. It was a rather well-maintained place, and as I pulled in, my first reaction was that it would be perfect. First impressions are not always correct, but over the years I had learned to trust mine. As I went through the door and approached the front desk, the young man behind the desk studied me carefully, and I almost detected a look of disdain.

"Do you have a reservation for Leroy Overstreet?" I asked nonchalantly.

He glanced at a book and replied in broken English, "I do. You are in room twenty-three, around the corner." I signed my name and paid for the week, as it had been reserved in cash. Then he said, "Señor, if there is anything you require, just let us know."

I thanked him, and I was actually in a hurry to get to the room and unwind. There did not seem to be very many people on the street in front of the San Lupe, so I eased my huge suitcase into the room pretty much without being detected. I couldn't wait to shower and just kick my feet up on the bed and call Madonna.

The phone rang about three times, and I heard that voice that I was already beginning to miss.

"Did you make it okay?" was the first thing out of her mouth.

"Yep, made it okay. Made the trip from Managua to Rivas fine, and I have checked in at the San Lupe and got my feet kicked up. I do have one small problem, though." I heard her catch her breath before I said, "I already miss you."

"Oh, you drive me nuts," was the reply. "Lela got her report card, and it was all A's, with the average being 99.23."

As our conversation continued, I further discovered that Lela had been worrying about me and wanted Madonna to call her as soon as she was finished speaking to me. Rye, on the other hand, was mad because he hadn't realized that I might be gone more than a couple of days, and now he wanted to know how many more days before I would be back home.

"Tell him I will try and find him a new knife to go with his growing collection."

Madonna seemed worried a little bit more than usual, so I asked her what was wrong. "Leroy, you be safe over there. I was watching the news this afternoon, and they had a report about an abduction and the killing of some college kids somewhere in Nicaragua."

I shivered a little bit and replied, "Don't worry. Manny will take care of me, and anyway, I am too mean to die."

She laughed, and that made me feel better.

The night passed quickly, and I slept well. I awoke at 4:00 AM without the aid of an alarm clock. It's one of those things that most people would like to be able to do and those who can think it is a curse. It was just me. At 4:30 every morning, like a programmed coffee pot, bingo; I turned on.

I woke up thinking about a cup of coffee, so I got up and made a pot. A slow rain was falling outside, and it was just too much for me—almost depressing. As I took the first sip of the coffee, I reveled in the steaming aroma of the strong, black liquid. I was already beginning to develop a taste for this Nicaraguan blend. As I sipped, I thought about how I might track Manny down. My first idea was to drive around a little bit as soon as the day broke to get a feel for the lay of the land, and then I would look for Manny. At about 6:00, I poured myself another cup and headed out the door.

Once in the car, I headed north and out of town. It didn't seem like I had gone much more than a half mile when I suddenly stopped passing houses. After that it was nothing but jungle and natural beauty. The roads were terrible, almost worse than some we had on the off roads at home. I continued about another eighth of a mile, and as I rounded a curve, I was exposed to a vast, beautiful lake on the left and what appeared to be a mountain on the right. There was a small place to pull off by the lake, and I pulled in just to take in the splendor of the lake and majesty of the mountain behind me. As I looked further south, I saw a few smaller mountains on the right, and the lake seemed to stretch about a half mile down the road to where it attached to a more modest mountain. One can travel all over, but the pure magic of water and mountains always grabbed me. It seemed to pull at my very soul, and I felt at home.

I wanted to check this place further, but now it was time to find Manny. I turned around and headed back south towards Rivas. I kept thinking about that one little house I passed coming out of town. It seemed different; better kept than most of the other ones. It dawned on me that as soon as I had passed the last house that the telephone poles had also stopped. It appeared to be the end of electricity, and from that I deduced that the only thing past Rivas was jungle.

As I drove back into town, I saw the house that had caught my eye before. It had a small gate with a fence that wrapped around a well-manicured yard, and the house itself was small and intriguing. I looked behind me. With nothing coming, I stopped in the middle of the road and observed the home. To the left of the house was a car with a cover over it. The cover came down just above the back bumper, revealing a sticker on the left side that I could not quite make out but that looked vaguely familiar.

I got out of the car to get a better view, and my heart began to beat faster. The sticker said, "101st Airborne." That was Manny's old unit. I had found him without really trying. I got back in the car and pulled slowly into the driveway, looking for any sign of movement in the house. It was dimly lit, but I saw no sign of life. I eased out of the car, closed the door quietly, and walked up to the house and raised my hand to knock. The door swung open, and I found myself looking down the end of a double-barreled shotgun.

Manny laughed and said, "Laroy, you should know better than to surprise a grizzled old veteran like me." With that, he grabbed me and gave me a big old bear hug.

I could tell that Manny had been keeping up with his exercise and had not gone soft since he had left the service.

"Melinda, come quick. Old Laroy has snuck in on us. Have a seat, Laroy. Melinda will get the coffee going in just a minute or two. So how was your trip? When did you arrive?" The questions were flowing. As I looked at Manny, I thought he looked much older, and his hair was gray. He still looked as mean as a snake.

Melinda soon came from the kitchen with cups and a pot of hot coffee which she placed on the table in front of us. Manny poured us each a cup and asked me to tell him about Madonna and how everything was going in the States. As I recounted everything, I noticed Melinda paying close attention. I asked her, "Where exactly are you from?

Tell me about yourself. Manny and I sometimes get too self-absorbed in our little world to take in what is going on around us, and for that I apologize."

She smiled and said, "I am a native Minnesotan, and I grew up about fifteen miles from the Canadian border. We had a small turkey farm, plenty of food, and a loving family. I knew at an early age that it was not going to be my home. Every single Labor Day, after lunch, it was a custom for our family to go outside and scour the farm to pick up anything that was on the ground that we wanted to see before spring. That consisted of rakes, water hoses, toys, shovels, or anything of value had to be secured before it started snowing."

I shivered. Being a warm weather person myself, I knew it wasn't my kind of place. "How did you meet Manny?" I asked.

"We met in the service, and after a few years we were married." She looked at him and smiled as she said, "He's my soulmate. When Manny suggested that we move down here to his birthplace, I jumped onboard because of one thing: climate." I could tell that Melinda was comfortable here, and it seemed as though she would be satisfied to live out her life here in Rivas.

"Let me get some more coffee for you guys, and I know Manny will want to take you to his library to talk." I was sure she saw me raise my eyebrows when she said "library."

"Manny with a library? That's about as probable as a snowstorm in South Florida."

Manny laughed, and we got up and headed down a hallway. Manny pushed open a door at the end of the passage and stepped inside. I followed and closed the surprisingly heavy door behind me and then turned around to view the library. It was anything but a library. In fact, I didn't see any books at all. The room was full of guns and enough ammunition to start a war. On further observation, I saw a couple of chairs and a small table that had a couple of magazines and two books on the bottom shelf. I walked over to see more closely. It was two old issues of *Sports Illustrated* Swimsuit Issues, and on the bottom was a Bible and a book titled *Nothing New Under the Sun*.

I couldn't help but say to Manny, "I love your library." His laugh was one that I had heard many times. "Manny, I know you didn't bring me down here without a plan, so let's get after it. How is this going to come down?"

"You never change, Laroy. You always cut to the chase. When Melinda and I moved back here, it was my goal to help the people who I was born and raised with as a child. You have seen enough to know that this is indeed a developing country with poor ways. We were cautious the whole time to be non-political, and my goal was to find out who the good guys and the bad guys were without portraying any animosity toward either one. I think we have succeeded in that, and most people just consider us a couple from the States, here to live out our retirement peacefully."

A slight tap on the door interrupted Manny, and in walked Melinda with a tray of sausage biscuits and coffee.

"You guys don't mind me," she said. "I thought you all would enjoy these."

Manny said, "I hope you like wild boar. It is how I keep my aim sharp while providing us with some pork."

The biscuits were homemade and excellent, and the sausage was delicious with a sweet taste like I had never experienced before. I knew Manny had a lady that could cook.

As Melinda left, closing the door behind her, Manny continued, "You remember me telling you about the attack on the police station. It changed my perspective on things, and I now realize that something is up that needs to be addressed before a lot of people get hurt. It got personal for me with that attack. One of the men killed was my best friend when I was small. We played together every day. His family became good friends of ours when we moved back here. Stephan was the only guy who knew what I was doing, and he assisted me in many ways. It did not hurt that his wife and Melinda had become terrific friends. It pains me about what is going to happen to her and the kids now that Stephan is dead. She has no family to speak of and is going to have to move in with a distant relative in Managua. Stephan's family was his pride and joy, and it is what he lived for. They were his whole life."

I detected that look in Manny's eyes that was designed to hide anger.

He continued, "There is a lake about a half mile down the road where I go and fish on Tuesday and Friday."

I interrupted, "I know the one. I checked it out this morning by accident. I was just looking around."

Manny looked at me with a faint smile and said, "I guess you also saw the mountain on the other side?"

"I sure did. It's beautiful, just like the lake."

Manny lowered his voice just a bit and said, "I am pretty sure those who attacked the police station have congregated in that mountain, and I really think there is a lot more to this than meets the eye. That is where you come in. I have fished enough at the lake to observe enough activity to tell me that a lot more is going on up in that mountain than what most people suspect. Here is what I think we should do. Tomorrow morning, I will go fishing down at the lake at my usual spot and my usual time: 9:00. I want you to come around ten and go to the south end of the lake. I will be fishing on the north end." He paused before adding, "Did you bring that old camera with you?"

"I sure did. I still even have that old zoom lens I bought at the PX."

"Does that thing still work? It is critical for you to stick out like a sore thumb. You know, a tourist with an attitude." We laughed. He and I both knew that I would have no problem with that.

Manny said, "Let's go for a walk, and I can give you a better lay of the land."

It sounded good to me, as I was full and had plenty of energy that morning. The nervous kind of energy I get when I feel like something exciting is about to happen. I got up to head towards the door, and then I realized that Manny was not following. I stopped and turned around. Manny was moving the table and leaning down to the area of wooden floor below it. I watched as he lifted a small section of the floor away to reveal what appeared to be a makeshift tunnel.

Manny looked up and grinned. "Follow me."

Once inside, I saw that the tunnel was very solid despite its crude construction. Manny had a light and began to walk down the tunnel as if on a morning stroll. I suddenly realized it was time to pick up the pace, as I didn't have a light. We had been going for a couple of minutes, when it came to me that this was not your ordinary tunnel. It just seemed to keep going,

I wondered why Manny had built it. It was constructed out of 4x4 posts on four foot centers, with a piece of plywood holding up the top. We had been walking for over a half mile, when Manny suddenly stopped and pushed a steel plate up to flood the opening with sunshine. He placed a small ladder through the opening, and we exited the tunnel.

After a moment, Manny said, "Are you all right, troop? I seem to remember that you are slightly claustrophobic."

I laughed and took a deep breath, and then I took in all the beauty in front of me. We were about fifty feet off the road on a little rise that gave a good view of the lake, and to our right, the mountain began its majestic rise to the top. We were basically at the base of the mountain on the north side, and across from us was the north side of the lake, which extended past us about four hundred feet, but we could still see from our viewpoint.

Manny said, "Tomorrow, this is the only help I can give you. As you work the lake, you will be in my constant view, so try not to venture up in the mountain. If you go up, I will lose you quickly and only know that you are up on the mountain, and that will not be good. Most people who have ventured up there have not been heard from or seen again."

I looked at Manny and gave him the good old American thumbs-up. "I got it loud and clear," I said with my most confident voice. "Manny, how can so much beauty be involved in something this bad?"

I looked at that beautiful lake and stared up at that magic mountain. I knew the view from the top must be breathtaking. When I glanced back at Manny, he was staring intently up at the mountain as if he was searching every inch of what was before him. His eyes never stopped moving as he answered, "It is much like life. Beauty is in the eye of the beholder." He sighed then said, "We should head back. I bet Melinda is fixing lunch, and I told her that you were an old southern boy that could eat like a racehorse."

I was trying to guess what Melinda was cooking for us. It did not seem to take as long to get back to the library, as I guess my mind was preoccupied with lunch. As we popped up inside and Manny fixed the library back to conceal the tunnel, I asked him, "What's the purpose of the tunnel? Did you build it? And if you did, how did you do it without arousing suspicion?"

"In due time, my friend," Manny said as he pushed some ammo boxes back that would typically house library books. What emerged from behind the ammo boxes surprised me. It was a bottle of Jack Daniels with a couple of shot glasses.

Manny grinned and said, "How about a shot of Jack for old times' sake?" as he filled the glasses to the top. "Melinda does not want liquor in the house, and I comply, except for special occasions. If this is not a special occasion, I don't know what is."

I had done my share of drinking in my life, but as I had gotten older, it occurred less and less. It, however, was just what I needed to steady my nerves and provide a pick-me-up for what lay ahead. It was just then that I detected a smell that any country boy would recognize. It was fried pork chops. My mind instantly changed from the burn of the Jack Daniels to the smell of the meat.

"Manny, lunch will be ready in about ten minutes," said Melinda. It was like music to my ears as all those delicious smells wafted lazily into the library.

Manny sipped the last of his Jack and said, "Let's go wash up. I hope you are hungry."

As we entered the kitchen, my eyes eagerly scanned the kitchen to see the feast I could smell. I was not disappointed. On the table were fried pork chops, creamed corn, creamed potatoes, butter peas, and stewed okra with tomatoes. For this country boy, that was the ultimate in fine dining. We sat down, and the next fifteen minutes there was little conversation as we ate.

When I reached the point where I could not consume any more, I looked up at Melinda and said, "That was awesome, just awesome. How do you manage to put this kind of food on the table here in Rivas?"

A small smile crossed her lips, and she said, "My sister cans corn, beans, okra, and tomatoes in the States during the summer and sends them over to me. She has always had that knack to do it just right. My mother taught her, and she still does it. After Mother died, she moved to South Georgia and found her home, and we have remained close all these years." Then she turned to her husband and said, "Manny, why don't you take Leroy out and show him the cellar where we keep all this stuff?"

I was ready to go, but I wasn't sure I could move, I was so stuffed. I thanked Melinda again for one of the most wonderful meals I had eaten in months. She seemed genuinely appreciative of my words and began to gather up dishes as I lingered at the table for another moment to soak up that sweet smell.

Manny was already standing at the back door with a wide grin on his face; he knew what I was doing. As we made our way outside, I noticed that the sun was shining bright. This was much more to my liking. The first thing I noticed in the northwest corner of the property was what appeared to be a small Indian mound about six feet high. It was partially obscured by the foliage that is abundant in Rivas. As we approached it, Manny went around to the west side, and as I followed, I saw a couple of steps going down to a door. Manny opened the door and went in. I followed.

Once inside, he turned on a light to reveal a small structure that appeared to be much like the storm shelters we have at home to ride out tornadoes. There were the typical things you would see: lights, a small bed, and an ax. There were shelves all around the room, lined with jars of canned vegetables. Corn, peas, okra, and tomatoes, all from

Melinda's sister, I assumed. There were a few guns and some more ammo. Just as I figured, Manny was well stocked.

Manny reached up and said, "Here, keep this with you," as he handed me a pistol and a couple boxes of shells.

"I sure hope I don't get involved in that big of a firefight."

Manny just laughed and said, "You never have enough."

I pulled the pistol out of the shoulder holster to look at it and got quite a shock. It was a pistol that I was very familiar with, a .38 Spanish service revolver. I had one at home just like it that had been passed down to me from my father, who got it from my grandfather. It was one sweet shooting pistol that I had a lot of confidence in, and I could hit with it. These guns were made in the early 1900s, and were in service for many years.

"Manny, I got one just like this. It's a great shooting pistol."

Manny just shrugged and said, "It was my friend Stephan's. He was toting it the day he died. I guess you wondered where we disposed of all that dirt from the tunnel. Well this is a lot of it. It took Stephan and me almost four years to finish the tunnel, and I primarily built it to keep an eye on the comings and goings of people at the lake and the mountain and as an escape route for Melinda and me if it was ever needed. I wish I could give you more to go on, but I know if anybody can find out what is going on up there and what they are planning, it is you. What are you thinking about? And how are you going to penetrate those people and get the information out of them?"

I just laughed and said, "I got a plan."

Manny smiled. "I have got some fishing gear in the house I will give you before you leave, and just so you will know, it is great fishing. Tomorrow when you get there, work your way slowly down to the north end where I will be. When you are close enough to talk, do not even look at me. Just tell me if you saw anything. I usually go into the Café Teais about three or four times a week, and as I leave I will come by your room to find out what you need and what you saw that day. Is there anything else you can think of that we should discuss?"

I thought for a moment and shook my head as we headed out of the cellar. I could only think of what it must be like living here and marveled at the amount of work Manny had put into this place. We were very different. Manny was the planner, and, well, I just shot from the hip. But we were so much alike in so many other ways. As long as you live, you may never understand what makes the world turn, but even as it turns, you know there is some order, some justification for what is.

Once back in the house, we made a little more small talk, and I realized the day was passing too fast. I decided I needed to get back to the San Lupe and get organized for the morning. I thanked Melinda again, and Manny walked me outside with a couple of rod and reels in tow, a small, well-stocked tackle box in hand.

"Manny," I said, "what am I going to do with any fish I catch?"

"On your way back into town, throw them out by the gate, and I will take care of them for you. Besides, you don't have any way to cook them at the San Lupe."

"Gee thanks, Manny." I started the car and looked back at him as I said, "See you in the morning, buddy. I bet I catch more than you do."

CHAPTER 9

As soon as I backed out on the road, I realized the skies had darkened, and yes, rain was beginning to hit my windshield. I drove slowly and looked carefully at every inch of land my eyes could take in. I rounded a small curve, and on the side of the road stood a very dark-skinned man who appeared to be glaring at me. I glared back as I passed him and then thought, *What the heck? Maybe he just needed a ride.* I stopped the car and waved for him to approach.

He got in and said, "Gracias, Señor. Headed to the Café Teais." He was a tall, slim fellow, who had a nasty scar that extended from his ear almost down to the lower lip on his left side. "You are an American tourist," he said, matter of fact.

I just nodded my head and then I thought better of that. I blurted out, "Well, I am American, but I am visiting to see if I might want to relocate here. America is going to the dogs."

He laughed and responded, "You don't know dogs until you live in Nicaragua."

He said it with such conviction, I knew at that moment that this guy could tell me a lot in a short time. By the time we had that small verbal exchange, I could see the San Lupe approaching on the left and the Café Teais on the right. I stopped in front of the café, and he got out, thanked me, and said, "I hope you find what you are looking for, but I must tell you, change is coming to Nicaragua, and it is for the best."

As I pulled around to the back of the San Lupe, I couldn't help but think that he might be one of those in-volved in whatever was going on up in that mountain. Once inside my room, I had two things on my mind: a hot shower and a good, long nap. After the shower, I came back and stretched out on the bed. The rain beating endlessly on the roof told me that sleep was not far away. I remembered thinking, *When you get up, you need to unpack that big suitcase and get everything you will need for tomorrow's trip to the lake.*

In just a few minutes I was sleeping like a baby—full, comfortable, and warm. I must have slept about two hours when my eyes popped open, and I felt fresh and relaxed. I got up, dressed, and stared at the suitcase. I decided I might as well get started. The first thing I got out was a small sports bag to carry the things I would need. The camera came out next, along with that old zoom lens that I'd had for years. Then a small knife that I had bought for Rye but had had to put up because he'd cut his finger with it. The next thing I took out was a quart bottle of Patrón Tequila.

I shrugged and put it in the sports bag as well. Liquor can bring out the bad from the good as well as bring out good from the bad, so I reasoned it might come in handy.

I caught a whiff of that strong coffee I was beginning to acquire a taste for and thought that maybe I just needed to stroll over to Café Teais to get me a cup and check the place out. I pulled on a light windbreaker and casually walked across the street and inside the café. It was a small building with a counter and several tables. I walked up to the bar, and a plump lady behind the counter looked at me as if to say "What do you want?" I pointed to one of the coffee canisters and said, "Coffee." She brought me a cup that was steaming, and the smell was just right. *Why can't we get coffee in the States that smells this good?*

I glanced around the room. The place was about half full. It appeared to be mostly locals. At one table there did appear to be a man and woman who were probably tourists. At another table, two guys were talking loudly. They had British accents, and I assumed they were working in Nicaragua, perhaps with one of the major oil companies. In the very back corner were three men who were talking very low. They almost seemed to be whispering. I immediately noticed that the one with his back to me was the guy I had given a ride to that afternoon. I slowly sipped my coffee and decided I would not make conversation with anybody. I got a cup to go and headed back to the room with only one thing on my mind: call Madonna.

I dialed the phone, thinking, *Thank God for cell phones.* As it started ringing, I anticipated hearing Madonna's voice.

"Dede, where are you at?" Rye sounded excited. "How many more days till you get home? Nonna will not let me do anything. She won't put the Jet Ski in the water, she won't let me go hunting, and she won't do nothing."

"Boy, am I going to have to pull your ears when I get home?"

He laughed and said, "Just come on home."

It pulled at my heartstrings. "I will be home in a few days, and we are going to do a bunch of stuff. I'm also going to bring you a machete like they use over here in the real jungle."

"Nonna, Dede is bringing me a machete! A real one! Bye, Dee. Here is Nonna. I love you."

She sounded a little stressed, and the first thing she said was, "Are you alright? I have been worried sick."

I replied as convincingly as I could, "Everything is fine. I hope to be headed home in about five or six days. How are you doing?"

"Well, Penny had to take Lela to a softball tournament, and Rye came to stay with me. He is into everything. He has been pretty good, but he misses his Dede. When you get home, we are going to slow down and take a vacation." She sighed apprehensively before adding, "Rye got into trouble."

"What did he do?"

"He had one of those BB pistols in the house. He was playing with it and it went off and chipped a corner of the sheetrock. I took the gun away from him and put it up. Leroy, I am not going to let him have any more guns in the house."

"Put that boy on the phone."

When Rye got on the phone, I could sense he knew what was coming. I pounced on him pretty hard. "Boy, you know I have taught you better than that. You will not handle those guns until you can remember all that I have taught you. Do you understand?"

There was a pause, and then he said, "Yes, Dee."

I didn't let up. "What if you had shot Nonna? You could have put her eye out. Do you understand? Maybe you are not as responsible as I thought. We'll talk about it some more when I get home."

I waited for Rye's response. Finally, he said, "Dee, I won't do it anymore."

Madonna got back on the phone, and I said, "You know, out of all the women in the world, I am so happy that I found you, worry wart. I will try and call you in the next couple of days. By then I should know when I will be home."

I didn't sleep all that well that night. I was more preoccupied than usual with what awaited the next day.

The next morning I got out of bed and took a shower. As I was getting dressed I slowly went over everything that was in my sports bags to see if I could think of something else I might need. As soon as I stepped outside, I was greeted by a warm rain. I headed to the Café Teais for breakfast with one thought in mind, *Hungry.*

I stepped inside to find the place mostly deserted. The same lady that I had seen in there before was behind the counter, and I wondered if she ever got off from work. I ordered eggs and sausage, realizing the sausage probably wasn't U.S. Grade A, but I didn't care. I just wanted to eat. The coffee was just what I needed, and I began to feel like I was truly awake and alive. I didn't feel like having any conversation this morning, and it was just as well since the few people in the place apparently felt the same. As I paid, the lady looked at me with a bit of apprehension, as though she was beginning to wonder why I was even there.

I smiled a big warm smile and said, "Good day."

Once back in the room, I tried to think of anything except what I was getting ready to do. I pictured Madonna at home, sleeping late like she always does. I thought about Lela buzzing around getting ready for school and making sure she had everything just perfect. I thought about Rye just getting up, jumping into his school clothes, and charging out the door like a little bull.

It all came back to Manny, the lake, and that mountain. I knew that whatever happened, it was about getting into and off of that mountain in one piece and with the knowledge of what was going on up there. I got the .38 out and loaded it, placing it securely in the holster and strapping it across my shoulder. I then put on my light windbreaker to see if the gun was concealed enough. I kept looking at the clock, and it did not seem to be working. It was. I was just ready to go, and it was only a quarter to nine. I still had an hour before I needed to leave.

I just paced around the room like a caged animal. I always did have an abundance of nervous energy. I started laughing at that thought. *You think you've got nervous energy.*

What about Rye and his poor teachers at school? I would bet they have never seen a kid with that much energy. I decided to go out to the car and load my bag and check out that fishing gear that Manny had given me yesterday. It all seemed to be pretty typical. A few different lures than what I was used to, but I expected as much. Manny hadn't told me what I might catch in that lake, but perhaps that was by design.

I had a few minutes to kill, so I walked up to the front desk to grab a cup of that fresh coffee. As I walked in, I noticed an older gentleman behind the desk. He had a well-manicured mustache and appeared to be about my age.

The man looked up and grinned as he said, "Good morning, Señor. Welcome to the San Lupe." I nodded my head and thought this guy was a pretty engaging fellow. "May I help you?" he asked.

"No, I just want to get a cup of your good coffee."

He pointed to the desk where it was displayed. As I started to walk by him, I suddenly stopped. His name tag said "Castillo." How could I have forgotten? This was the guy Wango had told me about that knew everybody in Rivas.

I went ahead and poured me a cup and then turned around to address him. "Sir, did you ever know a guy by the name of Bill Parker?"

His face lit up. "Señor, are you a friend of Bill Parker's?"

"I sure am, and Bill told me if I came to Rivas to stay at the San Lupe, look you up, and be sure to tell you he said hello."

"Ah, they don't make them any better than Bill Parker," said Castillo. "He was here several times, and he was always doing things to help my country. Is Bill still with the IMF?"

"No, Bill is now serving in the U.S. Congress and doing quite well. Heck, he's even a grandfather and getting old like the rest of us." Something clicked. It was the right place and the right time. "Castillo, I need to ask you something."

"Please," he interrupted me, "call me 'Manny,' and any friend of Bill's is a friend of mine."

Two Mannys. What a coincidence. Must be a common name in this country. "I'm trying to find out what's going on around here. You seem to have had some trouble in the last few months."

His brow wrinkled, and I could see the wheels spinning. "Yes, we have our troubles. There is a group of thugs who attacked our police station and killed some of our finest. I don't think it will stop there. I am beginning to believe that it was just a probing attack and something bigger is about to happen. Are you with your government?"

"No, I am just here to help a friend," I replied. "Manny Diaz and I were in the Army together, and he asked me to come see if I could figure out what the rebels were up too."

About that time the door opened and a young man and woman came in and headed towards the coffee pot. Castillo motioned with his eyes as if to say "We will continue this later."

"Thank you," I said. As I headed toward the door, I knew I had found somebody I could depend on if I needed help.

As soon as I walked out I noticed the rain had stopped, and there were quite a few patches of blue sky. Blue sky always seemed to lift my spirits instantly. I glanced at my watch and realized I needed to get a move on. I always hated to be late for anything I was doing.

I cranked up and pulled out of the parking lot to head to the lake. I made it to the southernmost point where there was barely enough room for me to get my car off the road, but it was out of the way. Now, to pretend to be a lost tourist who was there to enjoy some of the local fishing? I knew that would not be a problem for me, because I was good at acting like a novice.

Once I had my camera and gear out of the car, I proceeded to zoom in on the lake and take some pictures before I started fishing. It was still a little bit nippy, so the jacket I had on felt very comfortable. I could tell this place has abundant fish life, and I wondered why nobody was fishing this morning. It occurred to me that when people had an abundance of certain things they didn't seem to enjoy what they had been given. After a few casts and changing lures a couple of times, I caught a nice fish. It put up a pretty good fight, and once I had it on land, I took a few pictures and released it back into the beautiful place from which it came.

I turned and began to survey the mountains with interest and raised my camera to shoot a few pictures. As I zoomed in, I caught some movement about eighty feet up, and as I panned back, I could see the figure of a man with a camouflage hat standing beside a tall tree. I could not make out much, except that he was staring straight at me.

I continued to scan the mountain, and I snapped several more photos before I headed back and began to move towards the north end of the lake. I kept this up for a couple of hours, and it seemed every time I turned to take pictures of the mountain that the figure of the man was looking at me.

I caught a few more fish, and each time I carefully photographed each one and released them. As I got closer to Manny, I was amazed that he never even glanced in my direction. It was as if he was alone and this whole lake was his. When I got within fifty feet of him, I continued to cast and work the water before me. I never looked at Manny, but I did talk out loud. "Manny, we got company. I caught some fish but didn't keep any, and I got some nice pictures for you. Come by after you go to the café tonight and I'll show you the pictures."

Finally I heard Manny gathering up his stuff, and he went straight to his car and left. Well, now I had the lake in front of me and my new buddy up in the mountain behind. For some reason, I did not like that feeling too much. After a while, it became apparent that this guy was not going to come out, so I gathered up my stuff and headed back to Rivas.

As I passed Manny's house, I observed how peaceful the place looked. I bet Manny was out back cleaning fish and fussing at me because I did not string up the ones I caught. I kept on going and soon pulled into the San Lupe. I went to the room and stored all the stuff and was beginning to think about what I had observed at the lake that morning.

A couple of times I had seen a wisp of smoke clearing the trees up in the mountain. If I had to guess, I would say that is where the thugs had made their camp.

Suddenly there was a slight knock on the door. Manny wasn't supposed to arrive until later. I pulled on the jacket to cover the .38 and opened the door. It was Mr. Castillo.

"Do you have a few minutes to talk?" he asked as he stepped inside.

"Sit down and make yourself at home. I'm glad you came by. I got some questions for you. Yesterday as I was coming back from Manny's, I picked up this guy who was walking in the rain. He had a bad scar on the side of his face. Tall and slim. Do you know him?"

Castillo said, "His name is Petey."

"What do you know about him?"

"The story of his scar goes back years ago when he was bad to drink, and his wife caught him in a compromising position and attacked him and the young lady with a knife. The young lady got away, but Petey got cut on the face. Some say he got cut below the belt as well. That she almost sliced it off." He paused for a moment before continuing. "I would understand if you feel suspicious of him. My concern is that Petey, for all of his unassuming ways, is involved with the rebels. For the last few years he's been occasionally disappearing for several days at a time."

"Do you think Petey is the leader?"

"No way. I would bet it is this guy who never shows his face in town and has lived off the land for years. His name is Comacho, and he is dangerous, so if you should cross paths with that guy, you need to realize he is a killer. Petey is more of a facilitator. I have come to believe that Petey is Comacho's eyes and ears in this town. A lot of people believe that Petey is harmless enough, but I don't trust him any further than I can throw him."

"Well, Castillo, I will tell you that I am going to cover that mountain, and I intend to find out what is going on for my friend Manny."

Castillo looked at me intently and said, "May God bless you, my son."

His words did nothing to soothe my nervous energy, but I could tell from his eyes that he too desperately wanted to know what was going on in the mountain. He reiterated what he had told me that morning. That he thought the attack on the police station was a probe for a more significant strike that harbored nothing but trouble for the people of Rivas.

I went for dinner at Café Teais as usual. It was good, and the place was about half full. I noticed that Petey was not in there, but the two guys I had seen him talking to were at the table in the back where I had seen them before. As I left the café a little bit later, I decided to stroll down the streets and do a little window shopping.

I came across what appeared to be a hardware store. In the window was a machete that had Rye's name written all over it. The sheath was leather with some intricate carving that looked like it had been done by a true craftsman. I couldn't believe the price. I decided not to haggle. I just knew I was going to get it and take it home for him.

Once I purchased it, I looked around for something for Lela, but I didn't see anything I thought she would like. The lady who was working the store was polite but seemed to be watching me intently. I laughed to myself. She was probably confused as to why I hadn't argued with her about the price of the machete. I left the store and walked a little further before deciding to head back to the San Lupe. I was terrible at shopping, and I knew it.

Once back in the room, I showered and watched some television. As I listened to the people on TV speaking to each other in rapid Spanish, I censured myself for coming all the way here without brushing up on the language. Typical. I didn't get much of what they were saying, but when they laughed, I laughed. I was beginning to get sleepy when I heard a knock on the door. It had to be Manny.

He stepped inside and said, "How many did you catch and why didn't you keep them?" Then he laughed and added, "Did you see anything important today?"

"Well, yes and no," I replied. "It was such a beautiful place, between picture-taking and fishing, I had trouble focusing on anything else." I observed Manny's face and saw disappointment. "One thing that I did notice as I worked my way down toward you, was that I was being observed by someone up on the mountain. Every time I turned to take a picture, as I zoomed in, I could see someone staring at me. They made no serious effort to hide, although whoever it was had on a camouflage jacket and hat. It seemed the closer I got to you, the further they descended the mountain, as if they were trying to get a better look."

"Okay," said Manny, "that is what I had hoped for. Now here is what I think we need to do tomorrow. I will take the tunnel and watch you from my viewpoint, as I told you the other day. If someone comes down to talk to you, I will have your back, but don't go up the mountain with them, regardless of what they say to you. Just feel them out and get any information you can obtain."

I looked at Manny and said, "Do you know a guy named Petey?"

He looked shocked. "How did you meet Petey?"

I told Manny about giving Petey a ride into town, and that Castillo had been to my room and filled me in on what he thought.

Manny laughed in disbelief. "You never waste time, Laroy. You have a knack for being in the right place at the right time. Petey is one of them; he has to be. I have observed that mountain from my viewpoint for months, and Petey is the one who comes and goes from the mountain most often. Castillo is a guy you can trust, and I value everything he says. He has been around this place for years. I never got too close to Castillo, because I sometimes think he may have thought that I might be a rebel since I left this country and returned years later. In fact, Castillo once asked me if I ever regretted immigrating to America." He shook his head. "I better leave now. You be careful tomorrow, Laroy. I will be watching."

CHAPTER 10

At a quarter till nine the next morning, I was ready with my sports bag packed and the .38 secure in the holster. I departed the San Lupe. As I passed Manny's house, I began watching the right side of the road to see if I could detect the spot where Manny would be. I should have known I wouldn't be able to as Manny could hide better than anyone I knew. As I got to the lake, I was concerned that a lot of people might be fishing today. The weather was absolutely gorgeous.

To my surprise not a single car or person was in sight. I went down to the south end and parked where I had the day before and got my gear out of the car. I caught a bunch of fish, probably about fifteen. I photographed and released each one just as I had done the day before. As I slowly worked my way down the lake, I thought that it had to be the most peaceful and beautiful place on Earth. I was startled when I heard someone approaching me from behind, as they were almost upon me. I turned around and saw Petey walking straight up to me.

"Yankee, are you here to fish or cut bait?"

I thought his question odd, so I just smiled and said, "I have a fishing addiction. I just love to catch them, but I never eat them."

The look of disdain on his face told me he thought I was crazy. It was noon. I reached down into my sports bags and pulled out a bottle of Patrón, cracked the seal, and took a big sip. I looked at Petey. He seemed startled as I handed him the bottle.

Petey laughed and said, "Yankee, you surprise me."

Calmly, I said, "My name is Leroy. What's yours?"

"Petey."

"How on earth did you get a name like Petey in Nicaragua?" I asked.

"None of your business, Yankee. Just none of your business."

I laughed, took another sip, and again offered the tequila to Petey, who, to my surprise, knocked a big hole in the contents of the bottle. Maybe I could talk to this guy after all.

"Why are you here, Yankee? Uh, I mean, Laroy. We don't have tourists that come to this lake and fish very often."

I looked Petey straight in the eye and said, "I told you the other day, I am looking for a place to make my home, as I no longer consider the U.S. to be my country."

Petey took another swig from the Patrón and said, "You think Petey is a fool, don't you, Laroy?"

"I don't know why, but I am going to level with you. Have you ever heard of NEXRAD?"

Petey shook his head, and I continued, "It is the company that I work for in the U.S. It stands for Northeastern Exploration and Resource Acquisition and Development. What we do is buy and develop mineral rights and oil exploration rights in foreign countries. I was sent here to seek out a possible working relationship with any group that we might be able to do business with since we have not been able to do business with the people in power in Managua. It occurred to us that Nicaragua is on the brink of a power struggle, and we are intent on getting in on the ground floor, even if it involves helping the rebels. We have been successful in Syria, Libya, and Iraq in the last few years, and we want to continue that success in Central America at all costs."

I took the bottle out of Petey's hand and took a swig as if to say "I am one of you." Petey looked puzzled as if I had said too much too fast. I don't think it all registered, but I could see the wheels turning. The Patrón appeared to have had the desired effect, so I pounced, "I hear the rebels are about to take over this country, but they need equipment and money."

Petey glared at me and said, "How do I know I can trust you?"

"Look, I don't know if you even understand what I just told you. I don't know if you even know the rebels, but money and equipment are what I can provide. In return, I need to know if we would get the oil and mineral rights if we were successful."

A light went off in Petey's head. "You know, a lot of people have come out here and fished this lake and never been seen or heard from again."

I nodded my head yes and said, "Those people offer nothing. They have nothing to give and are only here for their own enjoyment."

"Okay, Yankee, you come back tomorrow, and if I come down, I will take you up in the mountain. If I don't come down, you must leave this lake and never return." With that, Petey turned around and walked away, taking what was left of the Patrón with him.

I breathed and thought maybe, just maybe, I was on the right track. I made myself stay and fish for another thirty minutes, as if I was trying to convince myself that I was not in any hurry to leave.

I gathered up my gear and walked back to the car and thought maybe I would get out of here after all. As I turned around and headed north towards Rivas, I glance at that mountain, and it looked so peaceful, so serene, I just could not imagine what lay waiting for me if I got the chance to actually go up and encounter its occupants. I began to speed up. All of a sudden I felt dirty and in severe need of a shower. Just talking to Petey had made me feel dirty. I shuddered as the memory of sharing the bottle of Patrón with him crossed my mind. That old rationale kicked in to make me laugh: "tequila kills all germs."

As I passed Manny's house, I wondered what he must have been thinking as he observed from his viewpoint. I also would have loved to have known what Petey thought, and if he had gone straight back and told them everything I had said to him. I guess I would know soon enough tomorrow. I just wanted to call Madonna and talk, but I knew I couldn't. She would be able to detect that I was worried. I went to the front desk and poured a large cup of coffee. I wondered where Castillo was. I said, "Gracias," to the young man at the desk and headed toward my room for a long, hot shower.

After a shower and feeling half-way clean, I decided to grab a late lunch at the café. The café was almost deserted. Only a couple of guys were there. I immediately heard their accents and realized that it was the two guys I had assumed were from England. As I ordered, I noticed that they were talking in hushed tones.

The food was excellent, but my mind was on many other things. I thought about talking to the English chaps, but something told me to decline. I did look over and notice a patch on the sleeve of one of the guys. It said "RAF." Maybe he was a pilot. It stuck out to me for some reason. After eating, I paid my bill and left the plump lady a good tip, and she even smiled at me. I thought, *Man, if I can make her smile, I can do anything.* Not wanting to push my luck, I decided to leave well enough alone.

Once I got back to the room with a full stomach, I crashed. One thing I had always been able to do was sleep and think at the same time. I never dreamed, but I could run different scenarios through my mind and even evaluate and make some of my better decisions while I slept. I would often wake up and move forward with the conclusion I had reached. I was jarred out of my sleep by a loud knock on the door, and I saw it was 10:15 PM already. I had slept a lot longer than I meant too.

It was Manny. As he came in, he looked worried. "What went on with Petey? Did he tell you anything?"

"Slow down, Manny. It actually went pretty good I think. I told him I was with NEXRAD and that we were there to help the rebels with cash and material in exchange for the rights to minerals and oil if they were successful in getting hold of power."

Manny smiled and said, "What the heck is NEXRAD?"

I looked at him incredulously and said, "Why, it's Northeastern Exploration and Resource Acquisition and Development. You mean you have never heard of NEXRAD?"

I thought Manny was going to choke, he was laughing so hard. "Well, did Petey buy it?"

"He sure did, but it cost me a quart of Patrón."

"You beat anything I have ever seen. You could sell anything to anybody at any time without breaking a sweat. I sure as heck am glad you came down to help me, old friend. I would never get to first base with these people. Now the real work begins. What do you have planned for tomorrow?"

"Petey said if he came down to get me tomorrow, he would take me up to see the people I needed to see. Manny, if he doesn't show then, the stakes become much more difficult. If he comes out tomorrow, I will feel better about this deal, but if he doesn't show, I don't know…" my voice trailed off.

"What do you think the odds are that Petey will show?"

"I think it's probably better than fifty/fifty. Look, Petey said they need equipment and money, so what have they got to lose?"

Manny nodded. "So from that, you can see they are going to attempt to overthrow the government?"

"I would bet you they are going to attempt something one way or the other. It is not a matter of if, but when."

"I will be at my lookout. If Petey shows and you start up the mountain, hold up your right hand as if you are scratching your head. That will let me know you feel halfway comfortable. If you don't, I will try to work my way up the mountain and stay as close as I can." He waited as I nodded in affirmation, and then went on, "Be careful. I have seen you talk your way out of some tough situations, and that is what you will probably have to do tomorrow."

I laughed, "You really know how to comfort a fellow, Manny." There was nothing else to discuss, and there was nothing else to do. It was time to do what had to be done.

As Manny left, he stopped at the door and looked back. Grinning, he said, "NEXRAD. That is pretty good, Laroy."

I got up early the next morning, showered, and was ready to go by 7:00. I gathered up my jacket and closed the door behind me. No need to take the bag, as I would have almost guaranteed that my trusty old camera would be busted up if it went into the mountains. As I pulled out of the parking lot, I caught something out of the corner of my eye. It was Castillo waving his arms frantically.

I stopped, and he approached the car. "Mr. Overstreet, you be careful out there today. I brought you a thermos full of coffee."

I smiled at him and said, "Thank you. It is going to be a good day." I couldn't help but laugh. So much for not calling attention to myself.

As I passed by Manny's house, I kept thinking about those sausages and biscuits that Melinda made. I would have loved to have had one with the coffee. I thought about parking at the pull off about midways of the lake, but I decided against it and went to the far end where I had parked previously.

I got out of the car and got the rod and reels and cast a few, almost hoping I would not catch anything. I looked around a few times toward the mountain and saw no movement. Finally, I just set the rod down and started looking around as if I was bored. It did occur to me that Petey might not show, but I was still confident he would. After about another fifteen minutes, which passed by slowly, I began to get a little nervous. I was about to walk on down toward the north end of the lake, when Petey popped out of the woods and crossed the road towards me.

As soon as he approached, the first thing out of his mouth caught me off guard. "Yankee, you got any more of that tequila?" I apologized profusely, but Petey only laughed and said, "Let's go up. You better be good, because I had to do some talking to get you up to see Comacho."

Castillo had been right, it was Comacho. The only thing I could think of was what Castillo had said about Comacho. *"He is a killer."* As I crossed the road, I slowed a bit and raised my right hand to scratch the side of my head.

Petey looked back and said, "What's wrong, Yankee? Did you get some of those bed bugs at the San Lupe?"

I tried to laugh, but it wasn't real, because standing just inside the woods was another man, and he looked a whole lot more dangerous than Petey. As we entered the woods at the base of the mountain, we walked up to the guy, and Petey said, "Yankee, this is Elvio, a good rebel. He is going to take us up the mountain in case you have trouble climbing."

Elvio stepped up to me and started to frisk me for a weapon. He stared straight into my face with enough hate to last most people a lifetime. The first thing he did was remove the .38 from my shoulder holster and empty the shells on the ground, and then he placed it in his vest. He never quit looking at me as if he could kill me on the spot.

Petey said, "Okay, Yankee. Let's climb."

The climb up was worse on Petey than me. I began to think that maybe all that climbing up bluffs with Rye was good training. I could tell that this mountain had been fixed to aid people who climbed it. In areas where the rocks were pretty much vertical, rope ladders had been hung, and you could scale that as easy as climbing a ladder. The other places had enough trees that one could grab on and feel pretty safe as the incline of the rocks was not that difficult.

At one point, Petey said, "Let's stop for a minute." It was apparent that he was getting winded.

I turned to look down at the lake. This was probably the most beautiful place I had ever been too. I decided I would love to have a cabin on the exact spot I was standing on. At that moment, I noticed Elvio looking at the .38 he had taken from me. One thing that stood out about Elvio was his shirt. It was an ugly black shirt that had "Managua" in dark blue letters on the front. I started to ask him if he was from Managua but quickly decided against it.

Petey was rested enough and ready to continue our climb. We had already gotten about one hundred and fifty feet above the lake, and it seemed like nothing existed in that first leg except a few lizards and snakes. As I looked forward, I thought I could see a clearing, but I couldn't tell for sure from my vantage point.

When we got closer, I found it was indeed a clearing. It plateaued into a pretty level spot that was about ninety feet deep till you hit the back, and then it went vertical about one hundred feet. There in the center was an opening to a cave. The opening was about twelve feet high and ten feet wide. As we climbed over and stood, I looked on in disbelief. About ten or twelve little shacks were spread out on the plateau. The area stretched to about two hundred feet wide.

About six men came running over to get a good look at me. These were hungry men, and they looked like men who had been hardened by life on the mountain. Elvio seemed to be in charge, as he barked some orders at the guys and they all reacted. Soon we had some coffee and wild boar with some flatbread. Several stumps were used to sit on and were placed all around the plateau. I noticed that nobody seemed to be concerned about anything, and the mood was relaxed. A dog was chained by a hut closest to the edge of the plateau.

There were very few weapons on display. A couple of the guys were toting some old AK-47s and most had pistols strapped on their sides. I strained to look inside the huts but could not see any weapons. I noticed as a few more men exited the cave. I was trying to keep a head count, and I was up to about fourteen different guys so far. There did not appear to be any women or kids in the camp.

After Elvio ate, he got up and motioned to one of the men. He pointed at me then gave him some directions that I could not understand. Elvio then proceeded to enter the cave. I looked at Petey and wondered how this guy got involved with this bunch. He seemed relaxed and comfortable in his surroundings. After about ten minutes, Elvio came walking out of the cave with an older, balding guy, who had what appeared to be a German shepherd at his side. The dog was more ferocious looking than the man, and I was glad the dog was on a leash. They approached me, and as I prepared to stand, the guy behind me shoved me back down. I did not move. I just watched them approach while keeping one eye on the dog.

Comacho stopped right in front of me, and, with a high-pitched voice, he said, "Who are you? Why should

I not just turn this dog loose on you and watch him tear you limb from limb? My men like that kind of entertainment."

I started to speak, and Comacho bellowed, "Shut up! We know your kind, and you are not to be trusted. You better speak the truth and speak it quickly if you want to get off this mountain alive. Petey has told us what you say you can do, but we don't know if you can deliver, and you could be a plant by the government. So, measure your words wisely if you want to live, and get to the point."

I looked him straight in the eye without blinking. "I'm here to make a deal on behalf of **NEXRAD** and to feather my own nest. It will give you what you need to acquire the power you so desperately want, and in return, we get to help you develop the resources that your country has, to the benefit of all. If I were a plant, do you think I would have walked in here by myself? I am also looking for a place to call home. America is not my home any longer. The people are weak, spoiled, and couldn't fight their way out of a wet paper bag. America is doomed to fail. If we can strike a deal, I will be living right here in Rivas. I will advise you and assist you in any way possible. I am the only one who can make this happen for you and your men, but trust cuts both ways, Comacho."

As soon as I spoke his name, his mouth dropped open. His grip on the dog's leash seemed to loosen slightly. "Who told you my name, you damn Yankee? Who told you my name?" His nose was about six inches from my face, and his eyes were as red as a beet.

"We have our sources, sir, and my company would not send me into this place without extensive research. We know that you are planning an attack to take over the town of Rivas and use it as a springboard to take over the entire country of Nicaragua. We also know that you are desperate for money to acquire more weapons and ammunition. You, sir, are lightly armed, and we can provide the money to get the resources you need. We also know that once you take down Rivas, other rebels from Managua are prepared to join you and swell your numbers. However, you are going to need intelligence as to what the government forces are up to, their movements, and if they intend to attack you. We can provide this."

I stopped to breathe. I was afraid I had talked too fast, but old southern boys speak slowly, even when we speak fast.

It seemed to register. Comacho looked at Elvio and then turned and headed toward the cave. As they went inside, I wondered if they had bought it or if I was fixing to die on that mountain. The other guys seem to relax, and as they milled around, I noticed one of them drop off the side of the plateau. He had a camouflage coat and hat on. He must be the "lookout" I saw the other day. Some of the guys were cleaning their guns while laughing and talking. The laughter mostly seemed to occur whenever one of them pointed at me and made some comment. Man, I wished I had studied Spanish.

The time passed slowly. I wondered what was taking so long. It stretched past lunch, and then finally, some guy came out of the cave with a bowl of rice and meat. It was pretty tasty, but then again I was hungry. I began to think I had a pretty good count of the men, and I was almost sure that, counting Petey, there were twenty-two total. Not exactly a standing Army but enough to overwhelm the small Rivas police force, which was even less heavily armed.

It was just taking too long, and I wondered about Manny. I hoped he was not trying to climb the mountain to get closer to the action, but it would not have bothered me if he was close enough to help if this deal went bad.

After another twenty or thirty minutes, Comacho and Elvio appeared out of the cave, thankfully without the dog. Comacho walked up to me and said, "Yankee, I have survived all these years by trusting my gut. I am going to take your deal, but how does it come down, and what assurance do I have that you will live up to it?"

It was the opening I needed. "Good. The first thing we need to do is establish if I get the cash in your hands, can you acquire the weapons and ammo you need?"

Comacho smiled and said, "That is no problem. Our good friends from England will gladly supply us weapons for cash."

It hit me. The two guys in Café Teais that I had thought were pilots were actually weapons dealers. I had miscalculated them badly. They were Petey's connection.

"Okay, ten days from now, a person will appear at the lake at noon. Have Petey go down and meet him. He will have a suitcase with 100,000 U.S. dollars in it. When Petey approaches, the driver will set the suitcase down, get back into his car, and leave. You will have twenty days to acquire your armaments and prepare for the attack. Is that enough time for you to get it together?"

Comacho looked at Petey, and when Petey nodded his head, Comacho said, "Agreed."

"In the case will be a name and number. You are to call that number and let them know you received the cash, and you will tell them the exact day that you will take the town. After you have taken Rivas, you are to call the number again, and you will be given instructions as to what to expect from the government. That is the only time you are to call this number. The person you will speak to is named Corrina. She will help you, and she is to be completely trusted."

Comacho sneered and said, "Why should I trust a woman?"

I stared intently into his eyes and said, "Because your life and the lives of your men depend on it. She is in good graces with this government. She's well-connected and in our employ. One word of caution: if this whole thing falls apart and you fail to deliver, she will expose your plot, your location, and everything about you if you don't make the call when you get the money. Believe me. The government will hunt you down like pigs and kill you all if you don't abide by the terms of our agreement."

I stuck out my hand to seal the deal. Comacho looked at me for a few seconds and then grasped my hand firmly. "Yankee, it looks like we have a deal."

"I will see you again, Comacho, and I wish you the best. I look forward to building me a small cabin right here on this plateau within six months, while you, sir, may reside in the finest palace this country has to offer."

To my surprise, he nodded his head and then abruptly said to Petey, "See he gets down the mountain safely, and go into town and see if you can get your hands on some of that tequila you had yesterday. Tonight, we party. Tomorrow we prepare to fight."

Elvio walked up and returned my pistol; he kept the bullets. I felt a sense of relief. I almost felt as if I had this all in hand, but now I had to deliver.

CHAPTER 11

The trip down the mountain was uneventful, and when we cleared the woods at the bottom, Petey stopped and said, "Leroy, you are either the smartest man I have ever met or the dumbest jackass on this planet."

I laughed and said, "Which one do you think it is, Petey?"

He just shook his head. "I know full well they don't have Patrón in Rivas, so how can I deliver for Comacho?"

I thought for a minute. "Tell Comacho that when the money comes, we will have six bottles of Patrón in the suitcase. Tell him that was your idea since you knew you couldn't get it in Rivas."

"Ah, Yankee, I guess I would have to say you are the smartest."

"Come on, Petey, and I will give you a ride into town."

As we crossed the road towards the car, I stroked my head with my right arm vigorously to let Manny know it was good. As I pulled into Rivas, Petey said, "Let me out at the café. I want to get some real food."

I figured he wanted to go in and see if his buddies from England were in there. I mumbled, "The food was good, but I need to start making plans. I have to move quickly to get the money back to the lake on time."

Petey got out and said, "You take care, Yankee."

"You too, Petey," I said. I felt kind of sad, because I knew I would never see him again.

I was elated that I had gotten down off that mountain in one piece, but even more importantly, in just a few days I would be headed home. Back to Bluff Shores, my pier, and my old Gray Heron that fished across the creek from me while I sipped my coffee in the morning. I went back to my room and turned on the shower. As the water warmed, I noticed the machete that I had bought Rye. I picked it up and looked at it, making a note to get something for Lela when I got back to Managua. I jumped in the shower and scrubbed hard as if I was trying to scrub Comacho, Elvio, Petey, and the rest from my soul.

I was tired, but I managed to pack before I crashed. I would head to Managua first thing in the morning and complete the best part of my plan. I knew Manny would be coming by perhaps a little bit earlier tonight, and I was looking forward to telling him about everything that had transpired that day. It didn't take long before I was sleeping. It had started to rain. It sounded as though it was raining harder than it had been for my entire trip. It sure made for peaceful sleep.

I woke up hungry and dressed to head over to the café. I thought to call Madonna and let her know I should be home in two or three days and that everything seemed to be working out just fine. It rang, and after several rings the answering machine came on. I listened to my own recorded voice as the machine implored me to leave a name and number. I needed to fix that message; I sounded like I was standing on a hill with a megaphone. I assumed that Madonna had gone out to eat with some of her friends or perhaps even to shop.

"Hey there, bunny rabbit. I should be home in two or three days, and I guess you better rest up. I'll call you tomorrow when I get settled in Managua. You sleep tight and see you soon."

There was a pretty good crowd in the café, so I just grabbed a seat at the bar and ordered a plate of steak fajitas. As they were cooking, I looked around the place to see if Petey was in there. He was not. I figured he was already back on the mountain and that he and the guys were into the tequila. To my surprise, Manny was seated in the back corner and devouring a plate of rice and beans. He never looked up. The two British guys were there, and they were being kind of loud. I wondered if they knew they had made a sale. I finished and then paid the plump lady with a smile and another large tip. I headed back to the room to wait on Manny. It wouldn't be long.

Manny knocked before I got settled in good, and as I opened the door he bounded in and gave me a big hug. "I knew you could pull it off if anybody could! I want you to tell me everything you saw and exactly what all was said."

Manny reached into his pocket and pulled out a flask, which I knew was probably his private stock of Jack Daniel's. As he poured a couple of glasses about half full, he said, "Man, I was getting worried about you. I was so happy to finally see you come out of those woods, I had to bite my fingers to keep from letting out a big war whoop." As Manny grabbed a seat he said, "Now, tell me. Tell me from the beginning."

I described our climb up the mountain, told him about Elvio, and explained what I saw when we reached the plateau. "Manny, have you ever been up that mountain?"

Manny shook his head. "My dad would never let me go up there. He told me about the cave, and I figured if there was a group up there, that was where they were holed up. How many of them are there, Laroy?"

"Well, I got a good count, and I am pretty sure the exact number is twenty-two. They are lightly armed, but they all seem to be capable physically, except for Petey. They all seem to have the personality for death and destruction, and I would say based on what I saw that they are clearly dangerous."

"Okay, so now what is the plan?"

"Before I tell you, I want your promise that you will ride this one out and not get yourself killed." Manny looked at me, and I knew he understood that I meant every word of it.

"You got it, Laroy. I'm getting too old anyway."

"Manny, if this plan falls into place like I think it will, forty days from today they are going to come down from the mountain, take over Rivas, and declare martial law.

As that happens, a group from Managua is going to start towards Rivas to join them. They think the numbers are sufficient to repel an attack by the government. They also believe that as the word spreads, others will join their cause and that they will soon have an army big enough to defeat the government and take power."

Manny seemed somewhat dazed and looked at me as if he couldn't believe what he was hearing. "How do we stop this?"

"I'll get to that, but one thing we need to think about is how to protect as many of the people in town without alarming them about what is fixing to happen, and that is what you are tasked with doing. I think you should seek out Castillo to help. Here is how I set this up: in about ten days a man is going to show up at the lake at noon with $100,000 in a suitcase. Petey is to come out of the woods, and as he gets close, the guy will place the suitcase on the ground and drive away. I want you to be at your viewpoint and verify that this transaction takes place. That gives them twenty days to secure the munitions they need. It will give them nine more days to prepare, and on the tenth day, they will attack Rivas." I told him about the part Leanna would play and that she would be working under the name "Corrina." I explained that the phone number in the case would contact her, and the rebels would call to confirm the attack. "That is where the plan will go off track. They will never get a chance to make a second call, because they will all be dead."

Manny sat his glass of Jack, on the table and said, "What have you planned?"

"I have to move pretty fast. I am leaving in the morning and going to Managua to make the necessary arrangements for the money to be at the lake in ten days, per my agreement. They think it is being sent from NEXRAD."

Manny almost choked on his drink. "You got to be kidding me. You mean you sold them on good old NEXRAD?"

I nodded. "Yep, it worked, but here is some information I need to set their death trap. Do you know how they attacked the police station? I mean how they came into town?"

"I know exactly how they did it," he said excitedly. "I spent a couple of days up in the hills around Rivas, looking for how they came into town. It was pretty easy to figure out about. Five or six came in from the west side of town, while the same number came in from the east side. They had plenty of cover and were on top of the police station before the guys knew what hit them. From what I could tell, Stephan put up a terrific fight." Manny's voice trailed off as he said, "There was just too many of them..."

"The trick is going to be to have enough government soldiers ready and waiting for them as they enter Rivas. I don't know the person to make that happen, but do you know anybody from the Army that should be in charge of the ground operation?"

Manny nodded. "Yes, his name is Colonel Rios. I have known him for years. He and Stephan were good friends, and he attended Stephan's funeral."

"Good, Manny. You think you can get in touch with Colonel Rios and give him a heads up about our plan?"

"Yes. I will call a mutual friend in Managua. He will be able to put me in touch with the Colonel."

"I will be leaving early in the morning, Manny. We have to get this done." I knew it was time to say goodbye to my old friend. "You know we may never cross paths again, and at our age, we could be kicked upstairs at any time. I just want you to know that I have valued your friendship all these years, and every time we talk, it renews my spirit."

"I know, Laroy. I live with it every day. Our time may not be long. I do worry about Melinda, and I have told her over and over if something happens to me to get out of this country and go back to the States to settle close to her sister in Georgia. I think she would, but as usual, she doesn't want to talk or think about it."

"You tell her to call me if that time should arise, and if I am still alive, I will assist her in any way I can. Despite all of our escapades, we wound up with the best of the best."

Manny stood up and knocked out the rest of his Jack. "Goodbye, old friend."

The door closed and Manny was gone.

The next morning, a light rain was falling as I went out to the car and put that monster suitcase in the trunk. One thing I had learned during my stay was that April through October was Nicaragua's rainy season. I was lucky I had packed so much rain gear in my suitcase before leaving home. Even if the only reason I had done so was because it had looked so empty.

I started towards the front desk, not knowing what I would say to Castillo but that I couldn't say very much. The fewer people that knew about the plan, the better. Luckily, the young man who had checked me in was working that morning. I poured one more cup of coffee for the road, turned in the key, and bid my host goodbye.

As I turned toward Managua and Rivas departed in my rearview mirror, I had some time to think. Had I done everything right? Would Leanna be able to help pull this off? I was confident that she could get her government to act, because she had the contacts and was probably one of the most capable people in Nicaragua. I knew that there were holes in my plan that needed to be filled and accounted for, and I would run it by Leanna and get her input. The trap had been set, and now it was a matter of execution. The one piece that was missing was Colonel Rios.

CHAPTER 12

It wasn't long until I was on the outskirts of Managua, and the rain stopped. I wanted to get a room close to the U.S. Embassy, so I started looking as I got close. Just behind the embassy about a block north was La Clemente, a neat looking hotel that appeared to be just what I needed for the night. As I was checking in, I marveled at the architecture of the grand old place; it was simply beautiful. I wondered what kind of stories those walls could have told.

I got the number for the embassy and called. When I got Leanna on the phone, she was very professional but seemed a little distracted. "Laroy, you're back so soon. Did you accomplish what you wanted?"

"I think so, but I need your help."

"Where are you now?"

"I'm at La Clemente in room 316."

"I'll come over there at lunch and we can talk. Is 11:30 good for you?"

"That will be just fine."

As I hung up the phone, I thought about Lela. I still had to find my girl something. I still had about an hour before Leanna got there, so I decided to walk around a little bit and stretch my legs. I spotted a jewelry store and decided to go in and browse a little bit. The prices seemed to be very cheap, but then again, I knew nothing about jewelry. I saw a bracelet that had Lela written all over it, and I knew I had found her a present that she would love.

I also spotted a ruby ring that I had to get Madonna. I had often called her "Ruby" when we were first married. When she would get dressed to go shopping she would put on red lipstick. She looked so beautiful, so I would sing to her *"You painted up those lips, rolled and curled that pretty hair. Ruby, are you contemplating going out somewhere?"* We would always laugh about that, and she would say, "You should buy me a ruby ring." Well, now I had.

I was back in the room with fifteen minutes to spare, and at precisely 11:30, a light knock sounded at the door. In breezed Leanna, as beautiful and as confident as could be.

"Please sit down, Leanna. I've got a lot to tell you. Let me start by telling you that in thirty-nine days there will be an attack on Rivas. A group of rebels will use it as a springboard to take over your country. I'm not sure if they have enough manpower to attempt this coup, but they believe they can succeed."

As she listened, Leanna didn't flinch but just stared straight ahead.

"I need your help, and your country needs your help. I have a Plan A and a Plan B. I want you to listen to Plan A and then help me get to the right people to explore the option of Plan B. I know you have the contacts within the Nicaraguan government to get their immediate attention to this matter. Without your help, a lot of innocent men, women, and children will get hurt."

Leanna never hesitated. "You can count on me. What is it you need me to do?"

I recounted to her exactly what had transpired over the last few days in complete detail. I told her about everyone I had encountered in Rivas, I told her about Manny and the underground tunnel, I told her about Petey, the trip up the mountain, my meeting with Comacho, and the agreement I had made with him. She stared in disbelief.

"I need you to get your government to send a man with the $100,000 to the lake nine days from now, and that will solidify the trap. It will give you thirty days to prepare for the attack, and once they are encircled, every single one of those rebels will be eliminated. Your country should remain peaceful for years to come."

I noticed that Leanna's eyes were moist, but her jaw was jutted forward with the determination of a tiger. "My mother was raped and killed by the rebels when I was young. These people you encountered are the last remnants of that group. They are desperate killers, and you were lucky to get out of there alive. I will set the wheels in motion this afternoon, then you and I can meet later tonight to discuss how things will continue. Is there anything else you can think of that I need to do?"

"Do you know a Colonel Rios?"

"I do. He is one of the best and brightest officers."

"Could you possibly see if he could meet with us tonight? I want to present Plan B to him. My gut says that Plan A is the way to go, but Plan B needs to be examined by your military."

"I should go and get busy," said Leanna, "Let us meet at my office around nine this evening, and we'll eat in. You certainly are a unique individual, Laroy. I don't think I have ever met anyone quite like you." With that she closed the door and was on her way.

That night at about a quarter before nine, I made the short walk to the embassy. I was escorted to Leanna's office by one of the guards. I entered to find Leanna in an animated phone conversation. It ended with her slamming down the phone and looking at me with a smile. "I got it," she said. "A lot has happened since lunch. The money is arranged to be delivered as per your request, and Colonel Rios will be here any minute."

I asked Leanna how she ended up working at the U.S. Embassy instead of for the Nicaraguan government.

She smiled. "I was convinced by someone many years ago that I could do more for my country by helping yours. It has been gratifying, and I wouldn't trade my job for anything."

Just then, a slight knock came from the door, and in stepped who I assumed to be Colonel Rios. The first glance told me this guy was all business, and that he had no time for any foolishness.

"Leanna, it is good to see you," he said as he walked up and shook her hand. Then he turned to me and said, "You must be the mysterious American that Leanna told me about. I am Colonel Rios. Leanna has filled me in on your discussions, and she said that you wanted my opinion on a Plan B. Where do we begin?"

I liked this guy already. He was straight to the point.

As he seated himself, Leanna said, "Should I go ahead and have them bring something us to eat?" Colonel Rios and I looked at each other and we both shook our heads at the same time. Leanna just laughed and said, "Good, I am not hungry either. Let us get to the business at hand."

I asked Colonel Rios about his knowledge of Rivas, the lake, and the mountain north of town.

He wrinkled his brow and said, "That mountain has always been a problem. It's hard to climb, and it has a vast cave about three quarters of the way up with multiple exits. It would be an easy place to defend and almost impossible to assault."

"That is exactly why I think Plan A is the way to go. Colonel, how much knowledge of the attack on the police station in Rivas do you have?"

"I was away on a training mission when that occurred, and all I saw was a few reports. How did you come to know about it?"

"I came here at the request of Manny Diaz."

"I trust Manny. He is a sharp guy." He paused, "Manny and I have talked. We have a mutual friend, and he gave me the backstory on you. The U.S. Government has also given us their assurance of your honesty, integrity, and ability. Going into that den of thugs was admirable, but this is a job for the military and the country of Nicaragua. I will not stop until these vermin are eliminated. Do I make myself clear?"

I stared straight into the eyes of Colonel Rios. I knew I was in the presence of a warrior. I replied, "Manny told me he spent a few days up in the hills above Rivas, and he is convinced from what he saw that they came down out of the hills on both the east and west sides of Rivas. I honestly believe that is what they plan to do this time, only with double the number of men. Perhaps by stationing a platoon on the south of the city on each side of the hill, they would walk into a death trap. You could kill or capture at will."

I could tell the Colonel liked the plan by the gleam in his eye. I had seen warriors before, and this guy was a warrior. I went on to tell him about Manny's tunnel and the view it gave of the lake. "Colonel, if you had a couple of men at that viewpoint with night vision equipment, your guys would be informed of timing and numbers."

"Excellent," said the Colonel. "I believe that is exactly what needs to happen. I will pursue it with the higher-ups." The one thing, Colonel Rios said, that he was adamant about, was, "I think you can forget about the capture part of your plan. These vermin have to be eliminated."

I looked at the Colonel and said, "Manny told me that you were friends with Stephan. Is that the main reason you don't want to consider capture?"

"You obviously don't know the history of our country, or the pain these vermin have caused our people." Colonel Rios abruptly stood up and said, "Leanna, I will make preparations, and I would like to be the one to deliver the money." He turned to me, extended his hand, and said, "I bid you farewell, my friend. And thanks for all you have done for our country. Leanna, I will be in touch tomorrow." And with that, he left.

Nothing was said for a few moments. When I looked at Leanna, she was so striking, and the beauty could not hide her strength and determination. "Leanna, I want to thank you for all you have done for me. Your help has been invaluable. I will be leaving for home tomorrow. If you will jot down my email address and keep me abreast of any developments as they occur, I would be most happy to answer any questions that come up if I can."

Leanna got up and came over and hugged me. "Laroy, it is my country and I that should thank you."

I laughed and she smiled. As I started towards the door she said, "Oh, Laroy. Will you tell Bill Parker to give me a call sometime? Or better yet, tell him to plan a trip down here to see us."

"I sure will." As I walked back to La Clemente, I knew I had three calls to make in the morning: Madonna, Manny, and Leanna. I must have slept very well that night, because when I woke up I was rested, relaxed, and ready. Ready to go home, ready to get back to my world, ready to see Lela and Rye, and ready to sit on Madonna's porch with the pups for the rest of my life.

I decided to eat breakfast before making my phone calls, and as I entered the dining room, I was somewhat shocked to see the two British guys sitting at a corner table. I abruptly changed direction to avoid them and went over to the other side of the dining room, taking a seat in a booth with my back towards them. I wondered if they were there getting ready to make a move to supply the rebels with guns and ammunition. It was indeed a small world, and for me, it sometimes got too small. I heard them leave, and I was somewhat relieved. I ate slowly and enjoyed every morsel of the delicious food and thanked my lucky stars that I was going home.

I went back to my room soon after and called Manny. "You must have been sitting on it, Manny," I said after he picked up on the first ring.

"It's about time you called me, you old dog," he replied. "How did it go last night? Is everything set?"

"Yes. The call will be made this morning, and Colonel Rios will deliver the money to the lake at noon in eight days."

"Is Colonel Rios going to be in charge of preventing the attack on Rivas?"

"I think so, but that is being worked out. I think the colonel will be in contact with you about using your tunnel to observe the rebels' movements the night of the attack."

"That's fine," said Manny. "Are you flying out today?"

"Yep. I got two more calls to make, and then I am headed to the airport."

"I can never thank you enough. You know that. But from the bottom of my heart, I thank you."

"Don't worry about it. It was a piece of cake. Besides, you never know when I may need some help."

Manny laughed and said, "You go, old friend. And peace be with you."

The next call was to Madonna, and she answered right away. "Please tell me you are headed home."

"I sure am. Depending on my flight, I should be home before midnight as long as I don't run into any delays. How are you doing?"

She giggled. I hadn't heard that giggle in a long time. "Oh, I'm just fine, but I am ready for you to be home."

"What about the babies? Are they doing okay?"

"They're doing great. Just growing up and eating everything in sight. Lela calls every night and wants to know if I have heard from you, and she doesn't understand why you can't call me about three or four times a day. Rye got on the phone one night and said, 'You tell Dede to hurry up and come home. We are missing out on too much fun.'"

I laughed. That boy's life revolved around fun. Our lives probably would have been a lot better if we followed the same belief. "I got you something, Madonna. I think you'll like it."

"Leroy, you know I don't need anything except for you to come home."

"I am on my way, baby. Don't wait up, but leave the light on for me." As I hung up, I realized how much I missed her and how lucky I was to have her. I made a vow to myself to spend a lot more time with her. It was at that moment that I knew when I got home I was going to retire. Yes, there comes a time in everyone's life when they realize it is time to move on, time for a new direction, and my time was now.

As I called Leanna, I was thinking about whether to tell her about my suspicion of the two British guys I had seen at breakfast, but I decided against it. I had always believed that some things were best left unsaid, even if you were inclined to spill the beans. I had made a living by trusting my instincts, and I was too old to change now.

When Leanna answered the phone, I said to her, "Tell me something good."

She laughed, "You are one impatient American. It's confirmed that Colonel Rios will deliver the money in eight days, along with six bottles of Patrón Tequila and a note with the name 'Corrina' on it complete with a phone number that will be activated the day before the money is delivered." She went on to say, "The military is on board and planning sessions are being held this afternoon to begin preparations for the attack."

"Leanna, you are simply amazing. Will you promise me one thing?"

"What is that, Laroy?"

"Make it a point to come to America sometime and visit with Madonna and me. It would thrill me to death."

"You got it. Is there anything else I can assist you with today?"

"No. Just keep me informed as much as you possibly can, and I will look forward to your visit."

As we hung up, my thoughts turned entirely towards home.

CHAPTER 13

I was in the terminal in what seemed like just a few minutes. I had my luggage checked and ticket in hand, with only about twenty minutes before I was to board the bird that would ferry me home. I grabbed a coke and a pack of crackers, realizing I had already forgotten how good those things were. I looked around me at the people coming and going, thinking about how you never have enough time in this world, and you never know the life stories of the people around you. Each person walked by, oblivious to me, but then that was okay with me.

I heard them call my flight number, and soon we were taxiing down the runway. Once we were airborne, I could finally breathe easy. As we circled and headed north, we flew up the coast of Nicaragua. It was even more beautiful from the air than it was from the ground, and I knew I would never pass this way again.

I catnapped on the plane, and it only seemed like a few minutes until the ding-ding of the bells woke me and we began to approach Miami. *Ah, America, you don't know how much I missed you.* If only I had time to rent a car and run down to the Blue Marlin for one of their Cuban sandwiches. I chuckled to myself at the thought. I was always thinking about food. I looked out the window to where the ocean met the land, and I observed how flat it was compared to the place I had just left.

As I deplaned, I looked at my watch and figured I had enough time to grab something to eat before my last flight. Once I was fed, onboard, and airborne, I knew that I would be home in a about an hour and a half. I started going over a checklist of things I wanted to do in the next few days. It usually involved Lela and Rye, but this time it was different. The first thing I was going to do Monday morning was turn in my resignation. After college and two years in the Army, I had never not been gainfully employed, and now it was time to do some bumming around. It was time to do more things with Madonna, and, yes, it was time to enjoy watching Lela and Rye grow up.

Once my feet were back on the ground, I rented a car to make the short drive home. The one thing I noticed immediately was the difference in where I was to where I had been. Hot and dry. The heat felt great, and for once I loved the dry. I tuned in the radio, hoping to catch some down-home news during the 45-minute drive home. The closer I got to home, the more excited I got. I just could not wait to be home.

As I turned into the driveway, the Southern Whitehouse appeared to be just like I left it. Bluff Shores was indeed where I needed to be. Madonna had left all the outside lights on—her sign that she had indeed missed me. As I went in the house, I tried to be quiet and not wake her, but as I slowly closed the door, I heard that voice. "Leroy, is that you?" We didn't sleep much that night, as we spent the hours talking and making up for lost time.

I got up late the next morning and stumbled into the kitchen to make a pot of coffee. Soon I was on the back porch and checking out the creek. The bluffs were bathed in sunshine, and the sun danced off the leaves and the water. I glanced at the waterfall, and there stood my old Gray Heron as magnificently as if he were indeed the king of this place. As I watched him patrol for breakfast, my mind started to turn to what I needed to do that day, and I caught myself. I needed a down day. One of those days where I just didn't get anything done.

Yep, it was time to charge the batteries, and that in turn made me think about the golf cart. With Rye sure to be coming to get his machete, I knew that golf cart would see some action. My two-year-old springer spaniel, Trouble, bounded up to me, and I got up to get him his treat. I couldn't help but notice the look in his eyes, like he was saying "Where have you been?" He was proud to see me, and it was all the welcome I needed.

I decided that after breakfast I would go ahead and call my old boss, Lyndon, and tell him of my plans to retire. I somehow dreaded calling him, but I was confident that he would understand. Tough as a ten penny nail, the one thing to know about Lyndon was that he was fair and understanding. I had always believed that people tended to get so caught up in work that they sometimes forgot to live. But, honestly, I'd never bought into that at all.

I heard Madonna stirring around in the kitchen, so I sneaked up behind her and put my arms around her, giving her a big kiss on the back of the head.

"Leroy, I know you are up to something. What are you not telling me?"

As she turned around, I was holding that big, red ruby ring in the palm of my hand. Her eyes told it all. They became moist as she slipped it on her finger.

I sang to her, *"Ruby, are you contemplating going out somewhere?"*

"Leroy, you didn't. You are impossible, but I love it!"

The phone rang as we were eating breakfast. It was Rye. "Dede, did you know I am out of school, and I can come stay a bunch of days with you?"

I laughed. I had to teach this boy about negotiation, but now was not the time. "Well, what are you waiting on, Rye? You're letting grass grow under your feet."

"You know I can't drive out to your house, and Mom won't bring me."

"You put her on the phone, boy. We will get to the bottom of this right now."

As Penny got on the phone she was laughing. "He has been driving me crazy while you were gone."

"I bet he has. How about Lela?"

"She has been just as bad but in a different way. She was so worried that something bad might happen to you, and Rye would pick at her and call her a worry wart. I'm glad you're home, too. Did you have a good trip?"

I could tell in Penny's voice that she was asking one of those probing questions that she had learned to ask from Madonna. The women in my life should have all been attorneys. I answered her in legalese that amounted to affirmative, then I said, "Load them up and bring them on. It's time to get on the water."

After I hung up, I told Madonna, "Before the kids get here, I am going to the office and have a sit down with Lyndon and tell him that I am retiring."

"Good. You need to do that, and bring home all those pictures and stuff that you have accumulated over the years."

"We don't have to rush it. It will probably take me two or three months to clear out my backlog. I will still need to go in from time to time to take care of some details."

"Oh, Leroy, I am so ready for you to be home all the time."

"You just wait. It won't even be a month before you'll be wanting to get me out of your hair." Her laugh told me she was probably in 100% agreement.

It was a pleasant drive and a beautiful day. Blue sky galore and warm sunshine told me we were fast approaching summer, and I was ready. Everything at the plant looked just about as normal as when I had left.

"Lyndon, have you got a minute to talk?" I asked as I entered his office.

"Come in, Leroy. I wasn't expecting you back so soon. How was your trip?"

"It was great," I said while taking a seat.

"You know, I sometimes wonder what all you do when you go on these trips, but that is your business. You got something on your mind. I can tell," he said.

"Yes. I am hanging it up. I'm going to go fishing and play with the grandkids."

Lyndon leaned back in his chair and responded with, "Well I don't know what to say, other than, will you take me with you?"

I laughed. We had known each other a long time, and I knew this would not be sad or difficult.

As I began my retirement, my mind did not wander far from the situation in Nicaragua. The day for the attack by the rebels was fast approaching. I had gotten an email from Leanna telling me the money delivery had gone off without a hitch and that Colonel Rios and Manny were confident everything was going as planned.

A few days later I received a call from Manny. After a few pleasantries, he said, "I was out in the yard yesterday, and I saw a rather large van pass the house heading towards the lake. I rushed inside and raced through the tunnel. From my viewpoint I saw boxes of weapons, ammo, and a few grenade launchers being unloaded from the van. It appears they have received the shipment."

"Have you gotten with Colonel Rios and told him everything you saw?"

"Of course I have," said Manny. "The only thing that surprised me was the grenade launchers. I told Colonel Rios, and he said, 'I am not surprised. Just a waste of some good supplies.' Laroy, I did not realize how close Stephan and the Colonel were. He told me the other day, 'This one is for Stephan, and they will pay with their lives.'"

"We got the right guy to get these thugs. You stay safe, Manny. Give Melinda my regards, and call me back if anything pops up."

I knew how badly this needed to work out for the people of Nicaragua. For Manny, Leanna, and Castillo. It was one of those things that could make history.

The day before the attack, I was much edgier than usual. Sometime during the day, Madonna asked what was bothering me.

I answered by saying, "I just have the blues."

She knew that I was capable of hitting a dark spot for no apparent reason, and within a day or so I would be back to normal. That night I couldn't sleep. At 3:30 in the morning, I was up making coffee. As I sat on the back porch, my mind was focused on a beautiful lake, a mountain, and the hills that surrounded the little town of Rivas. I worried about why I had not heard a single word from Manny or Leanna, and I would almost bet that whoever went through that tunnel at Manny's house to the lake was accompanied by Manny. It seemed as though the sun would never rise. Finally, I saw the first hint of the sun's orange hue peek over the bluff, and I was still filled with apprehension.

I knew it was going to be a long day, but I couldn't keep my mind from racing over every detail of the plan. No matter how well you planned there was always the unexpected.

Staring at a clear blue sky, my mind slowly wandered back down to earth, and there stood the Gray Heron, as graceful as could be, and in complete harmony with his surroundings. I thought, *You old bird, you got it made.* I went back inside to refill the coffee cup and check on Madonna. She was sleeping as sound as a baby, so I decided to leave her alone. I went back to the porch to wait out that seemingly endless day as the events played out above the hills in Rivas, Nicaragua.

Over breakfast, I could tell that Madonna knew I was tied up in knots. I tried to crack a few jokes, but she would have none of it. "Leroy, I'm going to shower then go into town, do a few errands, and a get a little shopping done. When I get back, I want you to be in a better mood."

"You can't just turn this stuff off with the flip of a switch," I responded.

"You know I don't pry into everything you do, but something is going on. You won't talk to me about it, but I can tell you are deeply troubled about something. Does it have anything to do with your trip to Nicaragua?"

I answered her as honestly as I could. "Yes, it has everything to do with Nicaragua, but it's something I can't talk about. It will be just fine."

She threw up her hands and headed to the shower. I knew she wouldn't grill me about it anymore. Lord knew I loved that woman.

Soon Madonna was gone, and I walked down to the creek and sat on the boat for a while, just looking around and soaking up the warm sunshine that I so dearly loved.

I must have glanced at my phone fifty times, wondering when it would ring. It was already noon, and I wasn't hungry, could not eat, and was just as miserable as I had ever been. I tried to think of something I needed to do to pass the time, but I just kept drawing a blank. It was useless. I was hung out to dry, and that day was kicking me in ways that I wasn't accustomed too.

I finally went back in the house and turned on the television to kill some time. "Breaking News" flashed across the screen, and I thought about how everything now was breaking news. Those networks had worn that phrase into the ground. I was jarred back to reality when I heard the word "Nicaragua."

The commentator announced, "We have breaking news out of Nicaragua. There was an assault, early this morning, by a group of rebels on the small town of Rivas in Central Nicaragua. According to government sources, it was a well-planned attack that appeared to have the goal of taking over the town as an operating base to launch a much larger strike against the Nicaraguan Government. Our sources have told us the invasion was prevented, with dozens of rebels killed during the attack. The situation is now under control. We will update you as soon as we have further information."

I jumped up into the air and pumped my fist. A sense of relief came over me, and my thoughts immediately turned to the particulars. I wanted more detail. It suddenly occurred to me to check my email. There it was. An email from Leanna, sent to me forty-five minutes ago.

Leroy,

It went as planned. Colonel Rios and his men have eliminated the rebels. None were captured. From his report, they were all eliminated without loss of life from any of our government troops. He and his men are following up with identification, and they have gone to the mountain to assess the situation and gather any information they can find. I understand that the forward observers at the lake took a good head count this morning and came close to being detected as a group of the rebels went into the hills on the east side of the lake. The observers got into Manny's tunnel and were not detected. Also, your friend Manny was with the observers and was most helpful.

For my country, I wish to say once again, thanks. - Leanna

I felt more relaxed. Now I just needed Manny to call and tell me that everything was alright. But knowing Manny, I figured he had talked his way into going with them up to the plateau and the cave to inspect everything.

It was about a quarter before seven in the evening, and I still had not heard from Manny. Madonna and I had grilled some steaks and had a delightful dinner. We walked down to the pier and were just enjoying the water; it was very peaceful as the sun sank slowly in the west. My phone rang. It was Manny.

He seemed subdued, so I said, "Are you okay?"

"I am fine. Just tired from climbing the hills. I am getting to old for that kind of stuff. I went with the two observers to the viewpoint, and with their night vision stuff we saw them come out of the woods by the mountain. When they split, eleven went to west side towards Rivas and the other eleven went to the east side. The group that went to the east came within about twenty feet of the tunnel, but we were already back inside and were not detected. The lead observer called Colonel Rios and gave him the count and told him how they were armed. One heck of a firefight broke out at daybreak, but it was over in about twenty minutes.

"Then we got a call from Colonel Rios telling his guys to come on back into town, where they were in the process of identifying and recovering the bodies of the rebels. I came along to see if I could help with any identification. When we went into town, the people seemed pretty calm. There were a few who wanted to know what was going on, but Rios had them under control. I went up the west hill first and observed the eleven bodies; they never had a chance. Comacho has been identified, and I recognized two of the other guys. I had seen them in Rivas before, but they were strangers to me."

Manny paused, and I could tell something was wrong. "What about the east side?" I asked.

"When we crossed over to the east side and got to the bodies, the first thing I did was look for Petey since I had not seen him on the west side. Some of the bodies were pretty disfigured, there were several that had suffered headshots, but I thought I could identify Petey if I saw him. There were only ten bodies. There should have been eleven. Petey was not one of them."

"What, you mean Petey got away?"

"Yes. There's a group out looking for him even as we speak."

I couldn't believe what Manny was saying. Of all people, how could Petey be the one to escape? "What about the cave, Manny?"

"I couldn't make the climb. I tried, but I couldn't do it. As you probably figured, there was a treasure trove of information in the cave, and it was much more elaborate than anybody imagined. It will take a few days to piece all of this stuff together, but that work is underway. It appears that this Comacho guy was smart and well-educated. I saw enough to know that they had planned for this to be the start of something much bigger. One of the more interesting things that came out of this is that there appears to be a connection to the Middle East, more specifically Iran."

"I thought when I was staring Comacho in the eyes that I detected someone who was not stupid, probably fairly well-educated, and probably a zealot. Well, I'm sure a lot will transpire over the next few days, and I'm just glad it turned out as well as it did and that you are okay."

"You always manage to miss the fun, Laroy."

"You know me, Manny. I *do* always miss out." We both laughed, and I said, "You better get back to your library and have one for me. Be sure and call me as soon as you hear about Petey. That worries me."

"I will," said Manny. "Talk to you soon."

I slept that night, thinking that now I could put that ordeal behind me and move on with my life.

CHAPTER 14

Where does the time go when you are having fun? Summer was almost over, and it had been one adventure after the other. With Lela it had been a softball whirlwind. She was developing her game at a rapid pace, and her pitching had improved by leaps and bounds. The thing I noticed most over the summer was her timely hitting. It seemed that she was at her best with two outs, runners on base, and the game on the line. That girl was "clutch," which led me to start calling her my "clutch baby."

Rye, on the other hand, was all over the map. It was non-stop water action with him. We must have looked funny going down the water on our Jet Ski at fifty miles an hour, especially with me on the back and the six-year-old driving. He could pilot like he was born to race. It was even more ridiculous when I would sit on the front of the boat and let him drive me around. If the water patrol had ever caught us, I would have been in deep trouble.

One afternoon we were out cruising around in the street on the golf cart, and an approaching car came towards us. Rye pulled off the road to be safe. It turned out to be our local district attorney, who was going down to his weekend house he kept on the lake. I knew him very well, and he grinned and waved as he passed us. Rye got back on the road and we continued. I looked back and saw that Christopher had turned around and started following us with his hidden blue lights flashing.

I told Rye to pull over. He looked around and his eyes got wide as Christopher stopped his car and pulled out his badge. With a stern face, he said, "Son, I need to see your driver license."

Rye looked at me and then looked at him and then back at me. I shrugged my shoulders and said, "I don't know what to tell you."

He looked back at the imposing figure with the badge and calmly said, "You will have to call my mom. She has it."

It was said with enough validity to crack up the old, hardened district attorney, who had now seen it all. We all got a big laugh and talked a few minutes, but I could tell that Rye was glad when Christopher got back in his car and left. That was when I knew that boy could handle anything. He could just adapt to any situation, and his quick thinking would get him out of all kinds of binds. So I kept putting him in those type of situations, just to see how he would react, and, for me, it was a lot of fun.

With school back in session, Madonna and I planned a little excursion to just get away for a while and see some new sights. We both needed it. We decided to venture down to the Mississippi Gulf Coast. It was a place we had been to a few times but had never really gotten to check out. I was craving some good seafood with maybe just a touch of Cajun.

As we were getting ready to leave, I took a call from Manny. It had been several weeks since the ambush at Rivas. "Laroy, you wouldn't believe how much effort the government put in trying to find and capture Petey, but it seems that he has vanished into thin air."

"Have you seen any unusual activity at the lake or the mountain?"

"The only thing that's unusual is that more of the local people are going to the lake to fish and swim now."

I laughed, "Is that messing up your fishing?"

"It's terrible," he said, laughing. "It is a good thing. A place with that much beauty should be enjoyed."

I asked Manny to call me if he heard anything on Petey. As I hung up the phone, I had a weird feeling about the whole situation. What if he started to develop and assemble his own group of rebels? I shrugged off the thought. It was troubling to me that Petey could disappear without so much as a trace, and I thought surely he would turn up sooner or later.

Our trip was pretty laid back and very enjoyable. It was great to go to some of those little out-of-the-way places and experience the local environment. From Biloxi to Pass Christian, we enjoyed it all. Madonna was beginning to think we might like to move down to this place, until she thought about Lela and Rye. The week flew by, and we started working our way back home. We decided to spend the night in Philadelphia, Mississippi and go to the casino. We are not casino people, but we had been a few times— usually just to observe the other people there.

It always amazed me how people seemed to enjoy throwing away hard earned money. As usual, we saw a diverse group of people who appeared to be having a good time. They were somewhat rowdy, and to me it was a microcosm of America. It also seemed that every time we went to a casino, we ran into somebody that knew somebody. We were familiar with proving that it was indeed a small world. This time would be no different.

I was watching a lady play a quarter machine, and she appeared to be winning. Anytime I saw someone winning on a slot machine, I tended to stop and observe. She acknowledged my presence, and it did not appear that I bothered her by watching. After several spins she hit a small jackpot, which paid her $1,200. The casino host came and cashed her out. You can never wipe the smile off a person's face when they hit the jackpot. She seemed to keep eyeing me, and I figured it was because she thought I had brought her some luck.

With her money in hand, she walked up to me and said, "I think I know you. I have your picture on my phone."

I was obviously shocked. "You must be mistaken."

She whipped out her cell phone and held it out for me to see. As I glanced at the photo, I couldn't believe my eyes; it was Manny and me.

"How it the world do you know Manny?" I asked her.

She laughed and said, "Manny is my brother-in-law. He's married to my sister, Melinda."

I was speechless for a second or two, and I realized that Melinda had taken a picture of Manny and I as we were standing in the backyard by the cellar that day.

"Are you Dawn? The one from Georgia who cans all those wonderful vegetables?"

"Yes, and Melinda told me you have a pretty good appetite."

I began to wonder what all Melinda had told Dawn and started to feel a little nervous, but as the conversation continued, it became apparent that Dawn did not know very much about my visit to Nicaragua. Eventually her husband, Jack, joined our conversation. As it turned out, they usually took a trip to the casino in Philadelphia once a year. Usually in the fall after the crops were in and all the canning of vegetables was done.

"Leroy, why don't the two of you join us for dinner?" Jack suggested.

I glanced at Madonna, and her body language said "yes," so I agreed.

During dinner, I was able to find out more about Melinda and life growing up in Northern Minnesota. It became apparent to me that Dawn adored her sister, and as kids growing up, Melinda had been a doting older sister to

Dawn. It was getting late, so we thanked them for dinner and gave them an open invitation to visit us at Bluff Shores if they were ever in the area.

As we were leaving, Dawn said, "I can't wait to tell Melinda that we ran into Leroy at a casino."

I smiled. "Tell Manny that I won bigtime."

The next morning, as we prepared to leave on our drive home, I asked the valet if there was a quaint old place close by that might be of some historical significance. He looked at me with a quizzical look that said "I don't know about this guy." Then with a slight grin, he said, "Oh yeah, you might need to go check out Williams Brothers. It's been here longer than dirt, and they have some good fresh cut bacon and hoop cheese."

My eyes lit up at the thought of hoop cheese. I thanked him and we headed out. It was close to the casino. As we pulled up we saw an ancient building that looked like it had probably been built in the '20s. It was not your average grocery store. It had a porch across the front about ninety feet wide, and it had shelves that displayed all different kinds of honey, molasses, jelly, and some fruits and vegetables. On a bench sat two elderly black gentlemen who had on overalls. As soon as I walked up to the molasses section, one of the men approached me and said, "What can we help you with today?"

What transpired over the next fifteen minutes was an excellent education about the different types of molasses, local honey, jelly, fruits, and vegetables. I remembered thinking that this guy ought to be teaching agriculture in high school or college. His wealth of knowledge and the way he presented held my total attention. The old gentleman had a gleam in his eye that said he enjoyed his work and his life. I wondered if I had that gleam in my eye.

As soon as I stepped into the old store, it was very different from what I had first imagined. It probably still looked the same as it had on the day it opened. Two men were standing in the middle of the entrance, slicing fresh bacon and hoop cheese. It took me a few minutes to figure out how the system worked. It was customary to give them your order and then go do the rest of your shopping. Once complete and ready to check out, you picked up your order.

While combing the aisles for something unique, I encountered a lady who appeared to be in her mid-forties. I glanced at her cart and saw a package of fresh bacon ends. When I met her on another aisle, I asked her, "Miss, where did you find those bacon ends and what do you cook with them?"

I got another education from someone who had that gleam in their eye. She gave me a big smile and directed me to where they were in the store. Then she told me, "You have got to cook you a big pot of turnip greens and season them with these fresh bacon ends. It is the best eating in the world."

I thanked her for sharing her secret recipe. From what she said and from her ample figure, I assumed she knew what she was telling me.

As we walked to the car, Madonna said gleefully, "Look how much stuff we bought! That's a neat place."

I could not have agreed more. As soon as we were back in the car, I opened up one of the packages of hoop cheese, popped a top on a cold coke, and was ready for the drive home.

The day was beautiful, and the scenery was just what I needed. Madonna was listening to some soft music and was soon sleeping peacefully. My thoughts turned to my chance encounter with Dawn and Jack. When Dawn had talked about Melinda, I had seen her face light up and display a love for her sister and a bond that would never be broken. It appeared to me that sisters were often that close with each other, whereas brothers seldom were. I had to believe it was a macho thing between brothers that made it appear that they were never as close as sisters. I knew that Melinda and Dawn would forever be close no matter the distance or circumstance.

I recalled Manny saying something about him wanting Melinda to move to Georgia with her sister if anything should ever happen to him. I looked at Madonna. Where would she go if something happened to me? I laughed silently to myself. That Cherokee in her blood said that she would survive, she would endure, and I felt secure that Penny and Lela would see to her needs.

I was jarred out of my thoughts by my cell phone. As I glanced down, I saw it was Wango.

"Leroy, how in the world are you doing? Have you got a minute to talk?"

"Sure, Wango. How are you doing and what's on your mind?"

He paused for a second and said, "I want you to tell me what you can about your visit to Nicaragua, but more specifically, I would like for you tell me exactly how you were involved in what happened in Rivas."

"Oh it was nothing. You know, just a little favor for my friend. Why didn't you prepare me better for Leanna? She is an absolute jewel."

Wango laughed, "America is fortunate to have such a talented individual in their embassy."

"Amen to that, and for whatever it's worth, she would make a great chief of staff for any congressman."

"I know more than you think, but I wanted to get it straight from you."

"Manny Diaz smelled trouble, and he wanted me to nose around and see if I could find out what direction it was headed and so I did. By the way, did you ever visit that beautiful lake outside of Rivas?"

"I went there once. Castillo wanted me to see the place, and it is beautiful, but don't try to change the subject. What happened?"

I knew I should level with my friend. So I told him about the gist of my involvement without going into too many details.

Wango replied, "Yes, I heard about your adventure from sources within the government. You were lucky you got off that mountain alive."

"Well, I will admit to breaking out in a cold sweat."

"When I heard that a company called NEXRAD, which is short for Northeastern Exploration and Resource

Acquisition and Development, had a hand in destroying the rebels' planned coup, I knew you were involved."

I chuckled and said, "By the way, your old friend Manny Castillo said for you to come visit him. Castillo is a fine man."

"I am going to be back home in a couple of weeks. Let's do lunch and talk. I have a few things I need to discuss with you in private."

Red flags went up as he disconnected. I felt somewhat uneasy. NEXRAD had traveled from a mountain in Rivas to Washington way too quickly.

CHAPTER 15

The time was flying by so fast I could not comprehend what in the world was happening to me. Several years went by like a flash. Lela had just started high school and was still playing softball. At home the leaves were falling way too fast for me. The only thing I really liked about fall was football and the comfortable weather but both were harbingers of the cold to come. It was relaxing to spend time at home and contemplate all those projects I intended to do, and there were whirlwind weekends with Lela's fall ball and Rye's football games. A typical Saturday morning was to attend Rye's game at ten then charge to who knows where to see Lela play in the afternoon. It sometimes meant an overnight stay to see the follow-up games on Sunday, which were part of the championship bracket. Lela was beginning to acquire enough hardware that I jokingly told Jon and Penny, "You guys might as well prepare to build a trophy room."

Rye was in the fifth grade now and was as comfortable with a football as any kid you would ever see. He explained it to me very quickly, "Dee, when you're on offense, you push, and when you're on defense, you tackle."

I said, "What do you do when you have to run the ball?"

He gave me that look. "They better hope they don't have to tackle me."

I laughed, but he was right. Stout as a bull, fast as a gazelle, and smart as a fox. That kid was a natural, and I kept telling everybody who would listen that he was going to grow up and win the Heisman Trophy. I could see it in his eyes; he loved the game and was going to excel beyond everyone's expectations. It was going to be fun to watch, and I just hoped I lived long enough to see it. However, when that thought came into my mind, sadness crept into my heart.

As we were driving home one day, Lela said, "Poppa, which law school is the best one in the country?"

I was somewhat shocked that she was thinking in those terms, so my response was to answer a question with a question. "I don't know for sure, Lela. Which one do you think is the best?"

"I think it's Loyola University. That's where I think I want to go to college, but Mom says no."

"Why would Penny not want you to attend Loyola?"

"I don't know? I think she said something about it being too far away from home."

"With your grades, you can go to any school in the country, and if you decide to go to Loyola, or wherever, I will be one proud Poppa." I could see the wheels turning, and I knew she would make the right choice.

I was too busy to worry about the world's problems. Rye made sure of that. Between hunting and fishing it seemed I had very little time for anything else. We always had to have more supplies to make our next trip a success. That boy could think of more stuff to buy than a lady in her favorite department store during a buy-one-get-one-free sale. We had enough knives, shotguns, ammo, backpacks, tents, tree stands, and survival food to last a lifetime. There was something about that boy that was a lot like Lela. Prepare, prepare, prepare.

One thing that stood out to me was that Rye was succeeding in school better than I ever thought he would. He was serious about making good grades and doing the best job he could, and for that I was thankful. He was so personable and enjoyed having such a good time that I thought he would be one of those kids who would be more concerned about the social aspect of school rather than the intellectual aspect. In fact, I would have bet on it. His teachers were amazed at his progress, and as he continued to get glowing reports, my concerns about the education aspect of his life were somewhat relieved. I knew that kid was going to have fun in life, and to see him balance that with hard work made me one proud Dede.

Rye was still a couple of years away from junior high, and one of the things that caught me off-guard was a conversation with Penny. "I'm beginning to think about where we need to send Rye to junior high. What do you think?"

"Well, I hadn't thought about it," was my initial response. "I just assumed he would continue where he is. Is something wrong?"

"Oh no," said Penny, "it's just that we've gotten four calls already from different people wanting to know if Rye would be interested in going to a particular school."

Red flags went up. "Now let me get this straight, why would these people be interested in where Rye is going to school?"

Penny laughed and said, "They want him to play football for them."

I went off like a rocket. "My God, the kid is only in the fifth grade, and they're trying to recruit him to play football! I know America is football-crazy, but that is absolutely ridiculous!"

"Calm down," said Penny. "I think you would agree that Rye is going to excel at football and we have to think about his future. Where he goes to junior high and high school will affect his scholarship offers for college."

"Penny, you're going to have to let me think about this. What have you told those people that have called?"

"I thanked them for their interest and told them we weren't at that point yet and that they should check back with us in about a year."

I should have known that Penny would have handled it correctly. "Okay. You negotiate a good deal for Rye, but get them to throw in a nice retirement cottage for Madonna and me." We laughed, but we both knew that she had two kids that were going places, and we were just along for the ride.

One day, Rye and I were out on the boat doing some jug fishing. We had twenty-five plastic jugs floating in the water, and it was hot, just like I liked it. The boy was enjoying himself immensely. He made a game out of who could spot the jug that turned out to have the biggest fish. The prize, of course, was a trip into town and free ice cream for the winner. I would have to pay either way, but to Rye, it would taste much better if he spotted the winning jug. It was unusual that we caught so many. We had gotten up to twelve fish when another jug took a ride. It was moving down the creek at a pretty good clip. Rye had spotted it, and I smelled a winner at the end of that jug. When we finally caught up with it and got it in the boat, I guessed that it weighed about 14 lbs.

Rye was ecstatic. "That's the biggest catfish we ever caught. I guess I should win a double scoop of chocolate for that one."

I made sure that Rye got a good dose of cleaning fish and he never wavered.

"Dee, when are we going to cook these puppies?"

I laughed at him and said, "Rye, we will put them in the freezer, and as soon as you can get Nonna to fix some hushpuppies, we will cook them."

He smiled at me and said, "Don't worry. I'll get Nonna to cook them tomorrow night."

I knew that Nonna didn't have a chance. On the way into town to get that double scoop of chocolate, Rye said, "You know you always told me that when I got to be ten you would take me hunting on one of your trips down south."

"I sure did, and the first time I go this year you are going with me."

"When will that be? How much longer till we go?"

I looked into those eager eyes and said, "I'm planning on going Thanksgiving Day weekend. Do you think your mom will let you go?"

I did not tell him about that sweet 16-gauge shotgun I had bought for him. I knew if I told him he would not sleep for a few nights. Rye was ready. I knew he would do just fine because that kid had spent so much time in the woods. Every time I took him out, he would stay until after dark if I let him. That boy was comfortable in the woods.

As Thanksgiving approached, Rye became increasingly excited. With two weeks left, he and Lela came for the weekend. On Saturday morning after breakfast, I inquired what the game plan was for the day.

Lela said, "I was hoping we could go to a movie."

I usually took them together, but this time Rye didn't want to see what Lela did. "Ugh, Dee, that's a girl's movie."

Nonna spoke up and said, "Why don't I take Lela, and you and Rye do what you want to do?"

That seemed agreeable to everybody. I looked at Rye and said, "I guess you and I better go to the gun range. I need to sight my rifle."

That was all it took. After he ate like a horse and cleaned his plate, he was ready to go. As we were preparing to leave, I walked out with the 16-gauge, and Rye immediately said, "Dee, whose gun is that?"

"Rye, if you are going hunting, it is about time you had the right kind of gun. It's called a 'Sweet 16.' It's the first shotgun a young man usually gets when he is sixteen, and it shoots sweet."

"But I'm only ten."

"I know, but I would not have gotten this for you if I didn't think you could handle it."

He just had to hold it on the drive to the gun range. He rubbed it until I finally said, "Boy, you are going to rub a hole in that new gun."

He laughed, "I can't believe I have a real deer gun."

Luckily, there were not too many people at the range, which surprised me with it being so close to deer season. I showed Rye how to load and unload, and he was ready to fire. Gun safety was not an issue for him, as Jon and I had taught him gun safety since he was old enough to play with a toy pistol.

When he squeezed the trigger for the first time, his eyes were filled with excitement as he looked at the target and screamed, "Dee, I got it!" Rye carefully put the safety on, and we walked down to inspect the target. The shot pattern was about an inch left of the bullseye but otherwise right on target.

"Did it kick when you pulled the trigger?" I asked.

"Yeah, it's got some kick, but I did just like you told me too. I held it tight to my shoulder. Can I shoot again, Dee?"

"Yes, but from the looks of that first shot, you're not going to need much practice."

He shot about seven more times, and then he pronounced himself ready to get a deer. It was just a great day. Just a boy named Rye and me.

In a flash the weekend was gone, and I found myself back on the porch on a Monday morning with my coffee cup, staring at my old friend across the creek. I needed to get ready for my annual Thanksgiving hunting trip. My restless spirit was beginning to kick up, and the urge to go was getting stronger each passing day. I was trying to figure out how many years I had made this pilgrimage to Fort Boyd with my good friend Tony, and I concluded that this must be the thirtieth year.

Fort Boyd was an old cabin that was situated about two miles from the highway in a scope of woods that completely concealed it from view. I always marveled at how they got electricity back to the old house when there was not another house within miles. It was rough there. There was no running water, and it was complete with an outhouse that sat about ninety feet behind the cabin. Fort Boyd was beautiful to me, because it was the perfect place for my restless spirit to calm down, and my soul could connect with nature. I knew this trip was going to be much different, however. Rye was going to be all over the place and fired up. I was ready for that, and I found myself looking forward to the hunt.

Over the thirty years that we had hunted at Fort Boyd, Tony and I had gotten to the point where we were carrying young kids to let them enjoy the place. It occurred to me that over the years I had seen those young men grow up, and now they were married and had children of their own. It was also very satisfying that several of them still looked forward to coming back to Fort Boyd for a weekend of hunting. I hoped that Rye would enjoy the place as much as I had.

It was the quiet time in the woods and just the magic of the place that seemed to ease my soul. The sounds, the sun dancing off of the creek, each small animal at peace with its surroundings but ever vigilant, made my inner peace complete. I would never give that up; I would never forget the sound or that feel of my hair standing up on the back of my neck as the soulful call of a coyote pierced the morning air.

On the morning of our hunt, I awoke to rain. I groaned. This was going to make for miserable hunting conditions. The one thing about Fort Boyd was that the ground was rather flat and held water, so when we went out into the woods to hunt, we would inevitably have to wade through the standing water. I knew that would suit Rye just fine. He was so fired up he would have waded through a snake pit.

It was about a four-hour drive, towing a trailer with four-wheelers and all the gear we could carry. Tony drove as he always did, and we laughed and told Rye of our hunting adventures on the trip. He couldn't get enough. As soon as we would finish one story, Rye would say, "Tell me another one." Somewhere during the trip, Tony became Uncle Tony as far as Rye was concerned.

I laughingly told Tony, "I don't know how to say this, but you have been adopted."

Rye was utterly wide-eyed as we pulled off the highway and began the last two miles of our trip through the woods.

The place was just as I expected. We unloaded, ate dinner, lit a fire in the wood stove as it was a little nippy outside, and laid out our clothes for the morning hunt. I knew Rye would probably sleep very little that night. His eyes were constantly scanning the cabin as he took in every inch of all the deer heads that were mounted on the walls and as he looked at all the old pictures over and over and over.

He found one picture that he seemed to like the most. "Dee, come here and look at this picture. Your hair was brown." We all got a good chuckle out of that, and Rye perhaps laughed the loudest.

It was bedtime. I said, "Rye, we have to be up at 4:30 to cook breakfast and be in our stands before daylight."

Rye's eyes got big, and he replied, "You want me to chop up the potatoes in the morning like I do at your house?"

"We don't have potatoes in the morning. Just eggs, sausage, and toast."

"Well can I scramble the eggs?"

"Sure, why not?"

Tony looked at both of us and said, "You mean that boy can scramble eggs and peel potatoes?"

"He sure can. I've had him doing that since he was four."

Tony laughed, "He is going to fit right in at Fort Boyd."

You couldn't get the smile off of Rye's face as he snuggled up in his sleeping bag and drifted off to sleep.

The next morning after breakfast, we decided that I should take Rye to the back northwest corner of the property to the shooting house we called "29." I was pretty sure the boy enjoyed the trip through the mud and water in the side-by-side, because he looked at me with that big grin and said, "This is fun."

We stopped about two hundred yards short of the shooting house and slogged the rest of the way with Rye getting mired up in his boots a couple of times. Once in the house we began to get quiet as daylight approached. The first thing to pop out on us was a very fat and noisy armadillo. It was Rye's first time to observe how funny they were in the woods and how much noise they could make. I marveled at how still that boy was and how focused he was on what he was observing.

About 7:00 that morning, two wild pigs came rambling through the woods, headed to bed down in the pine thicket behind us. They were too far away to get a shot for Rye, but he got a good look at them. "Those suckers were big," he said.

I smiled and said, "Just wait. We are just getting started."

It was about a quarter before 9:00 when I caught a slight movement out of the corner of my eye. A small, young doe popped out of the pine thicket. She nervously surveyed the woods and kept looking back into the thicket behind her. I didn't move. I glanced at Rye. He had already picked her up, and he didn't move a muscle either. The doe eased into the woods to our left and looked back as if she was giving the all clear. A small button buck popped out, and he was as frisky as could be. He would run and throw on the brakes, throwing his nose up the air like he was smelling for something. His little tail was going up and down faster than he was running. His mom looked on with the caution that only a mom can display.

Shortly, they were out of sight, and Rye whispered to me, "Dee, that was the prettiest Bambi I have ever seen. I wouldn't shoot him for nothing."

I smiled. "I am proud of you, boy."

Nothing happened for over an hour, and I was beginning to worry that Rye would get restless, when I picked up something black about a hundred and fifty yards out in front of us. It was coming straight toward us; I knew it was a wild pig. I poked Rye and pointed in that direction. As it approached, I saw it was a wild boar, and I felt Rye was fixing to get a shot. I glanced at Rye, and he placed his gun upon the edge of the house window and began to home in for his shot. When the wild boar got within forty feet, he slid the safety off and fired. The hog dropped as if hit by a rocket. I looked at Rye in amazement, as he had executed the shot as if he was a veteran of many hunts. The calmness he displayed shocked me, but then again, it was Rye.

"Dee, was that a good shot or what?"

I laughed and said, "Boy, you are something else."

In about twenty minutes we got down to get a close look at the wild hog. By Fort Boyd standards it was pretty nice. My guess was that it was about 80 to 90 lbs.

You couldn't get the grin off of Rye's face. "Take a picture and send it to Dad!"

"I will, boy. We are going to have to cook some tenderloin tonight."

He laughed, "You're always think about eating."

"Well you will be ready to eat after we get this hog out of all this mud, get it cleaned, and get it ready to grill."

I don't think the boy quit grinning all day. What a day it was. That night as we ate our tenderloin and baked potatoes, Tony said, "That kid is something else."

I replied, "You should have seen him, it was so natural. It was almost as if he had done it many times before."

"Perhaps we need to teach him how to skin one out and cut it up. What do you think?"

"Well, he has already asked me if he could skin out the next one we got. Old folks always need some young buck to step up and take over the work while the old ones supervise. That's what I am thinking."

Tony smiled and said, "We're always on the same page."

The hunt the next day went well. Rye saw more deer, and he passed on all of them, as he explained to me, "I am waiting for a big one." The next day we packed up and headed home, and I knew that Rye had had an experience that a lot of kids never get and that he would always remember.

CHAPTER 16

Once back home, the holidays came roaring fast and furious. It was a constant barrage of parties and the usual things that accompany the Christmas season. I was into it now more than I used to be since I was no longer working. Suddenly it was New Year's Eve, and another year was gone before I even realized it. I just wanted things to slow down. Just a little. We were into January when I got a call from Manny. Usually we didn't talk until around spring.

"Laroy, how are you doing, old friend?"

"I am well, Manny, and how are you and Melinda?" I quickly detected that something was wrong.

"Well, I have some bad news."

I braced myself. "What's wrong?"

"It is Colonel Rios. He was on a training mission, and his chopper went down. He is gone."

I was shocked. I could still visualize the colonel exactly the way he had looked that day I met him. "How did this happen?"

"It was raining very hard. They think the crash was weather-related. All nine on board were lost. Hector was a very good man, and I thought you would want to know."

"I appreciate you calling. It is just heartbreaking. Manny, I did not even know his first name. From what I could tell, Colonel Rios was so professional, so focused, and very dedicated."

"Yes. Nicaragua has lost a true patriot and a great soldier."

We talked for a few more minutes and then agreed to talk again in May unless something else came up.

It was my struggle with time that was beginning to gnaw at me. It was like an hourglass. If you are a grain of sand at the top, it goes pretty slowly, but as you work your way down to the narrow opening, it goes faster and faster. I was kept fairly busy going to and from sporting events. If it wasn't Lela playing softball or volleyball, it was Rye playing football and basketball. School was not what it was when I went, and I kept thinking it may not be the best thing for our kids, what with everything they did. A normal school day was nearly twelve hours, including all their extracurricular activities. But Rye and Lela were loving it and seemed happy, and that was what was important to me.

The day arrived when Rye entered junior high school. Lela would be a senior the following year. The recruitment of Rye, to see which junior high he would attend, went to the Russellville Generals, a local school that had supplied more scholarship athletes to colleges than any other school in the area. The coaching staff was well regarded by all the major universities.

Rye was the little man on the totem pole, but it didn't take long for him to climb to the top. By the second game, he was starting running back on a team that was dominated by ninth-grade boys, and Rye was still only in the seventh grade. In his second game, during the second play from scrimmage, Rye came around the corner and turned up field, and there was that blinding burst of speed he possessed. Eighty-five yards later, he crossed the goal line, and everybody in that stadium knew they had just seen something special. The kids and parents at Russellville would get to see that scene repeated for five more years.

The season passed quickly, and as fate would have it, the last game of the year was against another undefeated team, the Lee Golden Tigers. It was football weather, as there was a cold nip in the air. It was a great game, and with less than two minutes to go in the last quarter, it looked like Lee had the game on ice. The score was 17-13, and Lee had the ball. Rye was playing defense at the outside linebacker position.

Then it happened. Rye broke through the line and put a tremendous hit on the quarterback. The ball popped out, Rye scooped it up without breaking stride, and ran fifty-five yards to win the game for Russellville. It was a chaotic scene as he was mobbed by his teammates, and the crowd went absolutely nuts. Rye was a gem, and he was destined to excel on the football field or anything else he attempted.

It was soon Thanksgiving and time for another hunting trip to Fort Boyd. Rye was packed and ready to go. I thought about letting him hunt by himself this trip, but I just couldn't make myself do it. Rye, for his part, did not seem to mind, and he didn't ask me to let him. He got a nice eight-point on the second morning, and it was very wet and cold. As we were dragging the deer out of the woods, I felt a sharp pain in my lower back.

"Hold up, boy. I got to rest a minute."

Of course, Rye's adrenalin was flowing, and he was not the least bit tired. "Come on, Dee. Let's get this deer back to the cabin and then you can rest."

As I rubbed my lower back, I said, "You don't understand. Dee is old, and old people have to rest sometimes."

A big grin came on that face, and he replied, "You're not old. You just look old." That boy always knew how to make me laugh. "Dee, how many old people you know that climb bluffs, jump waves like crazy on the Jet Ski, and drag a deer out of the woods in all of this kind of mud? You're the toughest old man I know."

I had to laugh, but laughing made my back hurt worse. No way was I going to tell Rye though. In about an hour we were back at the cabin, and I got to sit down in front of a warm fire, complete with a tube of muscle rub.

It was approaching Christmas when I got a phone call from Lela. She was all excited. She had taken her ACT earlier in the year in preparation for college. "Poppa, I got a 35 on my test, and I'm so happy! What do you think?"

"I knew you would score well, Lela. You're the smartest girl I know." It was wonderful to see that girl take so much interest in her school work. I asked, "Have you focused in any more on which college you are going to?"

"No, I've just been so busy with school and sports. I'm really not worried about it too much. I remember what you told me a long time ago, 'take care of the present and prepare, and then the future will take care of itself.'"

"That's my girl. And I will just have to get you something special for Christmas."

"You know that bracelet you brought me from Nicaragua years ago?"

"I remember as if it was yesterday."

"Well, I still have it. In fact, I wore it to school today."

I laughed, "Girl, you will not do. Maybe I need to get you a new bracelet for Christmas."

"You can if you want, and you know I will love it, but I will always keep this one. It's very special to me."

"Are you going to get to come this weekend or have you got plans?" I asked.

"We have a volleyball tournament this weekend, and then the school will be out of session next Wednesday. I'd like to come and stay three or four days with you."

"You just plan on it, Lela, and we will make up for some lost time." My girl was growing up.

I was in the throes of winter's grasp, and the blues that encompassed me at times were circling as if they were about to swoop in and make me their prey. I could feel it coming, and I knew I had to move. I called Tony and proposed that we take off on a week-long hunting trip to Fort Boyd. It had been a long time since we had made that kind of trip together.

It was miserable and cold. Tony replied sarcastically, "Sure, the weather's perfect. We might as well get out and get used to it. Have you lost your mind?" Tony paused for a second and then said, "When do you want to leave?" Tony had always had this joke about how he and I only had a few clicks left in us before it would be over, and so the reasoning was to enjoy it while we could. It was agreed we would leave the next day.

A week at Fort Boyd without running water always required a trip into the closest small town about every three days for a motel room, shower, and somebody else's cooking. It had been several years since we had visited our favorite steak place. It was the only steak place within driving distance of the motel. And, actually, it was pretty good.

We pulled up to Diamond Jim's, only to discover it was no longer Diamond Jim's. We went inside and everything was different—the menu, the help, and even the décor. I asked the waitress what had happened to Jim, and she said, "He opened a new Diamond Jim's at the beach. He started making so much more money down there, that he closed this one and moved there permanently."

From the conversation, I figured we weren't going to get a good steak, so I ordered the chicken wings. Bad choice. Really bad choice. Back at the cabin, I spent more time in the outhouse than I did in the shooting house. Tony laughed at me until I recovered. What are good friends for if you can't laugh at each other?

Back home, I settled in to ride out the balance of winter. I would sit in the glassed-in back porch, which was warm and comfortable in the mornings, as I watched the Gray Heron perform his daily search for breakfast. He was oblivious to the cold, and it just didn't seem to matter to that old boy. The days were slowly beginning to get longer, and with each passing day I found myself searching for signs of spring. Those signs were always vital to me as they meant victory was at hand, that life was about to return to what was intended, and that winter had once again been dealt a defeat.

I was beginning to worry about Madonna, as she was starting to have one health problem after another. So far it was nothing serious, but it was like it was a warning that rough seas were in front of us. It was hard for me to accept that we were getting old. It helped to have Rye and Lela around. They kept us going, and the house was full of laughter when they were around.

I was on the way into town a few weeks later, and as I rounded a curve, there as plain as day on the side of the road was a beautiful clump of buttercups. I wanted to get out and pick them and take them home to Madonna, but I reasoned that I should let other people enjoy them, as I was sure this bunch was the first clump to be found. I laughed at myself. *You really are ready for spring if you can get excited about a few buttercups.* I called Madonna, and I couldn't hide my excitement.

She laughed, "Leroy, you are just a kid. You be careful and watch your driving."

I was in a good mood all day. Buttercups could defeat the blues.

That afternoon the phone rang. It was Rye. "Dee, you think it'll be too cold to go fishing this weekend?"

"What kind of fishing you got on your mind, Rye? If you are planning on us going ice fishing, I don't think it's going to be cold enough."

Rye laughed, "You're getting crazy in your old age. I was thinking we might go stripe fishing. I heard they were hitting pretty well."

"I'll check it out, and we will try to go," I replied.

As soon as we hung up, I went to the building where I stored my boat and started rounding up rod and reels, replacing the string on the reels, and just otherwise getting ready, because I was fixing to go stripe fishing whether it was cold or not.

Lela was heading towards a state softball championship. Her team was excellent, and Lela was pitching exceptionally well. As they entered the playoffs, we fully expected Lela's team to win their region and advance to the state finals. As it approached, I was looking forward to spending some time with Lela. It had gotten to the point that the only time I got to see her was when she was on the softball field. She had already attracted quite a bit of interest from several colleges and had been offered full scholarships to six different schools, with more sure to follow. Lela was not a nervous wreck anymore when it was her turn to pitch, and she was, in fact, the model of confidence. She was still having fun playing the game, and that was what was most important to me.

The week of the state championship came down to a final two out of three between Russellville Generals and a team from the southern point of the state called the Brewton Bears. The Bears were undefeated, and three players on that team that had already committed to play for major colleges. They claimed the best pitcher in the state and had two of the best hitters. Lela was picked to pitch the first game against their best pitcher. Once the game started, she was as calm as could be. She was almost perfect. The other team's two top hitters were one for five between them, with the only hit being a single to right field. She shut them out and pitched a two-hitter. The Generals won 2-0. The next game, however, was won by the Bears. They scored early and often, with the final score being 10-5. That set up a final game for the state championship.

Lela was ready to go for the championship, and it was fiercely contested. The Bear's pitcher was even better in this game than she had been in the first. It was a ballgame where the best girls' softball teams in the state were on display. A couple of errors in the bottom of the fifth inning allowed one run to score on a close play at the plate, and that was the way it ended. The Bears had won the state championship, and my heart broke for my Lela.

As we were driving home, not much was said. I glanced in the rearview mirror to see Lela holding her "red map," which was what they gave to the second place team in the state championship. I was not going to say anything. I was going to wait until Lela was ready to talk.

Finally she said, "Poppa, I know you're worried about me, but I'm alright because I know I pitched my best."

"You sure did," I said. "I couldn't be more proud of you."

"We should win next year. They're going to lose about seven players off their team and we'll only lose two. I know we're going to be better next year."

"That's my girl, and a red map is better than no map."

She laughed and said, "Yes, but I wish we had gotten that blue one."

After her performance at state, I knew the offers from colleges with good softball programs would only increase. It was summer, their school was out, and Rye was at our house about four days a week. It was amazing how fast that young man was growing. He was getting taller, stronger, faster, and adding weight. He was beginning to work out with weights, which I thought he was still too young for, but he assured me he was not.

We now had two Jet Skis, and we would go on long rides. One day Rye was down at the pier, waiting on me to come down and ride, and I noticed two girls about his age come by on their own Jet Skis. They slowed down and waved at Rye. When he waved back, they pulled over toward our pier. I delayed my walk and just watched. It was funny to me, and I just wanted to see what would happen.

In a couple of minutes, Rye came bounding up the steps. "Dee, is it okay if I go riding with those girls up to Goose Bottoms?"

I laughed and said, "Yeah, you go ahead. My back is hurting me a little bit, and I probably don't need to be jumping waves today anyway."

There was that grin again. "Okay. I won't be gone long."

As they sped out of sight, I thought, *Oh Lord, my Rye is growing up.*

Lela, on the other hand, was getting ready to go on a mission trip to Haiti. It had been her idea to go on this trip with her church group. Penny and Jon were dead set against it at first, but after talking to a lot of people, they finally gave in and let her go. Some of the college teams that had already offered Lela a scholarship had been helpful by telling Jon and Penny that it would be great for Lela and would not affect their offer.

Lela was so excited. Not so much about going to Haiti, but more important to her was the possibility that she was going to be able to help people that had less than her. There wasn't anything to not love about that girl, and I had no doubt that she would get a lot out of the experience. She was going to be gone for fourteen days, and that worried me, but I knew the adults going with her would see to her safety. I didn't have much time to think, because Rye kept me busy every day, and on top of that, the fish were biting.

CHAPTER 17

When Lela returned, I could not wait to hear all about her trip. Madonna and I took her to her favorite steakhouse to get the full scoop. It didn't take long for me to realize Lela had just had a life-changing experience. She told us all about Haiti, and the one thing she continually stressed was the abject poverty she had witnessed.

"I held babies that were malnourished," Lela said. With tears in her eyes she explained how they would look into her eyes with what could only be described as hope. I knew my girl was hooked and that she had found her calling in life. As we were finishing up dinner, she calmly said, "I volunteered to return to Haiti next summer for a two month mission."

Although I was thrilled for Lela and the direction her life was taking, I had that sinking feeling in the pit of my stomach. What if something happened? What if she was not happy? I dismissed it as one of the things you have no control over, and my optimistic side kicked in and assured me everything would work out for the best.

With school back in session, I was excited about the upcoming football games for Rye. He was excited too and was working hard. Lela was deep into preparing for her final year at school and was beginning to focus in on where she was going to go to college.

It was late on a Tuesday afternoon when I got a call from her. "Poppa, I've been selected as a finalist for the National Merit Scholarship Award! Can you believe it?" It was starting to come together for her, and I couldn't have been more proud. "I'm getting these scholarship offers from everywhere. Some for softball and some are academic."

I had to laugh. "You know all that stuff I bought you every time you got a report card?"

Lela giggled. "What's that got to do with it?"

"That's why I bought you all that stuff; I was hoping you would get these offers, get a good education, and one day pay me back."

We both laughed. "Aw, Poppa, you always make me laugh."

"Seriously, Lela, you just keep digging, keep working, and study those offers very carefully. The one thing I want you to promise is that when you decide where you are going to college, I want it to be a decision that makes Lela happy."

"You know I will. You've always told me to pursue happiness above wealth since I was little. I've never forgotten."

"Life is a balancing act, Lela, and it doesn't hurt to have a little money to go with the happiness."

"I love you," she said as we hung up.

As I reflected on what Lela had just told me, it did not surprise me that she was a National Merit Scholarship finalist. That kid was always so focused and intelligent, and nothing she achieved would surprise me.

Rye was quickly establishing that he would be one of the best football players to come out of this part of the country in decades. He thoroughly enjoyed going to practice, the games, the camaraderie with his teammates, and he was becoming a good student of the game. As I watched him play that year, I saw a determination to succeed and a desire to excel that you don't see very often in kids. I often wondered where his gift came from, although I knew part of it was heredity. Jon had been one of the best running backs in his high school, but this kid was going to break every high school record in the country.

In the back of my mind I worried about Rye getting hurt. I wondered what would happen if he suffered a knee injury and had to go through rehab. Over the years I had seen plenty of talented kids suffer injuries, and for the most part they never seemed to get back to 100%. I kept my fingers crossed, and Rye just kept running and running. It wasn't long before Jon and Penny started hearing from college coaches, and even some big-time names began to pop up. I couldn't get over the fact that it had started at such an early age. Recruiting a kid still in junior high must have been the new norm. I wondered if twenty or thirty years from now they would be recruiting kids playing pee-wee football.

One day in early February, Lela called. She was so excited that her words were mumbled together, and I couldn't make out what she was saying. I thought something was wrong. "Poppa! Poppa! I got it! I got it! Can you believe it? I got it!"

"Slow down, Lela. What did you get?"

"It came in the mail. The one I've been looking for. It came, Poppa, it came." It must have dawned on Lela that she was incoherent, because she suddenly said, "Hold on a minute." After a brief pause, her voice came back on the other end of the line, sounding much clearer. "I got an official scholarship offer from Loyola."

I was stunned. Her happiness flowed through the phone, into my ear, and down to my toes. "Oh, Lela, I'm so happy for you. I can't think of anything that has made me this happy in years. Well, are you going to accept?"

"I think I am. Mom and Dad and I are going to sit down the first of May and look at everything and decide. I think I'm going to do what you always told me: seek happiness. I love you, Poppa. I have to go. I have pitching practice, and I'm going to get that blue map to go with the red map I got last year," she said happily.

It was time for state playoffs before I could turn around. Another road trip for Madonna and me, and we thoroughly enjoyed our experience. We got to meet some of the coaches that were feverishly recruiting Lela, and I wondered if they knew she already had a Loyola scholarship in her pocket.

Lela pitched her heart out, and the other teams couldn't touch her. What surprised me was her hitting. She hit three homeruns during the playoffs and was named MVP of the state championship. Lela rode home with us after the tournament, and she held that blue map with pride. I saw a young woman that knew what she wanted and was ready to start a new chapter in her life.

"I know what I'm going to do. I am going to accept the Loyola scholarship and start there this fall. In the meantime, after high school graduation I'm going to leave for the mission trip to Haiti."

"Does your mom and dad know?" I asked.

"Yes, I told them last night. They were good with it. They said I had earned it. Mom is still fussing that it's too far from home, but she hugged and kissed me about fifty times and told me how proud she was of me."

"Lela, your life is before you. I used to worry a lot about you growing up, but I don't worry as much anymore. You are probably better prepared for Loyola than Loyola is for you."

"I'm going to miss you the most, Poppa."

"That means a lot to me. You will always be my girl."

I saw that Madonna's eyes were moist, and she said, "Lela, what am I going to do? I'm worried sick. I just wish you would stay home, but I know you're doing the right thing."

"Nonna, you'll be worried sick about me when I'm forty years old." Lela and I were both laughing as we turned into Bluff Shores.

Graduation night arrived, and as we were getting ready to go, the phone rang. It was Manny.

After exchanging greetings, he told me was currently in Managua.

"What, did Melinda finally talk you into a vacation?" I asked.

"No, I'm in a hospital," he said somberly. "I had to have bladder surgery."

I cringed. "I can't believe that. Are you okay?"

"Well, I am fine now. The doctors tell me I am as good as new. I should be able to go home in a couple of days. This getting old crap is for the birds. I called because Melinda and I are going to be in your part of the world in November. We are going to visit Melinda's sister in Georgia."

"Well, well, well, Manny! You had better make some time to stay a few days with Madonna and me."

"Oh, we will, Laroy. I will get back with you, and we will firm something up. I just wanted to let you know so you would keep that in mind."

"That's great, Manny. Tell Melinda I can't wait for her to meet Madonna. I'm sure she will take Melinda shopping and spend a ton of your money."

Manny laughed and said, "I was afraid you would say that. I have got to go. The doctor just came in, and I am going to twist his arm and see if he will let me go home in the morning. I will talk to you soon."

Another week went by, and we carried Lela to the airport to board her flight for her two-month mission in Haiti. As she boarded, I saw a beautiful and intelligent young woman who was utterly convinced that her life's purpose lay straight in front of her. Penny and Jon were hopeful that this would be one of the last missions she would volunteer for, and they reasoned that once she got into the swing of college life that she would be more focused on her future career.

I asked them why Rye hadn't come to see his sister off. Penny smiled and said, "Dee, in case you haven't noticed, girls are now his number one priority. He got invited to a swim party over at a girl's house, and when I questioned him about it, he told me there was going to be about twelve girls at the party. I had to pump him for more information, and he finally owned up that he was going to be the only boy there."

I laughed and said, "I hope you didn't embarrass him about that. I told you all a long time ago that Rye was going to break all kind of records."

It was well into summer and Lela was expected back in a couple of weeks. Rye asked if he could have a few friends out for a lake party. I reluctantly agreed and asked him, "Are you inviting those same twelve girls that you went to the swim party with earlier this summer?"

His face turned red. "No, Dede. It will be about four guys and five girls."

I could tell he had given the party some thought. I asked, "Are these four guys guards and tackles on the football team?"

"Why would you ask that?"

I smiled and said, "I just wanted to know how much food to buy."

His laugh told me he approved. "Only two of the guys play on the line, and, yes, they eat a lot."

On the day of Rye's party it was beautiful, not a cloud in the sky, and hot. The kids started showing up around noon, and it didn't take long for them to hit the water. I noticed that Rye took one of the girls on a Jet Ski ride, and I thought to myself that she must be the one that was his sweetheart.

I fired up the grill after a while and cooked what I was sure was way too many hamburgers and hot dogs. When everything was ready, Madonna and I served them on the patio down by the pier. Man, I have seen kids eat, but those two kids that played in the line consumed enough food to make even me shake my head.

Rye was laughing at them and kept saying, "Eat all you want, we have plenty, but you better block well for me this year."

Madonna and I moved back up to the porch after lunch and just observed. It was an afternoon of abundant laughter and continuous plunging into the cool waters of Bluff Creek. I could tell they were having fun, and as the evening wore on, I decided to load up the pontoon boat and take them up to Goose Bottoms. Once I was anchored down, they all offloaded and began to play, swim, and do what kids that age do. The laughter was continuous as the evening sun slowly started to sink in the west.

At one point, Rye and I were the only ones on the boat, and he said, "You know, they say I'm going to get a scholarship to play football. They're already trying to recruit me."

I nodded my head and said, "Boy, there's no telling where you are headed. You will be as good as you want to be."

"Do you know if Army has ever won a National Championship?"

I was stunned by the question. "Well, I don't know for sure, but I know they haven't in my lifetime."

"That's where I want to go to college. I want to help them win their first National Championship."

"That's good, Rye. That's good."

The little honey-eyed blonde that Rye had taken for the Jet Ski ride suddenly appeared. She climbed up the ladder and said, "Come on, Rye. Let's swim."

He smiled at me and said, "We'll talk about that later."

CHAPTER 18

A few days later it was time to meet Lela at the airport. Jon and Penny called and asked if Rye could ride with us. On the way to the airport, we talked about old times, and Rye kept us laughing by telling Madonna some of the stuff he and I had done and never told her. She pretended to be so upset that we would do such outlandish things. Rye just laughed and laughed. I could tell that he was ready to see his sister, and that made me proud.

As Lela came out of the plane and into our view, I saw that something was different about her. She had the bounce of someone who knew where she was heading in life. That jaw of hers was jutted out with a look of confident determination. Her smile was engaging, and you could tell just by looking that this girl was happy. She grabbed Rye and gave him a big old hug, and he lit up like a Christmas tree. After hugging Penny, Jon, and Madonna, she approached me.

"Poppa, I wish you could have been with me. You would have loved it. I got to meet some wonderful people, and I got to help some wonderful little kids who have nothing. I think my time and efforts will help some of these kids. It's all about hope."

On the day Lela left to make her trip to Loyola, it was pouring down rain. We all gathered together in the terminal at the airport, and Jon said a small prayer asking that God watch over Lela and give her safety and success in her studies. It was especially tough on Penny to see her baby girl spread her wings and fly from the nest. Even Rye seemed a little downcast. I knew those two could sometimes fight like cats and dogs, but they were there for each other, and in many ways, I felt that they were even closer than any of us knew.

Lela was as upbeat as she could be. Before boarding, she hugged Penny and said, "Mother, don't you worry. I'm going to be just fine." I saw a few tears in Penny's eyes, but I also saw confidence.

When it came to Madonna, Lela laughed and said, "Nonna, I'm not even going to ask you not worry. It won't do any good."

I felt a sense of sadness that I had never experienced before. It was as if I was burdened by the thought of something that I knew I could not accept. As I hugged my girl goodbye, it dawned on me what that sadness was. It was life.

Soon it was time for Rye's first high school football game, and he was ready. A ninth-grade kid starting on his high school football team is pretty unusual, and I could tell Rye wanted that honor, but it was not to be. On Thursday, the coach gave his team the starting lineup, and a senior who had started the previous year got the nod. I called Rye on Thursday night and we talked about it.

"Don't worry," I said. "You'll get your chance. That young man who's starting has paid his dues, and by being a senior he deserves the honor."

"I just want to play," Rye replied.

I laughed, "You came into this world wanting to play and play you will. Now be patient."

"I hear you, Dee. You're always telling me to be patient."

I got to see Rye before the game, and I was somewhat surprised at his demeanor. The boy was as calm as a cucumber, and he displayed a quiet confidence that I didn't often see in him.

The first quarter was an excellent defensive battle with neither team being able to move the ball. Midway through the second quarter, with the score still 0 to 0, Russellville took over the ball at their 45-yard line. As I looked down on the field, I saw #34 trotting out toward the huddle for his first high school snap. I poked Madonna in the ribs and said, "There goes our boy."

The first snap was a pass out in the flat to the wide receiver, and it was overthrown. On the next play, the quarterback handed the ball to Rye, who broke through the line. The middle linebacker was in perfect position to make the play, there was a collision, and the middle linebacker went sprawling backward. I leaped to my feet as Rye cut to the outside, and the race was on. I screamed, "Go!" The safety had the angle on Rye, but the safety was no match for #34's speed.

A 55-yard touchdown run on his first carry in high school, no wonder the colleges were already recruiting the kid. As I looked around the stadium, I heard a "buzz," and it was like the people were in shock and not quite sure what they had just seen. Rye got to play a few more snaps and busted off a couple of good runs. The final score was 7 to 0, and it was a game that would mark the beginning of an unbelievable journey for a young man named Rye.

Lela was getting settled in at Loyola, and about twice a week I would get an email from her, keeping me up to speed on what was going on with her school work. Lela would always end her emails with *P.S. - Send money. Ha!*

I knew she was having a ball by the tone of her emails. I got a rather lengthy email from her one particular day that got more into the nuts and bolts of her life on campus. The bulk of it had to do with professors.

Poppa, I have some professors who to me are just plain radical, and I sometimes get upset when I'm in class and have to listen to what they're teaching. I've met quite a few of my classmates who feel the same way. How do you think I should handle the situation?

I had to laugh at that. She was a clean-cut, all-American kid going to Loyola, and she was surprised to have radical professors? Lela was getting an education in more ways than one. She didn't know it yet, but she didn't need my advice, because she had been prepared well in advance. I could tell she was enjoying her time at Loyola by the way she described the beauty of the campus and by the way she wrote about some of the people she had met.

I decided to answer her email with a short reply.

To My Girl: When in Rome, do as the Romans do! Love, Poppa.

P.S. - Please find money enclosed.

I knew that would make her laugh. She had always liked people that were short and to the point.

It was closing in on Thanksgiving, and we were somewhat disappointed that Lela was not going to get to come home. We had all been ready to have her home for a few days. Manny called. He and Melinda had arrived in Georgia and were enjoying their stay at Melinda's sister's house. I invited them to come over before Thanksgiving and stay a few days with us. In the back of my mind, I figured if I could get them to come over before Thanksgiving, I could take Manny hunting at Fort Boyd and Madonna and Melinda could go shopping for a couple of days. It's funny how a devious little mind functions.

Sure enough, they came on the Monday before Thanksgiving with plans to stay for five or six days. Madonna and Melinda hit it off immediately, and Manny and I were soon free to do as we pleased. Pretty soon we were gathering up stuff to get ready to leave on Wednesday.

Rye called. "Dee, are you packed and ready?"

I told him about Manny, and Rye became excited. He had heard me talk about Manny and knew he was retired Army. "You mean I'm going to get to hunt with Manny? That's great! I'll see you all tomorrow."

It was all set. Another Thanksgiving hunt, and this time with my good friend Manny along. As Manny and I made the drive to Fort Boyd, our conversation was all over the map, and we caught up on old times.

It was a sunny and beautiful Thanksgiving morning at Fort Boyd, and I was in my little world. As I sat in a shooting house looking over a small creek, I was watching two young beavers at play when I heard two quick shots. I knew it was Rye. It wasn't long before I heard my old 270 fire. I had loaned it to Manny to hunt with on the trip. It was that one shot that I heard so many times before. It told me that Manny had gotten a deer.

It was about 10:00 when it suddenly sounded like a small war had broken out. There was shooting going on all around me. Tony, Fred, Thomas, and Pierce were all shooting. As I glanced to my left, four hogs came charging through the woods and were about to cross the creek. I readied my gun as they plunged into the water. The biggest one caught my eye, and I fired. It collapsed right in the middle of the creek. With all the game we were harvesting that morning, it was a good thing we had Rye and Thomas along to do the skinning.

About fifteen minutes later, Tony showed up on his four-wheeler and said, "Man, it's a good thing we got Rye and Thomas with us."

I laughed and said, "That's just what I was thinking."

"By my count, we got eleven hogs, two eight-point bucks, and three coyotes. Your friend Manny got one of the biggest eight-points ever to come off of this property, according to Fred."

I looked at Tony and said, "Well, we might as well get on with it."

I knew we were going to be so busy that it would lead to another bologna sandwich Thanksgiving Day at Fort Boyd.

When we got over to where Manny was hunting, Rye was already there and Manny was beaming from ear to ear. "Laroy, this is one sweet shooting 270 you let me hunt with."

I laughed and looked at Rye. "Boy, what did you get?"

Rye replied, "Two coyotes and two wild hogs. I saw that old buck that has a twisted and gnarled up rack, but I let him walk."

"That deer must be old as the hills. How it still lives I don't know. Well, let's load up and go over to where Fred, Thomas, and Pierce are and get the rest of the low down."

As we approached the area where Thomas was hunting, I saw Thomas, Fred, and Pierce standing in a small opening by their four-wheelers. The closer we got, I could see a mass of black behind them. It was seven wild hogs. I noticed that on the front of Thomas's four-wheeler was a nice eight-point.

We were all standing around, talking about what we had just experienced, when Rye said, "Thomas, I heard you shoot at about 10:15, and then about ten minutes later I heard a pig squeal. What was that all about?"

Thomas laughed and said, "I shot a small boar but just wounded it, and it got into the brush before I could finish it. After a few minutes I came down out of my stand and went over to investigate, and it charged me, so I pulled my bowie knife and stabbed it."

Rye looked at Thomas in shock. "You did what?"

We all got a good laugh. That young man was a hunter. Thomas had been a lot of help to Rye and had taught him a lot about hunting and preparing the game for the freezer. In the process, they had saved Tony and me from a bunch of work.

Fred chimed in, "Let's go back to the cabin and get the small trailer for the hogs and coyotes."

That sounded good to everyone else. It was getting close to lunch, and we had a lot do before the evening hunt. After eating our traditional Thanksgiving Day lunch of bologna and cheese sandwiches, Rye and Thomas took the trailer and went back into the woods to retrieve the rest of the game.

While they were gone, Manny remarked, "They are kind of like... what you always say, Laroy? Two peas in a pod."

I laughed and said, "You haven't seen anything yet, Manny. Just wait until they get back. Watch what they do."

The boys were not gone too long, and when they got back they went straight to work. It was automatic, almost like a game with no wasted motion. Rye and Thomas hung those wild hogs and skinned them in what seemed like no time at all. The long knives were flying, and each motion was a precision cut that seemed to require minimal effort.

Manny could not believe what he saw. "Man, I would hate to tie up with those two in a knife fight."

The next couple of days passed without a whole lot of action, and soon it was time to pack up and head back home. As always, for some strange reason, I felt depressed as I left Fort Boyd. This time I finally decided the reason why. I knew that someday this would all end.

CHAPTER 19

When Manny and I got back home, it was evident that Madonna and Melinda had been having a great time. I looked at Melinda and said, "Did Madonna give you enough help in spending some of Manny's money?"

She laughed and said, "Oh yes. Enough so that when I get back to Nicaragua, I may have to get a part-time job."

The next day Manny and Melinda had to return to Dawn's house to prepare for their trip back home. As we were saying goodbye, Manny said, "Laroy, that boy Rye is something. He is going to be a great soldier. He is the closest thing I have ever seen to a true warrior. You are truly blessed, and America will be in good hands with him as a member of the Armed Forces."

I was somewhat puzzled, and Manny could tell. "You mean you didn't know he plans to make a career in the military? Rye told me he wants to join the Army and be a member of the Special Forces."

I thanked Manny for telling me, and I decided that I was not going to say anything to Rye. I reasoned that he would tell me in due time. As I waved goodbye to Manny and Melinda, I couldn't help but wonder if I would ever see either one of them again.

The next few days I spent reflecting on our hunt and what Manny had said about Rye's ambition. I was still puzzled as to why Rye had not mentioned it to me. Then I remembered our conversation on the pontoon boat during Rye's lake party. That must have been his way of saying to me that he was thinking about making a career in the Army. Although I had plenty of reservations about him being in the Army, I knew that sometimes in life things seemed to be just true destiny.

It was evident that the recruitment of Rye to play college football had begun when I got a phone call from Penny. "It seems like every day a new letter arrives in the mail from a different university. We're getting letters from all across the country, and I don't want him to get distracted by all this attention. I want him to stay focused."

I laughed and replied, "Penny, my dear, the last thing you have to worry about is that boy being focused. Just put those things up in the closet, and in a couple of years, when the time is right, get them down and go over them with Rye." I didn't have the nerve to tell Penny that I suspected Rye's mind was already made up about his future anyway.

A couple of days later an email showed up in my inbox from Lela.

Poppa, I'll be home the 17th of December for Christmas vacation. I'm learning to do as the Roman's do, and my grades are quite well, thank you for asking. Love, Lela. P.S. - Send Money. Ha!

That girl was getting wiser by the day.

On the 14th of December, we had an unusual weather event for our area. Bluff Shores was blanketed by eight inches of snow. It was beautiful to look at as I sat on the glassed-in porch with my coffee cup and surveyed that wonderful little place I got to call home. And there he was in his usual spot, the old Gray Heron, with the surrounding bluff and waterfall covered in snow as he fished for breakfast. I was at peace with my life and blessed that my marvelous journey had given me so much happiness. Lela and Rye made it complete.

Lela's plane arrived, and my girl got off and bounded out with that spring in her step that told me she was glad to be home. She was so busy during the holidays with friends that I didn't get to spend as much time with her as I would have liked. What was enjoyable to me was the closeness that I saw between her and her brother. Rye acted as if he was Lela's sole protector, and he insisted on going everywhere with her. She was only able to go and do things by herself when she put her foot down and told Rye he was not going. However, she had learned how to do it diplomatically. One day in particular, she dropped Rye off at the house. She and a couple of her former teammates were going shopping and to a movie.

I took the opportunity to question Rye a little bit about his future. I went straight at him, "Rye, are you planning on joining the Army after college?"

He gave me that disarming grin and replied, "I think you know I'm all about fighting the bad guys. The problem I have is that some of the kids at school are saying I'm going somewhere like Alabama, Auburn, Ohio State, or Michigan. I've even heard some say I'm going to USC. I don't think they're going to like it very much when I go to Army University."

I laughed, "Boy, don't worry too much about that. You do what you think is best and listen to your mom and dad."

"I will, Dee, but I already know that Mom wants me to go to Auburn and Dad wants me to go to Alabama."

I just smiled and said, "Dee, wants you to do what is best for Rye."

"You know I always listen to you." That was all it took to make my holidays happy and bright.

One day after Christmas was over, Lela called. "Poppa, I want to spend the night before I have to go back to school tomorrow. Would you take me to the airport to catch my flight in the morning?"

She knew the answer to that before she asked. I knew this would be our time to talk and I couldn't wait for her to come over. Penny brought her, and we had a long, enjoyable dinner and spoke of the good times we'd had while she was growing up. We laughed a lot, and soon Penny had to go. She hugged Lela, and I saw a bond between a mother and a daughter that was pure and strong.

As the night wore on, Lela opened up and started telling me all about Loyola and her experiences in her first semester. "It was a big adjustment at first. Everything seemed to be so much faster than what I was accustomed. The other students come from everywhere, and all the different backgrounds and life experiences are much more varied than you would imagine. I love the school, and I know I've complained about some of my professors, but all in all, it's just what I want in a college."

"That's great, Lela. Now tell me something about the boys!"

"Poppa, you're impossible!" she said, getting flustered. Then, with a slight grin, she said, "I have met some very nice young men. Some of them I think you would like, and some of them I know you would put on the road in a heartbeat."

I laughed, "You can tell them all you got this old crazy poppa that will light them up if they mess with my girl."

She changed the subject. "I'm going to have a nearly perfect grade point average this semester. When you told me 'When in Rome, do as the Romans do,' it helped me, and I just wanted to thank you."

I could have cried. Here was a young girl, who was much smarter than I would ever be, praising an old man for being himself. I could tell she was getting sleepy, so I suggested she get some sleep. I could have stayed up all night talking to my girl, but I knew I was telling her right.

After taking Lela to the airport the next day, I came home and began the process of hunkering down to ride out the death throes of winter. The older I got, the more I questioned the validity of January and February. It just seemed to me those two months were a total waste of time and counter to any progress for humanity in general. I had tried for years to convince myself that it was a necessary downtime for all people. I even made the argument that it was impossible not to respect these two months, for one marked the beginning of the year and the other marked Valentine's Day and all the expressions of love.

That argument always failed me when I remembered that February would leap every four years, as if to signal that it was sick of itself. At the end of each February, I celebrated that I had succeeded in making it through another winter, and my spirits automatically soared as I anticipated another spring and the rebirth of nature.

Rye was toying with the idea of playing baseball in the spring, and as usual, anything that boy decided to try did not surprise me in the least. I was somewhat upbeat about the prospects, as it would give me something to add to my to-do list, get me out of the house more often, and let me spend more time with Rye. I never knew exactly why, but I had always been partial to what we called "The Boys of Summer" back in the day. As a boy, I always followed the Yankees, and most of my weekends were spent in front of the television watching the exploits of my heroes. I was not alone. Many of the young boys my age enjoyed the game as much as I did. I looked back and realized I could have spent my youth on much less trivial pursuits. Ah, those days of my misspent childhood. I did miss those days.

It became pretty apparent after a few games that although Rye was blessed with an abundance of physical talent his lack of time in the batter's box would not be kind to him. He got better as the season wound down and made some incredible plays in the outfield. What was funny to me was that before the season was over, two colleges had offered him a scholarship to play both football and baseball. I found that amusing, but I had bigger fish to fry. The flowers were blooming, the weather was warming, and I could see summer. It was time to live.

School was rapidly approaching the end of the year for both Rye and Lela, and I knew I would get to see a lot of Rye. The phone rang that night. It was Lela, and I could tell by the excitement in her voice that she had something on her mind.

"I need to ask you something."

"Go ahead, Lela." I had no idea where this conversation was headed.

Lela's words came quickly, "One of my political science professors has encouraged me to apply for a summer internship in the United States Congress. He told me he would do everything he could to help me get the appointment. What do you think?"

"I think that's wonderful. I hope you get the appointment, but just remember a lot of kids probably apply and there are only a few slots available."

"Oh, I know, Poppa. I already have my application filled out, and it's ready to mail, but I just wanted to run it by you first. How well do you know Congressman Parker? Do you think you might call him and put in a good word for me?"

"Sure, I'll call Wango, uh, I mean Congressman Parker, and tell him you have applied and see if there is anything he can do."

"That would be great, and don't worry if I don't get the appointment. I will be just as happy to go back to Haiti and work with all those wonderful babies. I almost didn't apply because I would miss the mission trip."

I could feel the love coming through the phone, and I said, "Lela, you're a hopeless romantic, and I guess that's why I love you so much."

"Either way, Poppa, I'll be home in a few days and would you please grill some of those baby back ribs? I have been craving some for months."

"That sounds good, Lela. You be safe, and I will see you in a few days."

The next day I called Wango. He seemed to be doing well, and he sounded upbeat about the direction our country was headed. I told him about Lela's application and asked him what he thought. He was optimistic and said he would get his staff on it in a couple of days to see if he could get her assigned to his office.

"Leroy, you know full well how political this place is, and it might not be possible for me to pull it off, but you can bet I am going to try."

"I'm not asking for you to make a few more rubber chicken dinners to get her an appointment, but whatever you can do will be appreciated."

"When I leave this place, I will never eat a piece of chicken again as long as I live."

I hung up thinking about Lela being an intern in the United States Congress that summer, and I felt that it would be an excellent experience for her, especially if she worked for Wango.

It was a warm, beautiful day at Bluff Shores. Lela was home and worried that she might not get her appointment. I was not the least bit concerned. I was staring deep into my cup of coffee, contemplating what would happen in the world that day, when the phone rang.

It was Lela. "I got the appointment! My letter came yesterday, but Mom forgot to bring in the mail. I'm so excited! But I won't be home much longer. I have to be in Washington on June the 5th to start my internship."

"That's great, Lela! What exactly will you be doing? Do you know?"

"I'll be doing research and helping to compile position papers of upcoming legislation pending in Congress. I will be met at the airport by an aide in Congressman Parker's office. Poppa, I love you!"

That was one of those things that Lela could do, and she always knew how to melt my heart. "Girl, I hope to see you before you go, but if I don't, you know I will always be with you."

The summer was buzzing by faster than a yellow jacket on a sugar high. I tried to slow it down, but it was no use. One Saturday morning, Madonna and I went into town for breakfast. We had just been seated and were preparing to order, when Rye's football coach came in with his wife.

Coach Liles was what they called a player's coach, and just about everybody in the community respected him.

Coach Liles passed our table, and then turned back around and said, "Mr. Overstreet, do you mind if the wife and I join you for breakfast?"

"No, please. And please call me Leroy, Coach."

His wife was a pleasant looking lady who appeared to be a good bit younger than Coach Liles. As she and Madonna chatted, Coach Liles talked exclusively about Rye. It was Rye this and Rye that, and finally he said, "Rye is a natural born leader and a natural born..." his voice trailed off.

I was into his thoughts, so I finished the sentence for him, "A natural born warrior."

"Exactly, Leroy. The kid is phenomenal, and one day I asked Rye about you, and his response made me want to talk to you about him. He answered me as he always does—straightforward. 'Coach, Dee is not my grandfather, he's my great-uncle, but Leroy is not that to me at all. He's my brother.'"

I knew I looked embarrassed, and I tried to hide it, but Coach Liles saw right through me. "I just wanted you to know, that whatever you have done for Rye, I for one don't think he can ever repay you."

Very seldom had I found myself in a situation where I could not respond to any statement or question, but that was one of the few times in my life I was dumbfounded.

Coach Liles continued, "That boy has more ability, more talent, and more physical ability than any athlete that I have ever coached. There is very little limit to what he can achieve. He'll probably be the number one player in the state next year, and the scary part is that he's probably number one right now. To be a sophomore and be considered the number one athlete is mind-boggling. I have seen him do things in practice that defy believability. We are going to be very careful in how we handle this young man, as the last thing I want to happen is for him to get hurt. Rye tells me you've been challenging him ever since he could remember, and that you always pushed him to do his best, regardless of what he was attempting to do. The main thing you knew was just when to let off the gas and even apply the brake if needed. Leroy, you should have been a coach. I hope you will give me some input and some direction when it comes to making sure Rye is successful and achieves all he can."

I laughed and said, "Coach, I appreciate the kind words, and I have always tried to help Rye in any way I could, but you can't teach what is pumped from a warrior's heart."

I left that breakfast thinking Rye was lucky to have Coach Liles.

CHAPTER 20

It was mid-June before I heard from Lela. Her email told me all I needed and then some. She was living the dream in the halls of Congress of all places. She was enjoying her work and meeting a lot of wonderful people.

Poppa, Congressman Parker is so nice and such a good man. I'm working hard, and I really enjoy all this research work we are doing. It is so interesting. I do miss home though, and most of all I miss you. All of this political stuff they do in Washington does have a much greater impact on the lives of every single person in this country, and it also affects many millions of people around the world. A lady that I work with has introduced me to a group called "Quality of Life." You just watch, they're going to do great things for people all over the world. When I get home, I'll tell you all about it. Love you, Lela.

P.S. - This email has no request for you to send money. Ha!

That girl. There was no telling what all she had learned and how the experience would help her in the future, but

I was so glad that she had gotten the opportunity. It was something that most kids never got to experience.

As summer drew to a close, Rye was already involved in fall practice, and Lela was home for a few days, preparing to make her way back to Loyola. I bemoaned the fact that they were growing up so fast, but nobody was listening. I, true to form, did not lose much sleep over what I could not control.

One morning, I decided to drive into town and pick up some supplies. I would probably also look around and buy some stuff that I didn't need, but I figured I would do my part to help keep the economy healthy. My reasoning was not always sound, but then again, I didn't lose any sleep over it. I rounded a small curve in the road and saw something moving in the ditch to my left. I immediately recognized that it was a little deer. I pulled the car off to the side of the road and went back to check it out. It was a doe that appeared to have been hit by a car. It was in the grip of death, unable to move and in obvious pain. I realized at that moment how weak and vulnerable I had become as a person.

As I looked into those baby doe eyes, I was paralyzed by the pain and the fact that there was nothing I could do to help that poor animal. A grizzled old man, who had seen too much death and too much pain, was having difficulty dealing with a deer who had been hit by a car. I came to grips with the reality of what had to be done. I reached into my car and got my old .38 service revolver and put the poor doe out of its misery. I turned the car around and went back home. My day was ruined.

Oh, how quickly summer had escaped. I became immediately involved in Rye's football season. It helped me avoid the thoughts of winter. Just as quickly as summer had flown by, Rye's football season was winding down. Rye had broken the state record for rushing yards in a single game and was on track to break the state record for rushing yards in a season. The Russellville Generals were on track for a state championship. Coach Liles had been true to his word, and when a game was under control, he would pull Rye and make him sit. It was good for Rye, but it was also like not allowing a stallion to race.

I bumped into Coach Liles after the last game of the regular season, and he asked me, "Do you know about this obsession Rye has about going to West Point and playing for Army?"

"Rye hasn't said much to me, but we did have a conversation one afternoon where he asked me if Army had ever won a national championship."

Coach Liles laughed and said "That explains it. Rye is going to put Army on his back and tote them to a national championship. I've tried to explain to that young man that he is going to get offers from just about every major college in the country, and I hope he will give them due consideration."

I laughed and said, "I'm with you, Coach, but go Army."

He looked at me as if I was crazy, but then he smiled and said, "I get it, Leroy. That young man is going to make his own decisions, and what do we know, right? Rye would probably laugh at us right now if he heard our conversation."

"You just keep doing what you think is right for Rye. We're thankful that you're his coach, and we trust your judgment."

As we drove home that night, I told Madonna not to be surprised if Rye went to West Point and became an officer in the Army after college. Madonna was shocked, and her immediate response was, "Oh no. I want him to stay in state so he'll be close to us."

I knew that a battle was brewing over where Rye was going to go to college, but I was entirely confident that Rye would handle the situation as good as any warrior.

Rye's Generals lost the last game of the state playoffs and had to settle for second place. They lost to the English Fort Bulldogs, who had the best defense in years and still could only hold Rye to a season-low rushing total of 122 yards and two touchdowns. It was a bitter defeat for Rye, but I saw no grief. I saw nothing but determination, and I knew that Rye was going to work harder than ever to win that state championship. It was going to be a long year before Rye would once again take the field for his beloved Generals, but for the fans, it would turn out to be well worth the wait.

Lela was planning on coming home for Thanksgiving, and I was excited. Until Madonna reminded me that I would not be at home that weekend if I went hunting at Fort Boyd. I was saddened by that, and I considered writing Lela to tell her that I wouldn't get to be home to see her, but I just couldn't bring myself to write the email. It was about two weeks away, and Rye was already plotting and planning for the trip.

A couple of days later I got an email from Lela.

Poppa,

My plans have changed. I'm not going to get to come home for Thanksgiving because I am going to Vermont. A close friend of mine has invited me to spend Thanksgiving weekend with his parents. Don't worry. He's a great guy, and I trust him. In fact, I may even bring him home for Christmas if you promise not to shoot him. I'll talk to you soon. Love, Lela.

I was both happy and sad. Happy, because if Lela was happy, I was happy, but sad because if I ever needed evidence that Lela was now a young woman, it was right there in the email.

The back and forth between Penny and Madonna was funny to me as they discussed the possibility of Lela getting serious about a boy. It seemed to hurt both of their feelings that the first news of this supposed romance had been delivered to me instead of either of them. It was not unexpected that a young man would vie for Lela's attention, as she had many who had attempted to woo her during her high school days, and I was sure there were just as many at Loyola. A girl with her good looks and classic southern drawl had melted many a heart over the course of time.

It was finally decided that Penny would approach her and try to find out how serious this relationship was and get some background on this young man. I wondered at that point if Madonna had done much research on my background as I had just walked right up to her car as she sat in the parking lot of a local burger joint and asked her name and for a date in one breath. Well, nobody ever accused me of not being straightforward, and besides, when you are young, you are in a hurry. As I have aged, I have finally figured out sometimes it is better to sit back and let nature takes its course.

It was only a couple of days before we left to go hunting, and I woke up that morning with chills and fever. I had Madonna take my temperature, and it was 103, which scared me, as I had not been sick in years. I felt worse as the day wore on, and I began to suspect that I had a full-fledged case of the flu. A trip to the doctor that afternoon confirmed it. As it began to sink in that I would not be able to go to Fort Boyd, I felt even worse. I knew I had to call Rye and tell him.

I could tell he was really disappointed. "You go ahead," I told him. "Call Uncle Tony, and you all plan on going anyway. It's not the first time somebody has missed a hunting trip because of sickness."

"I will, Dee, but I would just as soon come out and stay with you this weekend in case you need me."

I laughed, and even that hurt. "Boy, you go. I'll be just fine. It's nothing Nonna's chicken broth and tender loving care won't fix."

Rye's response caught me by surprise. "Okay. I love you, and I'll call and check on you before we leave."

Before they left, I got a call from Tony to check and see how I was doing. "This is the first time I ever remember you being sick. I know I missed a couple of times and you made fun of me, but since you are old and decrepit, I'm not going to do the same thing to you."

I managed to laugh and say, "You are all heart, my man. I hope that Rye doesn't put you through too much trouble."

"He could never get me in any more trouble than you did. By the way, I got a call from 'Earl the Pearl.' He's planning on coming down for the hunt."

"That's great. Get Rye and Earl in a conversation about football. I almost wish you could tape that conversation for me."

Earl the Pearl had played football for the University of Kentucky back in the early 70s. He was a tough defensive end who loved to put a hit on running backs. I felt that Earl and Rye would have a lot in common.

I no sooner had hung up from talking to Tony when the phone rang again. It was Rye. "You sure you don't feel like going? It's not going to be the same without you."

"You go on and have a good time and be careful. We may try and make another trip down there when you're out for the Christmas holidays." I could tell my boy was looking forward to going, and I knew he would have a good time when he got there. I for one just wanted to get back to normal and get rid of the aches and pains.

I woke up that Thanksgiving morning slightly depressed. I missed being at Fort Boyd, and I missed the camaraderie I had experienced over all the years. I tried to picture which stand I would be in if I were there that morning. It was an exercise in futility, as nothing beat the reality of the peace and quiet at Fort Boyd.

I realized that I was somewhat better that morning and that I was on the road to recovery. I found that my appetite had returned to somewhat near normal, and I was hungry. I couldn't put my finger on what that peculiar smell was. It finally dawned on me that it was Madonna cooking Thanksgiving Dinner. It was something I had not experienced in over thirty years, and this was obviously going to be a very different day than I was accustomed to. I wondered if I would even miss my traditional bologna and cheese sandwich. I highly doubted that I would as I took a deep breath and inhaled the aroma of turkey and sweet potato casserole cooking in the oven. I was able to sip on a cup of coffee for the first time in a couple of days, and my thoughts turned to Lela and her whereabouts in Vermont. I hoped she was having a good time.

After a few days I was feeling a lot better, and Rye came out to check on me and tell me all about his hunt. I was not too surprised that he talked a good bit about Earl the Pearl.

"I had a great time, Dee. How well do you know Earl?"

"I have known Earl about twenty years or so."

"Did he ever tell you about the time he was a freshman on the football team at Kentucky?"

I pretended not to know so I could hear Rye tell it.

"Well, he was at practice one afternoon when their coach was trying to install this new play, and they had Earl lined up as an outside linebacker. They would pitch the ball to the running back, who would try and turn the corner on a sweep and break upfield. The coach told the offense to run the play until they scored, and then practice would be over. Earl decided that was a good time for him to make a good impression on the coach and the team. Every time they ran the play, Earl blew up the blocking and made the tackle. They ran it over and over, and each time, Earl made the tackle. Everybody on both sides of the ball were getting mad, and it got violent. People were getting hurt, and one of the tackles got carried off the field with a broken leg. The coach was screaming at the offense, 'What's wrong with you people? A freshman is making you all look stupid!' Finally, one of the defensive ends came up to Earl and said in no uncertain terms he needed to let them score so they could get off the field and hit the showers. Do you know what Earl told him?"

I shook my head as if I had never heard the story.

"Earl looked the defensive end in the eye and said, 'Shove it, sissy. I'm Earl the Pearl and don't you forget it.'" Rye's whole body shook as he rolled in laughter, and even though I had heard the story before, I couldn't stop laughing either. After Rye regained his composure, he said, "I learned something from that."

"What did you learn, boy?"

He gave me that sly smile and said, "I'm going to play from now on with the same intensity that Earl showed as a freshman. I'm not going to be stopped."

I went to sleep that night convinced that Coach Liles and the Russellville Generals were going to be state champions for two consecutive years.

CHAPTER 21

It was confirmed that Lela would be bringing Emanuel home when the fall term ended. Much apprehension was in the air, and his background was a much-discussed topic between Madonna and Penny. Lela, being her usual mischievous self, would not disclose too much about Emanuel. Instead she fended off each probing question by saying, "You will just have to wait until I get home, and then you may grill him all you like."

She knew that this approach made me laugh, as the women around me were abuzz about meeting the young man who had captured Lela's heart. I too felt a little apprehension, because I had never thought a single man existed that would be good enough for my girl. As that day approached, everything seemed to revolve around getting ready to meet Emanuel. Rye and I had many a good laugh about the situation. We even made jokes about how he might look and what he might sound like. Of course, we did so outside of the earshot of Madonna and Penny.

Rye and I decided we would volunteer to go pick Lela and Emanuel up at the airport, which was promptly vetoed by Madonna and Penny. I knew they were afraid that the initial shock of being interrogated by both me and Rye might prove too much for the young man to handle. It was decided that Penny and Madonna would go and pick them up, which quite honestly was probably the best thing for all concerned.

The day Lela was scheduled to arrive went slowly for me, and I waited impatiently on Madonna to return from the airport and give me the lowdown on Emanuel. When she finally got home, she came through the door, babbling the kind of chatter that she didn't display often. Having lived with her so many years, I knew that Cherokee blood was at a fever pitch. It was a pitch of happiness.

"Oh, Leroy, you are going to adore this young man. I hope that Lela will marry him."

I was speechless, and I couldn't slow her down to ask any questions.

"He comes from a fourth generation family of farmers from Illinois, and his mother is originally from Vermont. His parents just recently bought a place near her old hometown, and they relocated there, but they still operate a huge farm in Illinois. He is such a darling, so polite, so caring, and when he looks at Lela, he lights up like a Christmas tree." I tried to slow her down, but she kept rambling, "He's in pre-law, and that's how he and Lela met. They're just the perfect couple. You just wait; you'll see that I'm right."

Finally, I got a question in, "How was Lela?"

"She was beaming, just beaming. She really is happy. I am telling you, Leroy, that girl is happy."

Finally Madonna started to slow down, and I asked, "When am I going to meet this young man?"

"Penny is cooking dinner tomorrow evening, and she wants us to come over tomorrow after lunch and spend the evening with them."

I laughed, "Penny cooking dinner? I hope she doesn't burn the ramen noodles."

I had Madonna's attention. "How can you say that about her?"

"I was just joking, but I would bet a dollar to a doughnut that Jon and Rye will be cooking steaks tomorrow afternoon."

It was a peaceful night at Bluff Shores for Madonna and me; our Lela was home. The next day, as I patiently waited for Madonna to get ready. I got one of those short and sweet texts from Rye. "Dee, he's a pretty good boy." I laughed. Rye was giving me a heads-up. It did help relieve any tension I might have had about Emanuel.

It was going on 1:00, and the makeup was still being applied. I thought of what my mother had preached to me time and again as a youth: "Son, you need to learn to have the patience of Job." All my life I had sought the patience of Job, and every time Madonna had to get ready to go somewhere, I failed. I had to admit that I had gotten better at this patience deal over the years, but I assumed that was because I recognized even I was slowing down. It was something I had been struggling with for the last few years, and I was hesitant to even consider that possibility.

My thoughts only lingered there for a few moments, and I snapped out of it. I was not going to allow the clouds of depression to consume me. I had only to acknowledge that I was the most optimistic person that I knew. I loved the feeling that let me take myself to a better place, and I believed that many people would give up everything to have that capability. I was determined to see this life through to the end and enjoy the ride.

I was jarred out of my solemn thoughts by Madonna saying, "I'm ready."

I pounced like an eagle, ready to go and prepared to soar. I always enjoyed the ride out to Jon and Penny's, as it was close to my old stomping grounds, the place where my father had instilled a good work ethic in me and taught me to love the woods. It was also the place my mother had tried valiantly to teach me the patience of Job. I never really understood how Jon and Penny wound up buying the place they did, but I was proud they got it because it was perfect for Lela and Rye.

As we pulled into the long driveway that lead to the house, I marveled at how nice the place looked. "It looks like Jon and Rye have prepared the royal treatment for Emanuel."

Madonna laughed and said, "They might have, but it was only after Penny threatened them within an inch of their lives."

I could relate, as sometimes it was hard for even me to prepare for company. I glanced to see if smoke was coming from the grill, and to my surprise none was detected. I mumbled to Madonna, "It looks like we're going to have ramen noodles after all." She gave me that look.

Rye was the first one out the door to greet us, and his dog Roscoe came running up as if his sole purpose in life was to protect Rye. I couldn't help but notice how much that boy had grown, and he had the build of an Olympic athlete.

His smile told me he was happy. "You aren't going to believe this! Dad asked Emanuel if he had ever had souse meat, and I thought Lela was going to crawl under the table. What was even funnier was when Emanuel said that his family had it every year for Christmas dinner on the farm."

I looked at Rye and said, "Okay, boy, spit it out. What did you do?"

"Aw, nothing, Dee. I just asked Lela if she knew she might be kissing souse-lips."

I couldn't stop laughing, and Madonna was fit to be tied as we went through the door.

As we walked in, Lela and Emanuel were sitting on the couch. She immediately ran across the room and gave me one of those big hugs that I had been missing. Emanuel was right behind and extended his hand. "You must be Poppa. I'm very honored to meet you. Lela has told me so much about you and Mrs. Overstreet that I almost feel like I know you both." Lela was beaming, and I could tell she liked this young man.

As I sized the young man up, I replied, "It's nice to meet you. Lela tells me you are from Indiana. What part?"

"No, sir," he answered, "I'm from a little town outside of Springfield, Illinois."

"Is this your first trip down south?"

"No, sir. We have relatives in Pontotoc, Mississippi, and we visit them nearly every year."

I kept bearing down, not knowing what I was hoping to establish. "I know some folks in that part of the country. What are their names?"

Emanuel's response caught me totally off guard. "Clifton McDaniel is my uncle on my mother's side of the family, and he has a pretty good-sized cattle farm in Pontotoc."

"I've known Clifton for many years. He's one of the finest men I have ever met. We went to college together before there was such a thing as the internet, and we had plenty of good times together." I could see the young man brighten, but more importantly, I could see Lela breathe.

Rye had been right on target with his text earlier. Emanuel was a pretty good boy.

Jon came in to break up the love fest, "Well, it's time to fire up the grill."

I almost busted out laughing, but I contained my laughter just in the nick of time. I gave Rye a warning glance, but it was too late. "Oh no, Dad, why do we have to grill? I thought for sure Mom was fixing some of her ramen noodles!"

Lela's eyes were shooting daggers at her brother, but Emanuel was laughing. "Jon, I'll be glad to help on the grill. I've had my share of ramen noodles in my lifetime. No offense to you, Mrs. Calverti."

We all had a good laugh as Jon, Rye, and Emanuel headed to the back patio to burn some of the finest New York strips I had seen in a while.

It was indeed an enjoyable meal. Jon and Rye got the steaks just right, and Penny did a great job on everything that goes with a good steak. After dinner and about an hour of good conversation, Madonna and I departed for home.

Before we left, Lela said, "Emanuel and I want to come out tomorrow. I want him to see Bluff Shores."

I agreed, "We would love that, my dear."

"You didn't think you were going to get by without cooking me breakfast, did you, Poppa?"

"What time should we expect you, darling?"

Without the least bit of hesitation, she replied, "My normal time."

"Then it will be ready at 10:30 sharp." And with that, we bid them good night.

I was looking forward to seeing both of them the next day, and I hoped that I would get a chance to speak to Emanuel, man to man. The two of them came early, and Lela was still beaming. It was a cold day even though we had plenty of sunshine.

After we had talked for a little while, Emanuel asked, "May we walk down to the creek? I would like to check it out." I grabbed my coat, and Emanuel and I went outside while Lela and Madonna cleaned up the breakfast mess.

I always made a mess when I cooked, but nobody ever seemed to complain after they ate.

Once on the pier, Emanuel scanned up and down the creek with the eye of an eagle. I could see he was looking at every inch, just as any boy would do who had been raised on a farm. After a few moments, he exhaled as said, "Lela has told me a lot about this place, and I can see what she means. Growing up here had to have been a ton of fun. I bet when spring arrives, those trees across the creek just glorify the beauty."

I felt his words were sincere, and I replied, "Oh, Lela and Rye have enjoyed this place, but not as much as I do. You'll have to come back and visit when the place is alive. Summertime is where it's at."

Emanuel looked at me, and his face was far too serious for me. "Mr. Overstreet, I am in love with Lela. I want to marry her, but it's going to be a few years. Not on my account, but Lela wants to wait. She has this burning ambition after law school to go save the world, and I am beginning to understand, but I'm afraid I'll lose her."

"Young man, many young men would like to find a girl like Lela, but you have to understand that she has a free spirit, and you must let it run its course."

"I know, Mr. Overstreet. Lela has told me that, and she said she gets it from you. If the time comes, will you let me know anything you think I should know?"

I looked at him, and I saw in his eyes the same thing that had been in my heart so many years ago. I'd had that same yearning for Madonna that this young man had for

Lela. We returned to the house, and after a few hours Lela and Emanuel had to leave. It was too short a visit, but I knew they had limited time and Lela would want to see as many of her friends as she could. I hated to see them go.

CHAPTER 22

The months went by until another year had passed. I woke up one morning, gripped by fear. Was I losing my mind? I tried to recall the spring and summer months, Rye becoming a junior in high school, another football season, the holidays coming and going once again. Was it the onset of dementia? A cup of coffee and it all came back. The past year wasn't a total blank. I remembered the important stuff. Lela was in her junior year at Loyola, and she and Emanuel were still together and becoming more attached by the day.

I shook it off. It was in the depths of winter once again, and I was feeling that itch to go. To do. Nature was on my mind. I called Tony. "Are you up for a few days down at Fort Boyd?"

"Uh, I don't know. I've been under the weather for a few days, and I can't seem to shake this stuff."

"Come on, man. You know we may only have one click left." It was a standing joke that Tony had started several years ago. Now and then, I would call and tell him "We are down to one click."

We concluded that Tony should give it a couple of days and then decide. I was just bored, and when I got bored, I became like a caged lion. I paced the floor. Madonna knew the mood, and she was as patient as she could be, but with the cloudy, dreary weather, it only got worse.

In a couple of days, Tony and I departed for Fort Boyd. It was a bitterly cold day, and the weather forecast called for snow. The drive south was rather quiet between the two of us; it was a drive that we had made many times over the years. I wondered what he was thinking.

Finally, we arrived at the gate and drove through the woods to a cabin that had been so good for me over the years. The peace and solitude I had found there had cleared my mind and renewed my spirit many times. *Ouch*, it was cold. The first thing was loading up the old iron devil with firewood, which blew the hot breath of warmth into the cabin and thus the soul. Luckily there was plenty of firewood cut and stacked, and soon the cabin was warm enough to unload and settle in for a long winter nap.

It was almost 8:00 the next morning before I woke up and proceeded to put the coffee on. Gone were the days where the two of us were up at 4:30 and in the woods by 5:30. Tony was still sacked out, so I loaded the iron devil up and just stared at the blaze and soaked in the warmth. I laughed as I recalled what Madonna had said to me before

I left. "Leroy, you be extra careful. You and Tony are getting too old to be doing this stuff, and I will worry until you get back home."

I was trying to remember how many years she had said that same thing to me, when Tony stirred and got up to get his cup of coffee. "Man that was the best night's sleep I've had in months," he said.

I ventured out on the front porch to check the temperature. An old coke thermometer had been hanging there for years, and I always marveled at how accurate it was. I looked at the needle; it was dead on. 10 degrees. I shuddered and quickly returned inside. 10 degrees and the two old guys were down here to go hunting. "No, we're here to prove our incompetence," I mumbled to myself.

Tony was laughing, and I realized he was listening to what I had just said. He was getting dressed for the hunt and said, "If you brought it, you had better wear it."

I, for one, was never the best at having enough cold weather clothes, but I took his advice and put on enough stuff, and as a result, could barely walk. Once in the shooting house, I waited for the action to start. As the woods around me began to come alive, my mind started to wonder, and I began to relieve my soul of all the negative things that had been weighing me down the last several weeks.

I felt the sting of the cold air on my cheeks as I surveyed the sights and sounds of what was before me. I didn't know how long I was completely absorbed in my thoughts and the marvel of nature before me, when I heard the sound of Tony starting the four-wheeler. I glanced at my watch and saw it was already 10:30. The morning hunt was over, and I had lost all sense of time, but somehow I felt better even though I was frozen stiff.

The five days at Fort Boyd were over before they had begun. Tony and I were utterly exhausted, and we had battled the elements the entire trip. The second day brought an excellent snow shower while we were in the woods, which only magnified the beauty. It was only the second time we had ever seen a snowflake at Fort Boyd, but that particular time it resulted in the ground turning into a magical white blanket. After the snow stopped, the sun popped out to add even more beauty to the woods before us.

Neither Tony nor I fired a single shot during the five days we were there. It was as though we were only there to observe nature. Something happens to a man over time that is probably meant to be. You lose that edge, and you begin to be at peace with it all. It was the beginning of the end of a circle of life that many men have pondered but will never solve.

All loaded and ready to make our way back to the highway, I was a disheveled mess and in a state of depression. I tried to hide it from Tony, but then I realized he was in the same shape.

"Leroy, we're getting too old for this, don't you think?"

I laughed and said, "Well, the wives don't have to worry about us getting into to any trouble if that tells you anything." He laughed, and as we pulled up to the gate at the highway and I got out to open it, it dawned on me that this could very well have been my last trip to Fort Boyd.

As I closed that gate, it seemed much heavier than in times past. It appeared that the chain was all rusty, and I paused, feeling like something was telling me not to go. As I snapped the lock in place, I turned to see if Tony had noticed that I was lingering at the gate. Sure enough, he had.

When I got in the truck, he remarked, "We only got one more summer, don't we?"

It was enough to make me laugh, and I needed it. "Heck, I'm not sure we even have thirty minutes, the way you drive."

The drive home was almost over when Tony said, "There's something I need to tell you."

I looked at him; he was staring at the road with a look I had never seen before. "Tony, I don't know what you are fixing to say, but this can't be good."

He didn't laugh or smile, and his expression was stoic. "I've been keeping this from you, but I can't make any more trips to Fort Boyd. My time is short."

I found myself staring into the pavement in front of us as well. "How long have you known?"

"About a month. The doctor says I have maybe about four months. You and I talked about this on a few occasions, and we agreed if one of us got down, the other was to move on. I have pancreatic cancer, and it's bad. We had a lot of fun, Leroy. I have no regrets."

We pulled into the Southern Whitehouse, and Tony insisted on helping me unload my stuff. I was speechless. Tony extended his hand and said, "Goodbye, old friend. May peace go with you."

He turned and got into the vehicle to leave. It was with great sadness that I stood and watched him drive out of sight. I stumbled into the house, cursing old age and disease. Madonna instantly seized on what was happening. She looked at me and asked, "You want to talk about it?" I shook my head, and she said, "I know, Leroy. I know."

Settled back in at home, I became utterly absorbed in reading. I began to read everything I could get my hands on and then some. It seemed as though my days were consumed by turning page after page, and it drove Madonna nuts.

"What are you searching for? You always seem to have your nose stuck in a book. What is up with you?"

I didn't know how to answer her honestly. I had always been one to read, but never had I read so much. It was as though I had to find something, and I had convinced myself that the only way I could do it was to read. I was amazed that the more I read, the more I began to believe that what I had suspected was starting to happen, and other people were finally beginning to notice as well. The youth of America were becoming focused on the future. They were more united and more patriotic.

I had first picked up on it a couple of years earlier when some of Rye's friends were out at the house, and I overheard a conversation between them. It had been about patriotism, sacrifice, and it was about defending the country. I was not surprised that Rye would be talking about that kind of stuff, but it was coming from the entire group, and there was a lot of emotion. I had thought for many years that the youth of the country had gotten a bad rap, and maybe some it was deserved, but this was evidence of youth that I had never seen in my lifetime. Reading filled those winter days and even carried me into the warmer months, which were also becoming quieter for me.

One day during the following summer, Rye came out and took me fishing. He was about to be a senior in high school, and the young man's social calendar was very full. That meant his visits to Dede's were now few and far between. On that particular day, time seemed to slow down just a bit, and we had a broad and enjoyable conversation. The first thing I discussed with Rye was what I perceived in the youth of America and how encouraged I was.

Rye's response was, "Dee, you know everybody my age is tired of the arguing and all the negative stuff that goes on in this country. People think we're all spoiled, won't work, and won't ever amount to anything. I can tell you that all of my friends and I are not only ready to work to solve the problems of this country, but we are ready to fight for it. We are ready to bury the hatchet of division, and we are going to do it in our lifetime."

I felt a warm glow of optimism slowly envelope my entire body. It was the kind of youth that I had hoped to see in my lifetime, and this was the kind of youth that would make America and the world a better place.

I asked him about Lela. "I understand that Lela is off on another mission somewhere in South Africa with that group she keeps talking about, Quality of Life. What do you know about this bunch?"

Rye laughed, "You know, it's just Lela being Lela." His brow wrinkled up a bit, and I knew he was serious. "This bunch is funded by a group of extremely wealthy individuals, and they do great work, but they don't want a lot of praise for their efforts. I think Lela will go to work for them full-time as soon as she gets her law degree. The money this group gets isn't wasted. It goes straight to help people who have been dealt a low blow from nature. Whether by a hurricane, volcano, tornado, or floods, they get in and get things done."

I looked at the young man and smiled. I knew he cared as much as Lela about the young and the poor, and though his methods would be different from Lela's, he would help the world in his own way.

"Dee, you know that Lela and I are close, much more than people think. And Lela is a lot tougher than people think, but if anybody ever messes with her, they're going to deal with me, and it won't be pretty."

Looking at Rye, I saw a boy that had grown up right before my eyes. I laughed, "Settle down boy, we need to catch a few fish. I'm getting hungry." And there was that big, wide grin I had seen on Rye's face so many times in the past.

As we were making our way back to the house, I asked him, "Is this recruiting thing getting to you yet? I read yesterday that you are the number one ranked recruit coming out of high school next year, and that in itself is a big honor."

"No. Mom and Dad are handling a lot of that, and they do a good job of keeping me focused."

It seemed like a good time to ask, so I fired the shot, "Have you told any of these coaches that you are going to commit to Army when you graduate?"

Rye's eyes went wide. I had surprised him. "How did you know that? I haven't breathed a word to anybody! I can't believe you figured that out!"

As I studied that face, I saw a sense of relief slowly descend on it. It was finally out. The boy didn't have to hide anything anymore. Somebody besides him knew he was going to West Point. "Have you told Jon and Penny?"

The brow wrinkled again, and he said, "I just can't seem to bring myself to do that, and I know I should. How would you do it?"

My reply was direct. "I think you should sit them down and tell them your decision and explain to them why you want to go there. They know as well as I do that you like to climb a mountain, and you have picked a tough one, but we will support you and honor your decision."

I could see the wheels turning. "Thanks, Dee. I knew I could count on you, and as soon as I get home, I'm going to clear the air."

Once back at the house with the fish cleaned and in the freezer, Rye seemed in a hurry to leave, and I knew he was fixing to get something off his chest that he had been carrying around for a long time.

Once late fall arrived, Rye's football team was headed towards a state championship, and word somehow got leaked that Rye was going to West Point. It became an overnight story on all the sports channels, and it seemed to be a story that had very long legs. Some of the headlines would have placed considerable pressure on most kids, but with Rye, it was like water off a duck's back.

One headline in particular grabbed my attention. "Rye Calverti Committing to Army Hails a New Era for the Army Football Program." One of the major networks had already called and wanted to do a live interview with Rye about how he had arrived at his decision to attend West Point. Through it all, Jon and Penny were like a rock when it came to supporting and protecting Rye, and for that I was very grateful.

CHAPTER 23

I was able to attend Rye's state championship game, and it was phenomenal. Rye was unstoppable, and the game was not even close. It was the first time in over forty years that the Russellville Generals had won a state championship in football, and Rye had a Most Valuable Player trophy to go along with the main prize. Another thing that caught all the experts off guard was signing day, when Army's recruiting class came in at No.7, defying all odds. It was the first time since they had started ranking classes that Army had even been listed.

Of course, the talking heads tied it to the fact that in another year Rye Calverti would be coming to West Point. I laughed at all of the reporting. They had totally missed the point. What was happening in the country had a lot more to do with youth and determination to restore America to a beacon of hope, a beacon of light, and a beacon of peace.

However, the fact that Rye was going to play at West Point did have some impact on recruiting, and for that I was happy.

Rye handled his senior year as a true champion. I never saw him be impolite, and he was always courteous and gracious in victory. More important to me was the fact that he reached out to all of his classmates, he was accessible, and he would help anybody. The young man had a lot of demands on his time, and I marveled at how well he handled everything. What surprised me the most was how the power teams in college football had kept up their recruitment of Rye.

It got so crazy that Rye borrowed my phone to escape the constant texts and phone calls he was receiving. As a result of that bonehead move, when I finally got my phone back, I was besieged by texts and calls from young girls who all seemed so disappointed that he had been replaced by an old man. It was a mistake that I would not repeat.

Rye got a big laugh out of it. "Dede, you better watch out. If Nonna gets a hold of your phone and reads some of those texts, you will be in the doghouse forever."

I responded by saying, "Don't worry, boy. I'm erasing them as fast as they come in, but I ought to keep a log of all of this stuff. How many girls do you know?"

"You told me a long time ago not to close any doors or burn any bridges that I might need one day."

"I never dreamed you would pay close attention to everything I said. Now you better stay focused; you have another state championship to win."

With a second state championship and MVP award in hand, Rye was preparing for graduation. It hit me that this would be the first year without Rye being on Bluff Creek with me, and I was going to miss those times. He left the day after graduation to begin a new chapter in his life at West Point.

As we stood on the tarmac at the airport, Rye gave me a big bear hug. It was goodbye. I said to him, "I expect nothing but your best efforts, and I will always be proud of you." My best words of advice to Rye evoked the biggest laugh. "Boy, you will learn pretty quick when you get there that your dirty socks do not go under the bed."

Rye laughed, and I knew the boy was ready, but the pain in Penny's eyes told me she was sad and was struggling to come to grips with the fact that her baby was ready to spread his wings and fly.

After his plane departed, I asked Penny about Lela, and she responded, "She's supposed to be starting law school this fall, but she barely has any time to prepare for it. The tsunami that hit Japan a couple of weeks ago sent her into action with Quality of Life again. She was one of the first people from that group to have her feet on the ground. She loves it. It's always about the kids for her, and the satisfaction she gets out of helping those people is what drives her. It's who she has become." Then with a big sigh she said, "I am so proud of my kids. They make it all worth it."

I could only nod my head in agreement, but I too felt the sadness that I knew Penny felt. They were grown and gone.

Summer became hot and almost unbearable for the first time in my life, and it scared me that I felt so lost. It was one bad news day after another. I had the urge to call Manny one day and check on him. Manny answered quickly, and before I could ask how he was doing, he said, "Can I call you back later? I am in the middle of something."

I recognized that tone of voice, and coming from Manny, it was not good at all. I said simply, "Sure, talk to you later." I hung up and waited all day for the phone to ring so I could find out what was going on. The call did not come during the day. The sun sank slowly in the west, and it was dark and quickly approaching my bedtime when the phone finally rang.

Manny was very distraught, "Laroy, I am at my wit's end. Everything I have ever done and all the efforts to prepare for any eventuality will not help. It is Melinda."

My heart sank. "What's wrong? What happened?"

"She has been sick for a while, and I tried to get her to go to the doctor. It got so bad I had to bring her to a hospital in Managua. After doing a battery of tests, the doctor came in this morning and told us time is short. It is cancer, and it is terminal."

I had never been comfortable in those situations, and I was speechless. Finally I mumbled something to the effect of, "Manny, if there is anything we can do, just say the word."

Manny's response struck me like an arrow to the heart. "You and Madonna have been great. You two have given Melinda and me the one thing that means the most in this world, and that is your friendship."

I was choked up, I couldn't talk, and Manny was the same. "Let's talk again in a few days, and may you and Melinda find peace. Our prayers are with you."

"Goodbye, old friend. I will call you soon."

It was but a few days when Manny called back to tell me that Melinda had died. I could feel the devastation and grief. I felt so sorry for my good friend and so powerless. There's nothing one can say or do in these circumstances that can help, even though you try your best.

"What are you going to do, Manny?"

"Well, we had talked some about this day, and we agreed that if she passed before me, that she would be buried in a small cemetery in the hills that overlook Rivas. When my time comes, I will be buried right beside her. It is a beautiful place, and it is close to our house, so I can visit her grave each day."

"Are you going to be okay?"

"Sure, this old soldier is a survivor. I still fish a good bit, and you are not going to believe this, Laroy, but I have even taken up reading."

I thought about trying to bring some humor to the situation by suggesting it would not take long to go through his library, but I could tell it would not have much of an effect.

"Laroy, this getting old stuff is for the birds. I never really thought I would make it this long."

I tried to encourage my old friend. "It will take some time, but you'll see better days." It was of no use.

"I value your friendship, but I will only see better days when I am reunited with Melinda."

"I want you to make plans to come here and stay at least a month, or even longer if you would like."

He promised he would consider my offer, but as we hung up, I had a sinking feeling that I would never see my dear friend Manny again.

I needed to hear from Lela and Rye. I missed them way too much. The emails were few and did not contain enough information to satisfy my idle mind. I called Penny and asked her to fill me in on anything that she had heard from that wild bunch.

"Rye is so busy he hasn't had time to be homesick, but apparently he does miss the girls." I chuckled and she continued, "Lela is very busy trying to get everything done before she comes home, and I detected that she was hoping she would have a couple of weeks before she starts law school."

I felt somewhat relieved by the fact that I would get to see Lela before her life as a law student began.

Rye, on the other hand, was all wrapped up in football, and fall practice was coming up. I told Penny, "The next time you talk to that boy, you tell him he better call me or I'm going to come up there and pull his big ears right in front of all his teammates."

Penny laughed and said, "I wish you would. The pre-season polls are out, and for the first time in my life they have Army ranked in the top twenty. One poll had them at number fourteen."

"They haven't seen the determination and the heart of some of those kids, especially the drive possessed by that

#34. I figure that the college sports world is in for another shock. Go Army!"

It was time for Lela to be arriving stateside, when I took a call from Emanuel. "Mr. Overstreet, how are things with you and your lovely wife?"

I liked this kid, but he needed to be less diplomatic. I consented to his pleasantries, however. "Good. How are things in your world, Emanuel?"

"Sir, I need your help. When Lela left to go to Japan, she told me we needed some time apart from each other." His speech was rushed as if he was trying to get it all out in a nanosecond. "I'm lost without her. I'm losing her. Have you heard anything? Anything at all?"

I took a deep breath and said, "Young man, I know enough about Lela to tell you that if your relationship with her were a problem, she would tell you straight up. I'll tell you what I will do. She is supposed to be here in a day or two, and when I see her I will inquire about your concerns and call you back."

There was dead silence on the phone for a moment, and then, "You don't know how much that would mean to me, and I will be forever grateful. Tell Mrs. Overstreet I send my best regards, and I hope to get to see you all soon. One other thing: I've heard that Army is going to be good this year, and it seems that Rye is generating a lot of excitement. I know you're proud of him."

I thanked Emanuel and told him I would be back in touch in a few days. After I hung up, it crossed my mind that Lela was either fixing to dump this young man, or we were fixing to have a wedding to attend. I decided not to make my suspicion known to Penny or Madonna but rather let nature take its course.

Lela and Penny came out the next afternoon. My girl was all smiles, and her demeanor told me she was very happy. I had hoped to get a chance to talk to her, but they had different plans. Penny and Lela laid out a carefully made plan that came as a surprise to me. "Poppa, you know Rye's first college game is next Saturday and that they play at Syracuse University."

I nodded my head to let them know I was well aware. It was to be the early game on the sports channel.

Penny reached into her purse and pulled out an envelope which I quickly recognized as airline tickets. "Well, you're going to the game! We're leaving on Thursday morning. We have reservations at the same hotel that the team will be staying in, and we are not going to take no for an answer."

I looked at Madonna, and her smile told me she was in on the ruse. I knew that Madonna would not be going, as she would never fly anywhere. Lela and Penny were both grinning broadly. They knew they had finally pulled one on the old man. They somehow managed to get out of there without me talking to Lela about her summer and Emanuel, but I knew I would see her tomorrow.

The next morning I had a little bit more bounce in my step. I knew it was from the anticipation of going to see Rye's first college game. Before I started breakfast, I decided to do a couple of things. First, I checked the weather forecast for next Thursday through Sunday for Syracuse. I then went into my closet to search for the old suitcase that had traveled to many different places with me. As I dragged it out, it seemed like it had grown. I couldn't fly with that thing. It was just too big. I shoved it back in its place for someone else to deal with. Even the coffee smelled better that morning. I poured a cup and went on the back deck to check on my old friend the Gray Heron. There he stood with the same regal majesty that I had been so fortunate to observe for so many years. After I finished my first cup of joe, I went back inside to fix Lela a big special breakfast. I knew she would come early and be hungry.

I heard the *tap-tap-tap* at the door which could only be Lela. She had always preferred to knock rather than ring the doorbell. As I let her in and gave her a big hug, she said, "Is Nonna still asleep? I need to ask you something, Poppa."

"She is. You know she loves her beauty rest." Lela giggled as I poured her a cup of coffee. Well, it was actually a half a cup of that caramel vanilla crème with a splash of coffee. "Girl, here is your crème with a tablespoon of coffee."

She laughed some more but then became serious. "It's about Emanuel."

"How is Emanuel?"

"Well, before I left this summer, I told him I needed some time away to think about us and our future. He has asked me to marry him several times, and I wanted to make sure this is what I want. While I was in Japan, it all became clear to me. He is the one that was meant for me, and I can't put it off any longer. When I get back to school, if he still feels the same way, I guess, well, I think we're going to get married. I'm really happy, Poppa. Do you think this is the right thing to do? And don't tell anybody. I want it to be a surprise."

I laughed, and it was one of the happiest moments of my life. My girl was happy, and I was delighted!

After breakfast and an hour of conversation, Lela told me insistently, "We are going to town and getting you some new clothes for our trip to Syracuse. You're a lot of things, but a fashion guru isn't one of them!"

I had to concur, and, as usual, she got her way. The sweater she picked out was nice, but I did have one argument. "Lela, you do realize this is September? Why will I need a sweater?"

Lela just smiled. "We're going to Syracuse, and it could be cool. The last thing I want is for you to be cold." I realized she was right and nodded my head in agreement.

On the way home, Lela talked about Emanuel and their plans for the future. She seemed so joyful as she discussed her career with Quality of Life, marriage, and settling down to raise a family. The idea of a little-Lela startled me, but I was happy for her. When we got home, Madonna and Lela reminisced for a while, and then she had to go. One thing about Lela, she always had to go.

The flight to Syracuse was excellent. It had been awhile since I had flown. I always loved flying, but I was worried for Penny; she was a nervous wreck. Jon seemed a little bit uptight, but I concluded his thoughts were more about Rye than flying. Lela and I sat together, and we spent the flight talking about old times. As we deplaned in Syracuse, it occurred to me that Lela had been right about the sweater. Once we got checked in, I couldn't wait to see Rye. It was about an hour before there was a loud knock on the door, and when that boy walked in, I was shocked.

Over the summer, Rye had added about 20 lbs. He looked larger than life. We all hugged, Penny and Jon were beaming, and it was one happy reunion. Rye looked every bit the part of a West Point cadet. I knew by looking that my boy was in his element. After a few minutes, we were all laughing and joking; it was just like old times.

Jon asked Rye about his game and what had improved the most. Rye's response was, "I worked all summer on a spin move, and I think I've got it down. I hope I get to use it in the game Saturday."

After an early dinner, we all kind of split up. Rye had gone to the restaurant with us but didn't eat anything. He had a team meeting to attend, and then the team would have dinner together and go to a movie. Jon, Penny, and Lela were going to check out some of the local sights and sounds, and I was going to soak up the comfort of the bed in my room.

As soon as I got back to the room, I searched my phone for Emanuel's number and hit the call button. "How're you doing, Mr. Overstreet? I hope everything is well."

"I'm fine, Emanuel, and I'm sorry it took me longer to get back to you than I thought, but I just want to say you have no reason to worry. I suspect that when you and Lela get back to school, everything's going to work out just fine. I will let her speak for herself."

"Thank you so much," he said in relief. "This is the best phone call I've ever gotten. Lela and I have spoken several times since she got home, and everything seemed great, but hearing it from you means a lot. If you get a chance, tell Rye I'll be pulling for Army on Saturday."

"I certainly will, and you take care. I wish you and Lela the best." I hung up the phone and called Madonna to give her my take on Rye. Then, after watching some television, I slept like an old man is supposed to sleep. Like a baby.

CHAPTER 24

Friday was somewhat uneventful. We mostly just hung out, talked, and soaked up the atmosphere. After lunch, Lela and Penny departed to go shopping. They had been around Madonna enough for me to know that they would take all afternoon. Rye and the team left after lunch to go to the stadium for a walkthrough. Jon and I stayed in the lobby of the motel, and we got to meet some of the parents and supporters that were in town for the game. A couple of times during those conversations, someone would figure out that Jon was Rye's dad, and they would tell him about all the good things they had heard about Rye. Jon's face could not hide how proud he was of his boy, and that alone made the trip worth it to me.

About 4:00 that afternoon, I excused myself and ambled into the hotel bar. It had always been my experience that if you wanted football talk, you could find plenty in a bar. As I sat there, lost in a Jack and Seven, my thoughts turned to Manny. I was worried about him, and I knew I needed to call him.

Three men walked in and sat down at the far end of the bar. Of the three, one was very animated and loud to boot. Shortly, I was jarred out of my thoughts of Manny.

The loud guy said, "You wait! I've been watching Army practice some. They are for real. Now I know on paper, Syracuse is supposed to win this game big time. Heck, even Vegas has Army a 19-point underdog, but I put my money on Army. I tell you something else, they got a freshman that may well be a Heisman Trophy winner before he is through playing. This Calverti kid is going to be something special, and you just sit back and watch. That kid will make a name for himself tomorrow."

I had just taken a big gulp of my drink and was thinking about ordering another, when I felt a tap on my shoulder. "Poppa, we've been looking everywhere for you. Are you ready to go to dinner?" It was Lela, and I had been caught red-handed. As we left, she giggled and said, "What is it worth to you for me not to tell Madonna?"

The next morning I was up bright and early. I was antsy. I was nervous. I was an old man with pregame jitters. During breakfast, I told everyone about the conversation I had overheard in the bar, and there were grins all around. It seemed to help Penny settle down some, and I realized then that we all had pregame jitters. The cab ride to the stadium was hectic. I had never felt comfortable in a cab for some strange reason. Once at the stadium, I expected to see more people milling around, tail-gaiting, and talking to old friends. It was not as many as I expected, but then I looked at my watch and realized we were very early.

After nosing around a bit and checking out the place, we made our way into the stands to find our seats. It was a beautiful stadium, and the people were beginning to trickle in. All of our eyes were on Rye as Army came out for warmups, and I saw nothing unusual. Rye seemed loose and relaxed. Looking at Syracuse, they seemed to be physically bigger than Army, but then I had expected that would be the case. It was rapidly approaching kickoff, and the stands were filling up nicely. The noise was all for Syracuse, as one would expect, it being a home game for them. All of those Army Cadets in the stands made for an impressive sight, and they were fired up and ready for the game as much as we were.

Syracuse won the toss and elected to receive. Supposedly the offense for this team was explosive and was expected to be able to score a lot of points this season. The football was in the air, and the game was on. It was 0-0 as the first quarter was coming to an end, and it looked like Syracuse was finally going to be able to put some points on the board. They had gotten down to the Army 20-yard line, and Army's defense stiffened. It was 3rd and 7, an obvious passing situation for Syracuse, when Rye trotted out onto the field and lined up as the outside linebacker, a position he had played some in high school. The ball was snapped, the quarterback was dropping back to pass, but #34 shot the gap and put a huge hit on the quarterback. How the

Syracuse guy kept from fumbling the ball I would never know. A loud groan went up from the Syracuse fans. Rye's sack had taken them out of field goal range, and Rye had just introduced himself to Army football.

Jon and Penny were getting antsy; they wanted Rye to see action running the ball. I said to them, "Give it time. The boy is a freshman." I was pleased with how tough and gritty the Army team was playing. They were giving Syracuse all they wanted, and the Syracuse fans were getting restless. About midway through the second quarter, Army held and forced them to punt.

The ball rolled dead at Army's 33-yard line. I poked Lela in the ribs as Rye trotted out onto the field with that chinstrap hanging down. He had the gait of a stallion who had just been cleared to race. I could smell it; this boy was ready and in complete control. On the snap, they handed the ball to Rye, the All-American nose tackle for Syracuse met him in the backfield, and then there was the spin move. The All-American tackled nothing but a mass of air.

In a flash, Rye made the corner and turned up field. The explosion, and then that blinding burst of speed I had seen in the kid as early as the age of four. Seventy-seven yards later, Rye was in the end zone, and Army football was back.

The Syracuse crowd sat in stunned silence as the Army Cadets went wild. I reasoned that the cadets, many of them graduating seniors, had not had many opportunities to experience this at an Army football game. What happened next seemed to take the air out of the Syracuse fans completely. A loud group of about fifty or sixty cadets jumped up and chanted, "Rye, Rye, Ree! Kick 'em in the knee! Rye, Rye, Rash! Kick 'em in the ass!" The Army crowd went nuts. It was a great day for the Black Knights.

The rest of the game was something to see as Army scratched and clawed for everything they got. It was late in the third quarter, and Army was driving down the field. It was 3rd and 3 with the ball on the Syracuse 16-yard line. Rye took a pitch from the quarterback, circled left end, and was loose down the sidelines. As he crossed the goal line, I felt the game, for all practical purposes, was over.

With Army leading 14-0 and the fourth quarter coming up, Syracuse had the look of a team that was defeated. As the game clock wore down, Army added another field goal, and with less than two minutes left, Syracuse finally scored when an Army defender slipped and fell, resulting in a Syracuse touchdown. With the final score being 17-7, the Black Knights defeated the No.5 ranked team in the country, and it capped one of the most thrilling days of my life.

After the game, we got to spend some time with Rye, and he was upbeat but under complete control. That demeanor seemed never to change. It was a short-lived victory party as the team had to depart to head back to West Point. While we grabbed a sandwich in a small snack bar, the sports channel was blaring the highlights of the day's game. It opened with the upset of the day. It was Rye and the replay of his 77-yard touchdown run.

A smile crossed his face as he looked at me and said, "Dede, it was just like we use to practice in the backyard."

I laughed, "Boy, you better be thankful that big, 300 lb. nose tackle didn't put a lick on you."

We both laughed as he replied, "Not a chance, Dee. Not a chance."

Soon he had to leave. He hugged us all and told us it would probably be after the season before he could come home.

He looked at me and said, "You get that grill fired up, because when I get home, we are cooking ribs." And with that, the boy was off to continue living his dream.

The next morning, I was up early, packed, and ready to head home. I went downstairs to the restaurant, grabbed all the newspapers I could find, and settled in for a nice, long breakfast. I hadn't ordered yet when Lela came bouncing in and joined me.

"Was yesterday not great? I'm so proud of Rye, I can't stand it."

I glanced at her and said, "Did you tell him?"

"Of course not; it would just give him a big head." We both laughed, and she picked up one of the papers. "Poppa, who is Doc Blanchard?"

"Ok, Lela, time for a little football history. The last time Army football was a powerhouse was in 1944, 1945, and 1946. In those three years, they won the National Championship every year, and Doc Blanchard is considered by many to be the best running back to ever play for Army."

"Gee, this article compares Rye to this guy. Do you think Rye will go down as one of the best to ever play for Army?"

"I don't know, but you can bet they are going to know he has been here."

Lela suddenly looked a little bit down, and when I asked her what was wrong, she said, "I'm going to miss you. I miss you all the time. I worry about you."

I gulped my coffee and said, "Enough of that kind of talk. You know you will always be my girl."

After we finished eating, she hugged and kissed me and said, "I have to get going. My rental car is here, and I have a fourteen-hour drive ahead of me."

"I thought you were flying?"

She smiled. "Well, I was, but I changed my plans. I just wanted to drive and see some of the country."

"You be careful, and try to get a few more emails and phone calls sent my way."

When we arrived back home, I realized this old man needed a few days of rest. Too much of a good thing was not a good thing. Madonna was having a few health problems, and it seemed we were both having to visit the doctor a good bit more than usual. Madonna was having difficulty swallowing and had to be very careful when she ate. Choking on her food was a result of achalasia, and she had waited to late in life to have the corrective surgery. She was stubborn that way, but I loved her even more as we aged. I was determined to stay active, but I realized I was slowing down at a pretty good clip.

One morning, as I was beginning to stir around, I felt something unusual. It felt like a sharp pain was shooting down my right side. I had never experienced anything like that, and at first I dismissed it as old age. However, the pain began to occur more frequently, and I decided I had better visit the doctor to check it out. I scheduled an appointment for the following Tuesday and thought no more about it. On Saturday I woke up with a splitting headache. As I got out of bed and started moving around the house, I began to feel sick to my stomach, and I decided to wake Madonna up and get her to drive me to the ER. I stumbled into the bedroom, and I fell.

When I awoke some seven hours later, I was in ICU. I soon discovered that I had gone through triple bypass surgery and had seven stitches in my head. When I fell that morning, I had hit my head on the corner of the nightstand.

The next few days were ones of reflection and prayer. I always suspected that when death came knocking on my door, it would come fast and furious. Nothing ever prepares one for death, and I felt lucky to be alive. As I studied Madonna's face, I saw her pain, and I felt the unmistakable strain that living with a free spirit like me could cause. I knew then that what time I had left was going to be spent giving her as little stress as possible.

Penny came to visit and she too was worried, but she tried her best to be optimistic. She caught me up to speed on Rye's exploits at West Point and brought me a few newspaper articles to read which she knew would make me feel better. When she started telling me about Lela, I could tell she was holding something back, and I felt pretty sure I knew what it was.

Penny remarked to me before she left, "Lela is so happy and is doing great in law school. I never dreamed these two kids would accomplish so much in such a short time."

"Penny," I said, "you and Jon deserve a pat on the back. You two have done a great job. I am so proud of you, and I will always love you."

She turned away very quickly, but not before I saw a small tear in the corner of her eye. As she closed the door, she said, "I will always love you."

Once I was released from the hospital, I was sent home with strict orders on diet and exercise from the doctor. Old Doc knew me well enough to know to deliver his lecture in front of Madonna. My fate was sealed. "You're not only lucky, but you're tough. I want to see you in my office in two weeks with a signed report from Madonna saying you have been doing exactly as I told you."

I jokingly gave him the one-fingered salute, and Madonna's faced instantly turned red. I laughed for the first time in days.

"If you can't get Madonna to sign that report, I will let you pass if you bring me a couple of those tickets to the Army and Ohio State game that's coming up in about a month." Again I replied with my one-fingered salute. Doc just laughed and said, "Leroy, you must be one proud man. That boy is something else, and there's no telling what he will accomplish."

I got serious. "Doc, I'm going to tell you something about Rye. Everybody thinks that boy is all about football. They think that after four years he will go pro and star in the NFL. Nothing could be further from the truth. When he graduates, he's going to turn his back on all the money and go straight into the Army to protect the country he loves."

He looked at me in shock. "Are you sure?"

"Sure I'm sure, doc, and if you ever breathe a word of what I just told you, you will have both Rye and me to contend with."

Doc shook his head. "That's incredible. It just makes me feel great; it makes my day. You know, it's stories like that which make me think there is hope for this country. I wish we could hear more about the positive things that are happening out there." Then he laughed, "I wish some of this positive stuff would rub off on you."

I once again saluted the doctor as he closed the door.

After about three weeks I was beginning to feel my oats, and I had to remind myself that I was old and needed to slow down. We went out to eat one evening at our favorite place, and we could hardly swallow our food because of all the people coming over and talking to us about Rye. It seemed every week he was making the sports reel for something he had done on the field. They were fixing to play the No. 1 ranked Buckeyes, and the Black Knights seemed to be the rage of the town as well as all around the country. It was a good feeling, although I did not have such a good feeling about the game. Again, Vegas had Army as a big underdog.

The Buckeyes were ranked No.1 for a reason. They were a very experienced team and had eight players that were expected to go high in the NFL draft. I couldn't help but think Rye was going to experience defeat, something he hadn't experienced since the tenth grade, but I had no doubt he would handle it gracefully and treat it as a learning experience.

Ohio State defeated a stubborn Army team by the score of 23-14 in a game that Army could have won, except for a couple of lucky bounces that had gone Ohio State's way. Army finished out the year 10 and 1, got a major bowl, and was headed to New Orleans to play the Georgia Bulldogs. It meant that Rye was going to miss the bulk of the holidays, but I knew that boy was doing what he loved.

CHAPTER 25

Penny called. "Rye will be home for Christmas Eve and Christmas Day, and he asked me to call you."

"Is that all he said?"

She laughed, "No, he said one other word: ribs."

I got a good laugh. "I guess that means I'm going to cook ribs."

They were all planning to attend the Sugar Bowl, but my traveling days were done. I would have to settle for watching it on TV. Rye had received about every type of honor a freshmen football player could get except for the Heisman. I knew he would be in that race next year.

Penny made a big deal out of Lela and Emanuel coming home. They would be there for about two weeks and then travel to the Sugar Bowl with her and Jon. I knew what Penny was up to, but I kept my silence.

It was so good to see Rye relaxing on the couch and Lela running and bouncing around like a beautiful hummingbird while the smell of Christmas was in the air. Madonna kept saying to Lela, "Young lady, you are up to something, and I want to know what it is." For Emanuel's part, he could not seem to get the grin off his face.

The guys were all involved in some football game that was on the tube, when Lela came over and sat down beside me. "Poppa, would you be upset if I didn't move back home after I finish law school?"

"Lela, my dear girl, I sometimes think the world is your home, and I am but a drag on your happiness. You know, I have always stressed to you to pursue happiness over wealth, and I still believe that to be the best course for anyone."

The look on Lela's face was dead serious. "You have never been anything except the best, and I love you more than you will ever know."

I looked at my girl. "Lela, you are one of the few people in this world whose heart pumps love and truth at the same time in a way that the whole world can see."

We were interrupted by Penny. "You all come on. We're ready to eat, and it's on the table."

I made my standard joke, "I hope you guys like well-done ramen noodles."

After a wonderful dinner and some excellent dessert, I was stuffed and ready for a comfortable chair, when Lela announced, out of the blue, "I have something to say to everyone. Emanuel and I are engaged, and we are going to be married this summer. We want to be married here at the

Southern Whitehouse, under the same weeping willow tree as Mom and Dad."

I started to applaud, and as I looked around, I saw tears in Madonna's eyes. "What on earth is wrong with you?" I asked.

She looked at Lela and said, "Baby, I have never been any happier for you in my life. Of course you can be married under the willow, and we will plan the wedding down to the last detail. I am so happy for you and Emanuel!" Then she looked at Emanuel and said, "Welcome to the family! You have our blessings."

Rye, who had just been finishing off the last piece of carrot cake, said, "Emanuel, I hope you know how hardheaded she is, and you best be ready to lose a bunch of arguments."

We all laughed, and as I looked around the table, I was one proud Poppa. I knew the coming months would be busy for Madonna and Penny, as the wedding planning process would be slow and meticulous. I, on the other hand, would be left with plenty of time to do whatever my heart desired.

The next afternoon, as Rye was departing for New Orleans and the Sugar Bowl, he stopped in to say goodbye. I marveled at how big that boy had gotten, and yet in those eyes I saw the same laser-focused determination that had always been there. "We're going to beat Georgia. We found something in our game preparation that will give us the win, and your boy is about to throw his first college touchdown pass."

I looked at him and said, "Boy, are you telling me the game plan?"

There was that big smile. "I didn't want you to be shocked."

I couldn't contain my laughter. "You know how to get old Dee, but I will tell you this: if you overthrow the pass, I am going to come down there and pull them big ears of yours."

He shrugged and changed the topic. "Do I smell ribs?"

I smiled. "Let's go out to the back deck and grab a few of those ribs off the grill."

Rye chowed down and consumed quite a few, and way too quickly it became time for him to leave. As he hugged me, I sensed his strength and determination. I wondered if the Black Knights knew just exactly what they had.

In a few days, all the kids loaded up and headed for the Sugar Bowl. After the game, Lela and Emanuel would be flying back to Loyola, and Rye would be returning to West Point. It was quiet for Madonna and me. We were alone with our thoughts of what lay ahead for those kids as our battles with old age became the main focus of our time.

On game day there was nothing but football on television, and the last game of the night was the Sugar Bowl. I admit that I sat in that old recliner all day, soaking it all in. As game time approached, I was ready, and I was sure Rye was raring to go. It didn't take long for Army to catch Georgia in whatever it was that they had seen in game prep. It was the second play of the game when a pitchout went to Rye, and as he went outside he suddenly pulled up and stopped. Rye threw a long pass down the sidelines to a wide open #88, who trotted into the end zone. I smiled. The pass had been slightly underthrown, and I wondered if Rye was thinking about what I had told him earlier. It was not to be the only touchdown pass Rye would throw that night, as they caught them in the same scheme in the third quarter and ran the same play, resulting in another touchdown for Army. The final score was Army 34 and Georgia 21.

Rye had two rushing touchdowns, and, combined with the two passing touchdowns, the boy was named MVP of the Sugar Bowl. After the game, the commentators kept talking about the Army team and their potential for the next year to be in the hunt for a National Championship. I slept very well that night. In my dreams, I saw #34 racing down the field, just as he had done in the yards for years.

As winter flew by, Madonna and Penny were busy with wedding preparation, Lela and Rye were at school, Jon was busy at work, and I was pretty much alone with my thoughts. Oh, I had the old Gray Heron, but overall, I enjoyed the peace and quiet.

One morning I decided to call Manny. When he answered, I could tell from his voice that he was pretty upbeat. "Have you been catching any fish?" I asked.

"Laroy, I am catching a lot more than I can eat, but let me tell you about the one that got away."

As I laughed, my thoughts suddenly zeroed in on what Manny had just said. "Speaking of the one that got away, has there been any sighting of Petey?"

Manny turned serious and said, "It is perceived here in Rivas that old Petey was wounded and somehow managed to escape. It is also believed that he died from his wounds.

So much time has passed that people don't even think about what almost happened that day anymore. I remember a conversation I had with Stephan one day as we were working on the old tunnel, and Petey's name came up in passing. It seems that he was born and raised outside of a little place called Jinotega. I have often wondered if he didn't make his way back to his old home place. Jinotega is very remote and very poor. It would be a perfect place for someone to avoid detection."

"Do you have any news about Leanna Futrillo? Is she still with the embassy?"

"Yes, I made a trip a few weeks ago to Managua, and I got to see her. She runs the place and seems very happy. Doing quite well."

As we hung up, I had flashbacks to that mountain in Rivas and memories of staring into the eyes of Comacho.

Spring arrived. As Bluff Shores started to come to life, my spirits began improving daily. I had plenty to keep me busy, as I was working extra hard outside to prepare for the upcoming wedding. The date had been set for June 28, and everything seemed to be progressing smoothly on that front. Lela, for her part, was busy at law school, and I was sure that time was flying by for her. I had worried how she would handle not going on some "save the world" campaign that summer. She had told us that she would not be doing anything with Quality of Life that year. I knew Lela would miss helping the kids, but I could only surmise that Emanuel was breathing a sigh of relief. Lela had let it be known that once she had obtained her law degree, she was going to work for them for five years, and then she and Emanuel were going to raise a family.

Rye's focus began to turn more and more to a military career. I worried more and more about Rye, as it looked to me as though we were headed towards one of those protracted wars in a faraway place that had already cost America so much of its treasure. It was never gold and silver to me that meant treasure, but our youth. The youth had always been our country's greatest treasure. Sadly, it had gotten to the point for me where life seemed to be more about death than life. With nearly each passing day, I learned that somebody I knew had passed away.

One day during that spring, Emanuel called to give me some news. "Clifton McDaniel passed away last night, and I felt I should let you know. We are coming down to Pontotoc for the funeral."

After a brief pause, I replied, "If you all have time, I would love for you to bring your parents to the house. Madonna and I would love to meet them."

"Yes, sir, Mr. Overstreet. We would love too."

"Emanuel, it is time you and I get something out of the way. My name is Leroy, and I would feel much more comfortable if you addressed me as Leroy."

He laughed and said, "Thanks, Leroy. That means a lot to me."

"I don't know that Madonna and I will make the trip for Clifton's funeral. I would like very much to go, as I thought a lot of him. If we don't get to go, please give our regards to Mrs. McDaniel and the entire family."

"I will, and I will call you tomorrow when I find out the arrangements. Oh, I thought I would tell you, Lela sends her love. She's so wrapped up in school, as am I, and it sometimes seems like all we do is study."

"I am proud of you both, and we are looking forward to the time when we have some little Lelas and Emanuels."

There was a stunned silence on the phone and finally laughter. "I think that might be a while, Leroy."

After the funeral, Emanuel and his parents came by and spent the day with us. I was very impressed by both of them. I could tell that his dad was a self-made man, the type of guy that has made America great. Madonna and Emanuel's mother were soon on a first name basis and enjoyed a relaxed conversation about many topics. Most of their discussion centered on the wedding plans, and it was agreed that they should come down and spend several days with us before the wedding.

Emanuel's dad seemed very interested in talking about Rye, and he said something that I thought had been completely missed by the average sports fan. "From where I sit, Rye has done more to restore pride in Army football than any kid in my lifetime. I can't tell you how many times I have heard his name come up at the places I visit. Be it local coffee shops, restaurants, or just wherever people are talking sports."

I wondered if he had just said that to make me feel good when he concluded by saying, "This young man is destined for greatness, but I don't think it is necessarily on the football field. I somehow suspect that he will become one of

America's greatest warriors in a time where we are fortunate to have many."

I thanked him for saying those nice things about Rye, but I didn't tell him that I was sure he was right and that I had seen that in him since he was very young. It worried me more every day, but I always was able to put it aside with my belief that whatever he encountered he would be able to overcome.

It was just a few days before the wedding, and I was putting the finishing touches on the Southern Whitehouse. I surveyed the old place, and I realized that it was aging just as Madonna and I were. The more I looked around, the more I concluded that, much like Madonna, it had aged more gracefully than I. As I glanced across the creek at the waterfall, I wondered if the Gray Heron would be in attendance at the wedding. I laughed to myself and shouted across the creek, "If you don't show up for the wedding, you're fired!" I was indeed glad that nobody heard me, as my sanity would have no doubt been questioned.

Emanuel's family arrived in town, and it was agreed that Rye would take Emanuel's dad and me fishing the next day. I was pleased when Emanuel ended up coming along, and I was impressed that Ike had proved to be a very capable fisherman. He seemed to enjoy the time on the boat and looked to thoroughly enjoy his conversation with Rye. As for Emanuel, his nervousness about his approaching marriage to Lela was only enhanced by the constant ribbing from all the men on the boat.

Emanuel's dad got the biggest laugh. "Son, there is one thing I forgot to teach you. You will never be able to out-smart an intelligent woman, and from what I see, you don't have a chance."

On the morning of the wedding, we awoke to a pretty strong thunderstorm, and the usual panic ensued. A huge tent was erected down by the volleyball court where Lela and Rye had spent many a day playing. The old weeping willow tree was standing proud and beautiful, even though the rain was drenching its many branches. Madonna was fit to be tied until Lela called.

"Nonna, how hard is it raining out there?"

Madonna bravely replied, "It is raining pretty hard, but it looked like it might clear off in a little bit."

"Don't you worry one bit. Momma said it did the same thing on her wedding day, and the sun popped out about 11:00, and by 1:00 the sky was blue, and it was gorgeous."

We had forgotten about that, and it gave us renewed hope. As if by design, the rain stopped at about 10:30, and by 11:00 it was bright and sunny at Bluff Shores as the morning rain dried up quickly. As the guests began to arrive, I thought about how important that day was; it was the day when my Lela would begin her life's journey with her partner in life. It was my greatest hope that she and Emanuel would find the happiness and peace that Madonna and I had enjoyed for so many years.

The wedding ceremony went off without a hitch. It was beautiful, and all the planning that Madonna and Penny had done paid off. If there was a hitch, it was that Trouble, my now fifteen-year-old springer spaniel, decided he wanted to be part of the ceremony. He waddled up and lay right down beside the preacher as he cited the vows. There were a few giggles, but to me it was as typical as the Southern Whitehouse itself.

The reception under the big tent was excellent and the food was great. One thing that stood out was a gaggle of young girls surrounding Rye. Rye ate up all the attention and seemed to be able to make each one of the girls think he was paying extra attention to her. It was so funny to watch.

Lela was just radiant and seemed so happy. Emanuel had a look on his face like he had just won the lottery. As soon as the reception was over, Lela and Emanuel would be leaving for a week in the Caribbean. I gave her my last-minute instructions, which I was sure she had memorized by now: "Be careful and stay safe."

After all the guests were gone, Trouble and I got on the golf cart and toured the grounds to survey the damage. To my surprise, it didn't appear that the cleanup would be very difficult.

Rye came walking up. "Dee, I'm leaving to see a movie. I'll come back in the morning to help with the cleanup."

I laughed, "You go ahead, boy. No big deal."

I watched as he got into a car with five young women, and another car pulled right in behind them that appeared to have even more girls. I didn't know how the boy did it, but life was good.

CHAPTER 26

A year went by, and another summer was over. Before I knew it, Rye was preparing for his junior year at West Point and Lela was starting her last year of law school. Rye's football season went by quickly, and it appeared that they would play for a National Championship. Rye broke every single rushing record in Army history and earned an invitation to New York for the Heisman Trophy award. It was an exciting time for him, and he handled it with as much humility and honesty as one could expect. The kid from USC won the Heisman, with Rye coming in second. I knew he was disappointed, but nothing seemed to hold him back.

The playoff pairings were announced, and as it turned out, USC and Army would play in the semifinal game in the Peach Bowl in Atlanta. I thought about trying to attend, but my health concerns made me decide against it. Lela and Emanuel didn't come home for the holidays, as they went to his parents' house. I knew that Lela and Emanuel's full focus was on finishing law school, and I completely understood. Penny was not too happy about it, and I had a talk with her about how important it was for Lela. I don't know that I helped that much, but with Penny, it was always fun trying to convince her of anything. I often thought she should have been a lawyer.

The semifinal game was a nightmare for Rye and the Army team. Every conceivable bad bounce went in favor of the USC Trojans. It was a battle that came down to the very end. The Army quarterback dropped back to pass and was slammed by the Trojan defense. The ball popped up in the air, and a fleet defensive back scooped it up and ran untouched into the end zone. It was the deciding play of the game, and USC won 31-20.

As they interviewed Rye after the game, he was very gracious in defeat, and he concluded by saying, "We are going to go back to West Point and get back to work. I want to promise every Army fan watching that we will be back next year, and my teammates and I want to promise all of you that next year the Black Knights will be crowned the National Champions." It was one of those moments in the sports world that would linger in sports fans' minds for some time to come.

For Rye, it was not empty words, and it was that determination, that drive, and that warrior in him that made me so very proud. I had the feeling that what he had said would soon become a reality. As I went to bed that night, my biggest fear was that I might not be around to see his dream come true.

Spring came and went. Lela passed her bar exam and became a full-time employee with Quality of Life. She and Emanuel had made their home in a suburb of Virginia to be close to their work in D.C. I struggled with the fact that Lela and Emanuel were both working in the nation's capital. With all the terrorism that was going on in the world, I feared for their safety. It was just an old man's fear for the young becoming more and more relevant in my life, and I battled it daily. It was further compounded by my suspicion that the U.S. was about to become engaged in another foreign intervention in a country called Kyrgyzstan. One would think that after our recent involvements around the world that we would have learned to keep our nose out of others people's business, but I knew we were incapable and would soon be involved.

Rye came home for a few weeks, and I asked him what he thought about the situation. "Dee, I wouldn't be surprised if after I join the Army full time that Kyrgyzstan is my first deployment."

"Does that mean you are not going to apply for a deferment to continue your career in professional football?"

"I guess my last football game will be here before I know it. My only desire is that my last game for Army be in the National Championship, and then I will serve my country, which is the only thing I ever really wanted."

I looked at him, and I knew we were lucky to have such a boy who knew what he wanted and was 100% committed to giving back to his country.

More and more I began to hear good things about the work that Quality of Life was doing around the globe. They could respond faster than any other aid group and could allocate resources and get them to the affected area with lightning speed. Lela was happy in her work, but I worried about the constant travel to all of those out of the way places. It seemed to never end, and the world always seemed to be in crisis. It had gotten to the point that the Red Cross wanted to work with Quality of Life because of their response time. Lela was the point person for this group, and it was her boots that first hit ground when disaster struck. It was her courageous leadership which was helping to fulfill the goals of Quality of Life.

I had to speak to Emanuel to find out where Lela was and what she was doing. I never thought that Emanuel and I would be very close, but as time went by I began to appreciate him, and I knew that Lela had the best support that one could have in life. Lela was his life, and there would never be anybody for him but her.

One morning, for no apparent reason, I decided to call Emanuel. As the phone rang, I began to worry that it might be too early to call. I had always had the suspicion that folks in D.C. didn't get up as early as I did.

He answered and we exchanged pleasantries. I asked him about Lela and immediately sensed some apprehension in his voice. "Well, Leroy, she took on a tough assignment yesterday and left last night, and I don't know how long she will be gone."

"Where did she go?"

"She is headed to Kyrgyzstan."

My head exploded. "Has she lost her mind? How could you let her go? You have to know what is going on in that country!" I realized I was screaming at the phone. "Emanuel, let me call you back. I have to calm down." I slammed the phone on the table. For once I was mad at Lela and just downright mad at the world.

As I sat alone on my couch, I tried to envision what it must be like in Kyrgyzstan. I knew that anarchy, genocide, and all the terrible things that humans could inflict on one another were happening there. The world powers had seemingly turned a blind eye to this tragedy. NATO had largely become irrelevant. Over the years they had become nothing more than peacekeepers after the majority of the genocide was complete.

The thing nobody could understand was why Russia had not intervened. Everyone seemed to be waiting on Russia, and they showed no inclination to act. I knew that America would finally respond to stop the killing, and I suspected that we were just days away from an invasion. The last thing I wanted was for Lela to be caught up in a war halfway around the world. I wanted her home.

I decided I had calmed down enough to call Emanuel back and apologize for hanging up on him. He answered the phone as if nothing had happened.

"Leroy, I am worried as much as you are. I tried to talk her out of going over there, but you know how bull-headed she can be."

"You are learning. How long do you expect she will be gone?"

"I can't know for sure, but she indicated that she might be over there for six months."

"What exactly will she be doing when she gets there?"

"She is with a group of five people, and this is her first trip as the team leader. Their first objective is to secure co-operation from government leaders to allow them to safely bring in whatever supplies are needed and to secure help to get those supplies to the ones who need it. Lela is a natural at securing this cooperation from government officials. She can soften the heart of the most hardened dictator. You know, she worries about you constantly, and she tells me not to tell you all of this stuff, because she doesn't want you to worry."

"I appreciate your honesty, and I would ask that you tell me anything that you think I need to know. One thing I would like to know is how much longer until the U.S. Military intervenes in Kyrgyzstan? Do you have any idea?"

"I hear that an invasion is imminent."

My worst fears were confirmed. Lela had just landed herself in the middle of a full-scale war.

I impatiently waited for Lela to get back to the States. It was beginning to settle down in Kyrgyzstan, as the US Armed Forces had restored some semblance of order. I was now very anxious for Lela to be home. The daily reports of aid convoys being attacked did not help my feelings at all. The insanity of it all was just more than I could bear, but I knew in Lela's mind that it was all about the children.

Word came in an email from Lela herself.

Poppa, I am fine, and I hope to be returning home in about a month. There is so much to do. It has been one of the most horrifying experiences of my life, and I will tell you all about it as soon as I get home. With all my love, Lela.

Rye was closing in on his dream. They were ranked No. 2 in the nation behind a great Alabama team, and it appeared that they should make the playoffs. All the buzz was that Rye Calverti appeared to be headed towards a Heisman Trophy. I looked on with great interest and tried to figure out if Rye would play against Alabama. When Rye graduated high school, Alabama had put forth great effort into trying to get him to accept a scholarship. He was personal friends with several of their players, and I wondered if there was much talking going on between those guys.

USC, after an early season loss to Oregon, had been playing well, and it looked to me as though they would probably get one of the four slots for the playoffs, and Florida State would get in also. Rye was enjoying every single day. He loved the military, and he loved playing football for the Black Knights.

One day Penny called, all excited. She had just talked to Lela and had learned that she would be home the day before the National Championship game. She was trying to figure out if Lela needed to just plan on meeting the family in Palo Alto or fly on into D.C. If Army lost its semifinal game, they would not be going to the Rose Bowl for the National Championship.

"What should I tell her to do? Do you think Rye and his guys will beat Florida State?"

"Of course I do. You tell Lela to just plan on meeting you guys in Palo Alto and to hurry up and get home."

Penny laughed, "I don't know who wants to see her the most, you or me!"

I was feeling weak and just did not seem to have much energy, but with Lela coming home and Rye playing for a National Championship, I just couldn't let myself dwell on how I felt.

It was Heisman weekend, and Rye was in New York to pick up the award. To wind up on that stage for the second consecutive year was one heck of an achievement. As he stood before the assembled group, he showed very little emotion, but I recognized that small grin and knew he was thrilled.

His speech was inspiring and uplifting to the youth of the country, and Rye took the occasion to announce his plans to the sports world. "In accepting this honor, I do so on behalf of my teammates, the Black Knights. They are my life, and I don't intend to shirk my responsibility. I think this is a good a time as any to tell you about my plans."

I leaned forward in the chair to not miss a word, although I was pretty sure I knew what was coming.

Rye continued, "Most of you have assumed that I would apply for a hardship to allow me to defer my duty and enter the NFL draft. That is not my intention nor will it happen. My football days will hopefully end in a couple of weeks with a National Championship. I want my teammates to know that for those who graduate this year, I will be joining them on active duty, and I look forward to serving with them as we work to protect our country. It was always my dream—my duty. I always planned on serving my country, and with God's help, that is exactly what I will do. Thanks to all of the people who have supported me. Now it is my time to support you."

There was not a dry eye in the house.

Sometimes things don't go as planned, and the playoffs game was a perfect example. No. 1 Alabama lost to No. 4 USC; it was a huge upset. The Army team dispatched an excellent Florida State team, 33-21, and the game that Rye had longed for was now squarely in his sights. It was ironic that the team they would face was the same team they had lost to the year before, and Rye's promise to all the Army fans was to become a reality.

As Jon and Penny departed for California, I resigned myself to watching all the hype that leads up to the game itself. An aging Joe Buckman was to call the game. He had proven over the years to be one of the best sportscasters of all time. I marveled at how he had aged, and it made me realize how much time had passed. It was billed as the game of the Black Knights' attack against the Trojans.

One of the most important things that happened before the game was a phone call from Lela.

"Poppa, I am so glad to be home. I just had to call you. How are you and Nonna doing?" I told her we were doing fine now that she was home safe, and she went on, "I will be home for a week, and I'm going to come and stay with you for a couple of days. Emanuel said to be sure and tell you hello. We are going to the Rose Bowl parade this morning, so I have to get going, but I will see you in a couple of days."

With that she was gone, but my spirits were higher than they had been in some time.

As game time approached, I realized that this would be the last time that I would see #34 take the field for his beloved Black Knights. They constantly spotlighted Rye during warmups and showed clip after clip of his exploits on the field that had led to him winning the Heisman. As he stood at mid-field for the coin toss, that chin strap was hanging down, those shoulders were squared, and he personified the look of thoroughbred stallion, ready for anything.

The game was a defensive struggle, and it was 7-0 at the end of the first half with Army in the lead. It was another one of those trademark runs by Rye that Army fans had gotten used to. Sixty-six yards right up the middle, breaking tackle after tackle. As the second half started, I was concerned that depth might play a big factor, as USC had a lot more depth than Army. It was as if two heavyweights were going toe to toe. At the end of the third quarter, it was a 14-14 tie, and you could cut the tension with a knife in that stadium.

I knew Penny must have been about to pull her hair out, and I was glad I was in my old recliner. With three minutes left in the game, Rye got outside, and as he turned up the field, I tried to get up out of my recliner. He juked the defensive back and was down the sidelines with only the safety to beat. The safety was an All-American who had the angle on Rye, and there was a collision which resulted in the safety bouncing off like he had just run into a stone wall. Rye stumbled, regained his footing, and shot towards the end zone. At the 5-yard line, he pulled up. I knew that look; I had seen it several times over the years. Rye had pulled a hamstring and was in obvious pain.

With the touchdown in the books and Army leading 21-14, Rye was standing on the sideline. The pain must have been unbearable, but he was standing. As the defense took the field, the entire offense came to stand by Rye. His arms were around his teammates on either side. It was the only way he could stand. Army's defense held and forced USC to punt; the offense went back to work without Rye. As the defense came off the field, they lined up beside Rye, just as the offense had. It was indeed a proud band of warriors who were not going to be denied.

As they hoisted the National Championship Trophy at midfield, it was the most impressive thing I had ever seen at any sports event. It was America's finest on display for all of the world to see. As confetti rained down on the Black Knights, it was apparent that there would be no moment in the sun for Rye. He had already been carted off to the locker room and the attention of the medical personnel. I knew that it wouldn't bother him in the least bit, as the boy was not a publicity hound and neither were his teammates. That band of warriors was such a refreshing change from the usual sports team. They were all in for each other, and it was something that was spectacular to see.

As Joe Buckman signed off from the Rose Bowl, he said, "Ladies and Gentlemen, what we have just witnessed was one of the most thrilling and awe-inspiring performances I have ever seen at any sporting event. I am honored to have been your announcer." As he said goodnight, they showed Rye running down the field and into history.

The next morning, Penny called early and said, "Rye rested pretty well last night, but he is going to need to rest for a few weeks. His spirit is good, and he said to tell you he would call you later today and that he could not wait for you to try on his National Championship ring."

I laughed and said, "You tell that boy I may take that away from him if he is not careful."

"I will let you tell him. We are flying out this afternoon, and we will be home tonight. I hope you are ready, because Lela is planning on her and Emanuel coming and staying a week with you. She seems very happy, but this last trip took a toll on her, and I hope you will talk to her about her future with Quality of Life. She has, in my opinion, given enough to help solve the world's disasters."

"You forget she has a law degree and can prosecute or defend any case she so desires. If you doubt that, let me ask you when the last time was that you won an argument with her?"

"If anybody can reach her, you can. I have to go and get this bunch in gear, or we won't make our flight. I love you and will see you soon."

As I hung up, I realized my Penny had reached a maturity level that only comes with age. Madonna and I had often joked that Jon and Penny were just kids raising kids, but I had to admit, they had done an outstanding job.

CHAPTER 27

Lela came busting through the door as if she were Rye on one of his touchdown runs. She raced across the room and hugged me like never before. Then she and Madonna hugged for what seemed like ten minutes; it was so good to have my girl in the house. Emanuel was more relaxed than I had ever seen him, and his smile never left his face.

Lela was ready for breakfast and ready to talk. She dove right into talking about the war in Kyrgyzstan and what had happened and what had almost happened while she was on the ground in that awful place. "It was the most horrifying thing I have ever seen in my life. The cruelty, the absolute disregard for human life, and I saw enough murder of innocent women and children to last me a lifetime." As her voice trailed off, I knew she was thinking about the children. "How can humanity do those types of things to each other? I was not in any real danger, as I was somewhat protected the whole time I was there, but I did go out on several convoys to deliver food, medicine, and blankets. We were attacked, twice, and I did fear for my life, but thankfully we escaped without anyone getting seriously hurt. I saw many young boys and girls who had been disfigured by landmines. It was horrible, just horrible. Will the world ever find peace?"

It was the opening I needed. "Lela, in the history of man, there have always been wars, so I don't expect to ever see world peace. But we must hope, we must always strive for peace, and you, young lady, have done your part."

As we ate breakfast, Lela became more solemn, and I could tell she had a lot on her mind and wanted to talk much more in depth about everything in life. I sensed it was a good thing, because I felt we would need the time to cover all the things she wanted to. The bright side of the conversation at breakfast was their trip to the Rose Bowl.

"I so wish you two could have been there with us. It was unreal. To be able to go to the Rose Bowl Parade, to spend time with my brother, to meet so many truly wonderful people, and to witness Rye achieve his dream was just unbelievable. Rye and I had dinner one evening, and we talked about you and Nonna for about an hour. All the memories, all the good things, and all that you two have done for us over the years. I know your ears had to be burning. If they weren't, it could only be because you're getting hard of hearing."

"Huh? What did you say?" I asked jokingly.

Some of the pain Lela had experienced in Kyrgyzstan seemed to melt out of her eyes as that old sparkle took its place. "Poppa, one of the things that helped me when I was struggling with all the insanity in Kyrgyzstan was memories of my childhood. I had flashbacks to some of the funny things that happened to me growing up, and most of the time it involved you. I must have embarrassed you to no end. The one I thought about the most was of you taking me to dance class. I remember vividly coming off of the dance floor and seeing you sitting patiently with all the mothers and grandmothers as if you were one of the gang. It was so funny. Every time it flashes across my mind, I just have to laugh. You were obviously as lost as a goose, but you handled it better than any Poppa ever. During the depressing moments in that war-torn hellhole, I did my best to do what you would have done. I handled it."

I could not help but smile. "Lela, you are the one girl I have known in my life who can get me to do anything."

After breakfast, the girls left to go shopping, and Emanuel and I got the chance to speak openly. I began by asking him, "What has my hard-headed girl not told me?"

"A bunch of stuff. Most of it concerns her future with Quality of Life. She's told them that she won't go into a war zone again and that she will only go to areas that have been hit by a natural disaster. In two more years, I expect Lela will be ready to take up a normal life. I love her more every day, and I just hope I can make her as happy as she makes me."

"Lela is lucky to have a good man in her life, and we are thankful that it is you. I have always worried about her. She has always had such a big heart, I worried she might get it crushed. I hope that you two have a very long and productive life."

That night after dinner, Emanuel said, "I hope you'll excuse me. I have some research to do for a paper I have to submit at a committee hearing next week."

"Help yourself. You may use my study if you like."

As he headed to the study, Madonna said, "Leroy, I think I will go to bed. I'm tired after all that shopping we did today. Lela walked my legs off."

I laughed and said, "Goodnight, darling."

As I looked at Lela, I knew we were fixing to have one of our epic, mental sword fights, and I knew she was ready, willing, and able. Once we were alone, I tried to preempt her first thrust by saying, "Are you looking forward to getting back to Washington?" It was a glancing blow.

"Why would you think otherwise?"

"I don't know. I just thought maybe it was time you scale back on saving the world and get on with your career and family."

"But you always taught me to finish what I started, and I still have four years left on my commitment to Quality of Life."

"Lela, I'm worried that you might get hurt. That all the devastation you see might adversely affect you, and if something happened to you, it would be more than I could bear."

She laughed as if to say *touché*. "You think I don't worry about you? In case you haven't noticed, you're not a spring chicken anymore. Nonna tells me you haven't been following your doctor's instructions. Why does that not surprise me? I'll tell you why: you have always done things your way, and that is what you taught me, and that is what I am going to do also."

It was the end of the discussion, even an old man could read that writing on the wall. I laughed and signaled to Lela that the sword fight was now over, and she got up and came and sat down right beside me. She snuggled up just as she had so many times as a little girl, and I instantly melted just like I had so many times before.

The week went by very fast. I was lamenting that I was only going to have my dear Lela home for a couple more days, when we got a delightful surprise. A knock on the door early one morning made me remark, "Who can that be?" I went to the door, and as it swung open, right there in front of my eyes stood Rye. I almost croaked. "Boy, get in this house and give me a hug! When did you get home?"

He looked so big, and that grin was bigger and better than ever. "I got in late last night. I'm only going to get to stay a couple of days, but I wanted to see all of you before I have to go back. Did Lela leave me any breakfast?"

I was shocked as I looked at the young man standing before me, a National Championship ring on his left hand. Lela came running through the house and jumped in his arms. The love between a brother and sister was just what I needed that morning.

"You all sit down," I said. "I think I feel like cooking up a big breakfast for my favorite kids."

"I was hoping you would say that," Rye responded.

I knew this was going to be one of those happy days that unfortunately didn't occur often enough. The conversation at breakfast centered around the National Championship game, and hearing Rye describe the little things that you don't see or hear during the game made my heart swell with pride. Rye suddenly removed the ring and said, "Dee, I want you to put this on, because being with you today means more to me than this ring."

The tears rolled down my cheeks. It was embarrassing. I hadn't cried like that since I was a young boy, but I was overcome by the moment.

After regaining my composure, I looked at Lela and Rye and said, "I want you two to know that the joy and inspiration you have brought into my life is more than I could have ever possibly dreamed." It was without a doubt the most emotional moment in my life, and the only way I could think to relieve the emotion was to make them laugh, but the words would not come to me.

Finally, Madonna came to the rescue. "Leroy, you made the coffee too strong. After all these years you would think you could learn how to brew a decent cup of coffee." She had bailed me out. Laughter returned to the Southern Whitehouse.

Just as quickly as those two had reentered into my life, they seemed to exit even quicker. Lela and Emanuel had to leave the next day to return to D.C. Rye was only going to be there one more day, and I knew he was juggling his time to accommodate a few women. I laughed at him as he left to go into town that evening. He was all spiffed up, and when I inquired if that was how a Black Knight went styling, his grin was pretty much a dead giveaway.

The next morning, as Lela was getting ready to depart, she came in and gave me one final lecture. "I want you to pay extra attention to your diet, take your medication as you are supposed to, and get more exercise than you have been getting."

I smiled and said, "You need a houseful of kids, and then you would not have to go all over the world to be a mother."

She gave me a laugh and said, "I may just fool you one day."

"I am patiently waiting for you to do just that."

With Lela and Emanuel gone, Rye decided he wanted to take me into town for lunch. The more I thought about it, the more I decided that one of those juicy cheeseburgers from Staggs Café was exactly what I needed. I knew I wasn't supposed to have all the cholesterol, but what the heck? No one lives forever.

Lunch was enjoyable, and I got to see some folks I had not seen in quite a while. Everybody came around to congratulate Rye on the National Championship. It was more embarrassing to him than me.

It was on the way home that I said, "Okay, big boy, what's next for you?"

"I finish school in the spring, and then I will be off on active duty. I'm looking forward to the service."

"Do you know what you will be doing?"

His reply was short and to the point. "I'm going to Ranger School, then after that I will be involved in the Special Forces."

"Do Mom and Dad know?"

"Yeah. Mom is having a fit about it, but Dad's okay with it. It's what I've wanted to do since I was a kid. I don't know where the desire to serve comes from, but for me it's all about God and the good old USA."

I couldn't have been any more proud of him, but I also couldn't dismiss the fears of what was to come in the future. I volunteered to take Rye to the airport the next morning, and Penny voiced some concern but reluctantly agreed. On the drive in the next morning, Rye started laughing.

"What's so funny, boy?"

"You just blew that Mustang off the road. You may be old, but you still got it."

"Got what?"

"The need for speed. You still drive like you're heading for the checkered flag at Daytona. I bet there aren't even half a dozen old people in this county that can drive as good as you. It must be where I got my need for speed, because I have it too."

I laughed and said, "You still racing those dirt bikes?"

He winced. "No, not as much as I used to, but when this hamstring heals up I'll start thinking about it." As we approached the airport, both of us got quiet and seemed to be lost in our own thoughts. My mind was flashing through all the crazy things we used to do when he was small. I glanced at him, just thrilled to be with him and thrilled that he was content and happy.

CHAPTER 28

I tried to stay positive. Even though old age was an infirmity that I did not suffer well, I was glad to have made it that long. I couldn't escape the truth; my health was not good. One morning, as I sat on the back porch with my coffee and the old Gray Heron, I concluded that I was not going back to that old sawhorse I called a doctor. Sometimes you know when the heart is failing, and I was content to live out my final days without any lectures from Doc.

I couldn't help but wonder how many gray herons I had been through in my life, as I knew full well that it was not the same one. My best guess was that it had to be close to four different herons, but it amazed me that every morning one was standing beneath the small waterfall and looking for breakfast.

It had been relatively quiet for Lela, and Emanuel was making a name for himself in D.C. Rye was getting ready to go off on active duty, and I was still trying to find out where he was going to be stationed. Madonna was having more and more trouble with the curse of achalasia, and I feared that it would finally take her from me.

Rye came home after several months on active duty as a full-fledged Army Ranger, and as we talked it became apparent to me that he was heavily involved in the Special Forces. I hated for the young man to leave, but I knew he must. It was only a matter of days. One of those things that had the potential to shape history occurred, of all places, in Libya. Some extremists had taken over the U.S. Embassy in Benghazi and were holding nineteen Americans captive. America had some history with Benghazi, and the government was determined not to let this action go unanswered. America negotiated and got nowhere. It looked to me that, regardless of what happened, we were going to lose some of our finest in Benghazi.

It was a few days later when I awoke to find the news ablaze with what had happened the previous night at that embassy. The Special Forces had gone in and rescued the captives. The details were murky, but it appeared the extremists had been eliminated and all of the captives freed. A coldness come over me as if I knew that Rye was right in the middle of it. I didn't expect to hear very much, but as the day wore on and more details became available, it became clear that the rescue team had pulled off a very sophisticated operation. Over the next few days, America's national pride rose to new heights. I became even more convinced that Rye had been involved, because we had not heard a word from him, and all of our calls to his cell phone went unanswered.

After a few more days, Penny called to say that she had heard from Rye. He hadn't been able to say much, but he had told Penny that he had been on a little excursion and that he was fine. Penny said, "I know Rye was involved, I just know it. I want him home, but I know he will never come back to our home. What can I do? What can I do?"

"I know, dear. I have suspected since the story broke that Rye was right in the middle of it, but don't you worry. He's doing what is in his heart, and you can't change what pumps through a person's heart."

The thing that made me almost certain that Rye was there came in a news report about the raid. Over the years, the Special Forces had taken to assigning each team member a number. In this particular report, they stated that the mission's success was in large part a result of the actions by Team Member #34, who had put himself at significant risk to dislodge the extremists and ensure the success of the mission. I shuddered when I heard the #34.

Lela called a few weeks later. She was excited about an appointment she had received from a prestigious law firm in D.C. "They are going to let me do my work with Quality of Life as the need arises, and the job will enable Emanuel and me to buy our dream home. We have already started making plans to move, and in a day or two I will send you a video." I was excited for Lela, although not so thrilled about her choice of D.C. as her home. "Emanuel is working hard, and we stay very busy. I wish we could slow down a bit."

I laughed, "Lela, you know who you're talking to. You came into this world wide open, and you have not slowed down yet."

"I miss you so much. How is Nonna? And have you talked to Rye?"

I replied in the negative and inquired if she had heard anything.

"Yes. I don't know where he's been, but I could tell in talking to him that he's been involved in something really important. I almost think he was involved in that raid in Benghazi."

"I would not doubt anything that boy gets involved in, and you shouldn't either. Have you forgotten how your brother always pushed the envelope? You were always so careful and cautious, but Rye on the other hand, would jump off a bluff if you dared him to."

"I know exactly what you mean. I don't know what he's been up to exactly, but I'm glad he's back in the States."

One morning I awoke with a few more pains than normal, and I had to tell Madonna, "I feel like I needed to go in and have the doctor check me out."

She quickly responded, "Where are you hurting?" She called and got me set for a 10:00 AM appointment. One thing I could say about the old doctor: he always managed to accommodate me whenever I felt I needed to come in.

As we left the house, I told Madonna, "I hope he doesn't get on his soapbox this morning; I would hate to step on his toes."

"Leroy, you know full well all he has ever done is to try and help you. You better not embarrass me today."

I took that as the final word and minded my P's and Q's.

Doc was in a talkative mood and seemed jolly enough. "Leroy, from what I can tell, you seem to be doing okay, but your blood pressure is up a little bit more than normal, and it seems your sugar level is higher than it has been in some time. You been watching that diet that I have been preaching to you about for years?"

"Yes, sir. I have been doing well. You can ask Madonna."

"Where is Madonna?"

"She's out in the lobby. I told her there was no need for her to come back with me—that I would shoot you straight."

"You know I have never known when you are shooting me straight. Sometimes I think you are the most capable person of selling me a bill of goods that I have ever met. You will probably outlive me!"

"Well, Doc, you know what Willie Nelson said about old doctors. Maybe you should think about retiring before you become one."

He laughed, "I may just give that some thought."

Labor Day was fast approaching when Hurricane Isabelle came bearing down on Central America. As I watched the constant updates on the news, it appeared the brunt of the storm was scheduled to make landfall in Nicaragua on Labor Day. My first thoughts were of Manny. I had not heard from him in a couple of months. I was not too worried about him being able to ride out the storm, as I remembered the storm cellar in his backyard well stocked with foodstuffs and supplies. What did concern me was the massive size of the hurricane. If the predictions held true, it would make landfall as a category five storm, and the resulting destruction would be tremendous.

It gave me more pause when I considered that Lela would once again be right in the middle of another operation to help the children. I didn't know why, but even with all of the things she had done, the thoughts of her going to Nicaragua elevated my blood pressure. I dismissed those feelings as just being old and having a case of the worry-warts. I did not sleep at all that night.

The next morning I turned on the TV to news that Nicaragua had been devastated by one of the most powerful hurricanes in history. Hurricane Isabelle had made landfall right in the middle of Nicaragua's eastern coast and had torn through the country, destroying virtually everything in its path. Many deaths had already been reported, and the fear was that the death toll would climb into the thousands. As I poured my first cup of coffee, I couldn't help but wonder if Lela was already making plans to head down there.

I decided to send Leanna Futrillo an email to see if I could get through to her. I knew I probably could not, but I decided to try anyway. I knew it would be impossible to get through to Manny, because the cell phone service was out pretty much over the entire country.

Later on in the day, I got a call from Lela. She and her team were leaving in two days to get started with their relief effort. Lela told me that they would be able to get into Managua and that they would meet with the U.S.

Embassy to coordinate their efforts. At that point I said to her, "Your first point of contact should be a lady named Leanna Futrillo. She is the best, and she will help you cut through any red tape."

"How do you know this lady, Poppa?"

"I don't know if you remember or not, but when you were young, I had to go to Nicaragua on business, and I met this young lady. She is a go-getter and will help you immensely. In fact, I sent her an email this morning to see if she could give me an idea on the scope of the damage. I expect to hear from her at any time."

"You're always one step ahead of me," she said with a chuckle.

"Listen up. If you get anywhere near Rivas, I want you to seek out an old friend of mine. His name is Manny Diaz. He visited us here at the Southern Whitehouse several years ago on Thanksgiving. You didn't get to meet him because you could not come home that year. Manny is a lifelong friend of mine and can give you valuable information about the area. I don't have a good feeling about this trip, Lela. You keep your eyes and ears open and please be extra careful."

"I will, Poppa. I'll talk to you when I get back." And once again, she was gone.

Within an hour, I heard that annoying, high-pitched tone, alerting me of a new email, and for once I was glad to hear it. It was from Leanna.

Leroy, it is so good to hear from you. I had meant to stay in touch better than I have,, but I have been very busy. I have often wondered how you were doing. As I am sure you know, our country has been hit hard. The damage is beyond my comprehension. Please pray for us as we face a long and difficult recovery. We are in the early stages of assessing the damage. Initial reports that I have seen defy belief. We have many dead, and there is no way I can describe the devastation. I know of your interest in our country, and I will update as time permits. Yours truly, Leanna.

Heartbroken, I sent my reply.

Leanna, help is on the way in the form of my great-niece, who I consider my granddaughter. She is working for a relief organization called Quality of Life. Lela will be on the ground in Managua shortly, and I have taken the liberty of telling her to seek you out for guidance. Please be advised that she is very dear to me and reminds me so much of you. She is a person who gets things done. I ask for your support. Thank you, Leroy.

It was about an hour before I heard that horrible sound from my laptop again.

Leroy, I have received communications from this group, and we are anticipating their arrival. I have heard of the great work they have done over the years, and I look forward to working with your Lela. I will help in any way I can. She can expect my full cooperation. If it would help, please feel free to give her my phone number and email, which I have attached. I think the advance team from Quality of Life is scheduled to arrive here day after tomorrow and I will try to meet Lela at the airport. I am so busy, and we have so much to do, that I may not be able to, but please tell your Lela to contact me at her earliest convenience.

As I read this, I felt better for myself, for Lela, and for Nicaragua. I would have bet a dollar to a doughnut that if

Lela and Leanna teamed up, the recovery would go much faster than anybody imagined.

I emailed Lela to give her Leanna's contact info and told her to be safe. I figured she was airborne, because I didn't receive a response from her for quite a long time. I wondered about Manny. I wanted to talk to him, just to make sure he was okay.

As I waited for a response from Lela, Penny called with some good news. "Rye will be home a week from tomorrow on a thirty-day leave. He's back in the States, and he sounded just fine. He wanted me to call you and let you know. That boy is going to be the death of me. I worry about him all the time."

I laughed. That news was the only thing that could have possibly cheered me up, and I couldn't wait to see my boy.

It was getting late, and I was a little worried that I had not heard back from Lela. I was tired and sleepy; Madonna came into the den to tell me I needed to go to bed. God love that woman. Always looking out for me, she was indeed a blessing in my life. As I laid my head down on my pillow, it crossed my mind that I'd had to get old in order to realize how fortunate I was in my life. As sleep finally came, I flashed back to what Rye had once said. "You're not old. You just look old."

Early the next morning, I got a call from Lela. "I met Leanna Futrillo last night. What a wonderful lady. We talked for hours, and you were right; she is going to be able to help us tremendously. Managua is getting back to a semblance of normality, but the problems are huge. Nicaragua does not have the resources or the workforce to handle such devastation. Leanna said they have a group of soldiers leaving to go to Rivas to check out the damage and assess the situation there. She is trying to hook us up with them, and after a day in Rivas, we will head towards our objective: Jinotega."

"Slow down, Lela. Did you say Rivas?"

"Yes."

"I still have not heard anything from my friend Manny."

"I'll try to find him, Poppa. Our initial indications are that the biggest needs are water, blankets, and medicine. We brought a good supply of all three, and we are going to need it. I may not be able to communicate with you for several days. I don't know what we're going to find, but I suspect the worst. If I can find your friend Manny, I will try to get word back to Leanna to let you know about his condition. I got to go. There is so much to do. When I get home, we are going to have a little talk about your visit to Nicaragua all those years ago. I got Leanna to spill the beans on you, and what I heard did not surprise me one bit. Love you!"

That girl could hang up a phone quicker than Superman. I was feeling better about Lela's situation, but something kept pulling at my heartstrings. *Jinotega.* Where had I heard that name before? It just wouldn't come to me, but something kept saying, *Jinotega, Jinotega.* With my fingers crossed that Lela would find Manny doing well, I went out to the back porch to my coffee and the old Gray Heron.

CHAPTER 29

I spent the next day mostly scanning the news for any information out of Nicaragua. It became quite clear that the destruction was even more significant than had initially been thought.

Sometime during the afternoon, Penny called. She had just talked to Rye and learned that his thirty-day leave had been held up by paperwork. "He thinks it will be delayed by about four or five days."

"Oh, that's just great, Penny. That seems to be the way of life in the Army: hurry up and wait. I talked to your wayward daughter this morning, and she seemed in pretty good spirits. She said it was bad, but she was confident."

Penny sighed and said, "You tell that girl that she better call her mother."

I laughed, "Well, you know how she is, caught up in the moment and raring to get something done. I would say she is a lot like her mother."

"I'll be glad when she is through with Quality of Life and starts focusing on the quality of *her* life."

"Me too, dear. I'm always worried about your two kids. They are the world to me."

"Don't forget that you are the world to us."

I didn't hear anything else that day, but the next morning I got an email from Leanna.

Leroy, things are improving in Managua. Lela is in Rivas and Manny is as well. A few of our soldiers came back for medicine and water, and they will return to Rivas today. They are working on some road repair, and hopefully Manny will be back here in Managua in a couple of days. I am sure he will call and update you. Work is beginning to get cell towers operational, and I am not quite sure how long this will take. Initial reports from Rivas indicate that the town suffered a lot of damage. There were several deaths and multiple injuries. Please pray for us as we continue our recovery efforts. Respectfully yours, Leanna.

I was much relieved about Manny, and I just could not wait to talk to him and get his assessment of the situation as well as an update on Lela. I found myself wishing that Rye was home. Somehow I just knew that him being home would help my health and my heart.

Manny called from Managua at about noon the following day. "Laroy, I hate to say this, but your girl is sharper than you ever were!" With his ensuing laugh, I was relieved. Manny was fine.

"Why, you old scoundrel you, I taught that girl most everything she knows. Where is she and what is the situation down there?"

"It is bad. The town was pretty much destroyed, but by the grace of God, we escaped a lot of death. We have our share of broken bones and injuries, but by and large we were lucky. Lela and her group left yesterday to go further north towards Jinotega. I don't know what kind of progress they can make; the roads are a mess. We just need more people and equipment to get this stuff cleaned up. I don't know how long it is going to take. Lela and her group brought a ton of water, which was badly needed. She was able to leave some in Rivas, but I know they desperately need it further north. That girl is remarkable. A gem."

I sensed that Manny was struggling with the task that lay ahead, but, as always, he would rise to the challenge.

He then asked, "How is Rye doing?"

"He is well. He is supposed to be home in a few days."

"I always told you that boy would be the ultimate warrior." He paused before adding, "That Lela is a warrior for the kids. You ought to have seen her interactions with the young ones in Rivas. They instantly loved her and didn't want her to leave. I will be traveling back and forth between here and Rivas for a few days, and hopefully we will have phone service back up soon."

"Manny, before you go, where have I heard of Jinotega before? I think we talked about that place, but I can't remember the conversation."

Manny hesitated for a moment before responding, "The only conversation I can recall about Jinotega is about my suspicion of it being Petey's location. It seems that his family had a place in a very remote place not far from there."

"That's it. Now I remember. With all the crazy things that can happen in life, what if Lela crosses paths with Petey?"

"You worry too much. I doubt that Petey is even still alive."

"You're probably right. Let me hear from you as often as possible. I feel like I might as well be on another planet."

The next afternoon, Manny called back to tell me that he was again at home and that they now had phone service. The folks in town, though somewhat still dazed, were beginning to put the pieces back together. "There has been no word from Lela. I think tomorrow I may get to venture up that way with a team from Managua carrying supplies."

"Aren't you getting too old to be roaming around the countryside?"

Manny laughed, "All I will do is sit in the truck and ride. You can bet I will not do too much. I just wanted to get some news about Lela and see how things are going up there. While I am there, I will feel out some of the locals for any info I can get from them."

"Info? What kind of info are you talking about? The only thing that concerns me is making sure that Lela is alright."

"Oh, don't worry. I intend to see that Lela is doing okay and working with people she can trust. It is just that in all the years I have lived here, I have never been to Jinotega. I shouldn't be gone for more than a couple of days. I will call you when I get back."

I wished I could still get up and go like Manny. I had that uneasy feeling that one gets when a dark cloud approaches.

With nothing left to do but wait, I turned my attention to Rye. Four more days and he would be home. I could not wait to see my boy. As I waited, my time was spent like most old men who have been put out to pasture. I was pretty much alone with my thoughts as the television blared on about all the chatter of the day. It did not affect me; it was just noise to help me through the day. I was beginning to feel that I might not make it until Lela got home.

I knew I was approaching death, and, somehow, I was at peace with it. You go through life preparing, always preparing, and when you approach the end, you realize how foolish all your preparation was. It just didn't matter. I could still laugh at myself, and that was the only thing that was keeping me from plunging into the depths of insanity. I looked around at our house: all the relics, all the signs of a long life, and I could not help but wonder how Madonna would function after I was gone. It was with sadness that I realized that despite that Cherokee blood, it would not be enough to stave off loneliness. Well, it was going to be a long four days before Rye came home. I just had to make it, and I knew I would fight.

I was so restless. So worried. I knew that feeling. Something was wrong—very wrong. If Manny would just call and let me know that everything was okay with Lela. I stared at the phone, but it was no use. Its silence was so obvious, as if were screaming at me. It would not ring.

Finally, one day, it did ring. It was Manny. "Laroy, are you sitting down?" That urgency in his voice told me instantly that my worst fears were confirmed. "It is Lela. She has been kidnapped and is being held hostage."

I cursed the phone. This could not be. Why? Who?

"This morning a note was attached to the door of the mission in Jinotega. The padre opened the note and this was all it said: '*We have captured two of the invaders of our country. One was a man who was executed on the spot as he resisted capture. The other is a woman who goes by the name of Lela and claims she works for a group called Quality of Life. If we do not receive one million U.S. dollars deposited in this account within seven days, she will meet the fate of her accomplice.*' The note ends by giving the name of the bank and the account number. It appears to be a bank in the British West Indies, and the note says that once the money is withdrawn and their agent is safely allowed free passage, Lela will be released into the custody of the mission."

My mind snapped into action as the tears rolled down my cheeks. All I could think of was that beautiful child who had never done anything except help the children. "Talk to me, Manny. Give me input. Where do we go from here?"

"The padre is on his way to Managua with the ransom note. He intends to deliver it to the government and alert the U.S. Embassy. I rode back to Rivas with him, and we got to talk a good bit. As crazy as this sounds, I think it is Petey who has kidnapped Lela."

I cursed the phone again. "How can that be? It's impossible, right?"

"I described Petey to the padre and asked him if he had ever seen anybody like that in Jinotega. His expression was of total disbelief, and he nodded his head yes. He told me that an old man appeared in Jinotega about a week before the hurricane hit and bought an unusually large amount of water, food, and ammunition. The padre noticed the man, and after he had gone, he asked if anybody knew him. The owner of the store where he bought the water and food told the padre that the old man said he was from Rivas and was going on a hunting trip with a group from Managua. The owner said the old man gave him the creeps and seemed to know a lot about the area. I asked the padre if he remembered a couple that had once lived out in the swamp with a young son. I told him I thought their last name was Santiago. He told me that that had been before his time, but someone had mentioned to him about an old house in that swamp. To his knowledge, nobody had ventured out that way in years. It has to be Petey."

"Manny, let me think. I will make some contacts and call you back in the morning. Thanks for all you have done."

The first thing I had to do was call Penny and Jon. I would have rather taken a beating than make that call, but I knew I must. Penny answered, and I said to her, "I don't want you to be upset, but I have some bad news. I am afraid our dear Lela has been kidnapped and is being held hostage in Nicaragua."

I was met with stone silence and then a small cry. Jon was instantly on the phone. "Leroy, what are you telling us?"

I relayed the whole conversation to Jon and tried to be as reassuring as I could. "Jon, get in touch with Rye and tell him to call me. I am going to make some contacts and see if I can get some things working from my end, but I want to talk to Rye as soon as I can." As I hung up the phone, I could hear Penny crying softly in the background.

Madonna was stoic. There were a few tears, but to her credit, she knew that it was not the time for panic. I made a mental note to call Wango in the morning and see if he could get any information about the bank in the West Indies. As I prepared to send Leanna an email, I felt a calmness come over me that I hadn't experienced in years. The old me was beginning to function, and I was thinking clearly. It gave me confidence that I might could figure this thing out and get Lela back home again. I bowed my head and said a prayer, something I realized I had not done enough of in my life, and then I wrote Leanna.

Leanna, by now you have probably read the ransom note and understand the scope of the problem better than I, but it is imperative that I do everything within my power to get Lela out of there safely. I am sure that your government, Quality of Life, and the United States will do everything to secure my Lela's release, but I wish to be in the loop, and you are the only one I consider dependable. I am not asking you to do anything you are not supposed to do but rather to just give me any information and input that you can.

First things first. It would appear to me that your country's resources are stretched to the breaking point, and I don't know how capable your government would be at extracting her from her abductors. Second, I think I know who is holding her. Third, I would like to ask you to acquire some coordinates of a piece of property that is located northwest of Jinotega in an area that is one huge swamp. The coordinates will be like looking for a needle in a hay-stack. The only thing I can tell you is that in this place the only thing that exists is an old, rundown shack. If it has an owner, the last name would be "Santiago." I need you to buy time for Lela in any way possible. Thanks, Leroy.

I knew I would be up all night. The possible scenarios kept rolling through my head.

Shortly after I sent the email, Rye called. "I'm catching the first flight out in the morning. I should be home around noon. How are Mom and Dad holding up? And how are you and Nonna?" The calmness and the maturity that came through the phone helped me.

"We're coping, Rye, but this is hard to deal with. It is eating us alive."

"I know, Dee, but we will figure it out. I know you well enough to know that you already have a plan."

"I'm struggling. I'm an old man. Come on home, boy. I need you."

There was quiet on the other end, and then, "Don't you worry. We are going to get Lela home. I'm pulling together some stuff to bring home with me. Some stuff I got from…uh…through certain channels. Don't worry. I'm not going to get into any trouble. I will see you as soon as I get home."

I would not have expected anything else from Rye. If anyone hurt or threatened his sister, they got a massive dose of Black Knight Warrior.

I didn't sleep. It was crazy. Insane. I kept coming back to Petey. It had to be Petey, but what was the connection to the bank in the West Indies? As I noticed the first rays of morning light, I stumbled to the coffee pot and made my way to the back porch. As I glanced toward the creek, there, at the waterfall, proudly stood the old Gray Heron.

CHAPTER 30

It hit me hard. Rye was going to be the only one I could trust to pull this off and get Lela back home. I knew I couldn't depend on the Nicaraguan Government to do a successful rescue, and the U.S. Government would be too slow to react.

At almost noon, the back door opened and Rye bounded out on the porch. "Dee, before you get started, I have to tell you that I'm leaving in the morning. I am going to find Lela and bring her home. It *will* happen, and you had better believe me."

I couldn't help but wonder what the young stallion before me must think of the old bag of bones and wrinkled skin I had become. I looked up at Rye in amazement.

He sat down and said, "I was able to get some help from my commanding officer, General Mateus. I was able to bring home some technical equipment that will help me find Lela and secure her release. The government has full knowledge of what I am going to do, and I will be cleared through customs all the way to Managua. I know you have been planning her rescue since you got the word. Now let's get on with it."

As I looked at him, my mind drifted back to the first time I saw him as a newborn, with no fear in those eyes. The bond between us had been instantaneous. His thoughts were my thoughts, and my thoughts were his thoughts. It was as though we were intertwined with an invisible wire. Although I had known fear and had never been a warrior, it did not matter in the least. It was all about Lela now, and I felt certain that she would be home in a few days.

"Rye, do you remember the time we went down to Fort Boyd when a guy named Manny from Nicaragua went with us?"

"Sure I remember Manny. Your old Army buddy."

"When you land in Managua, I want you to go to Manny's. He lives in a little town called Rivas. I will talk to Manny tonight and tell him what we are thinking. I'm going to wire Manny $10,000 to buy anything you need while you are there. Also, before you leave, I've got $5,000 in cash here at the house that you need to take with you. If there is anything you need in the way of guns, Manny has a well-stocked arsenal."

"I knew you would have a plan, but I shouldn't need any weapons or ammo. I brought what I need along with the tech gear."

"Get on home and see your mom and dad and try and get some rest. You're going to need all your strength."

"Okay, Dee. Don't worry. Everything's going to be okay."

As he rose to leave, I said, "Wait. Let me give you the money." I went into the closet which had been our fort when Rye was little.

"Man, this room brings back some memories," he said as I fumbled through some stuff to find my old suitcase. As I pulled it out, Rye said, "Wow. I had forgotten about that big thing. Can I take that with me? It'll help with all the gear I have to take."

I managed a smile. "Of course. This old thing has been to Nicaragua once before, but that story will have to wait. Hell, I never knew why I bought the darn thing anyway."

I showed him the compartment where I had stashed the money. Then, suitcase in hand, he went to give his Nonna a big hug, and he was off. I was tired. Dead tired. I eased out to the car and secured a pack of cigarettes that I kept hidden from Madonna. I wanted a drink of Jack Daniel's and a quiet smoke. I reasoned that it might help. I knew it was not what I should do, but then I was used to going against conventional wisdom.

I was once again on the back porch. I felt the smoke burning my lungs from the cigarette, when that irritating sound from my email went off. It was from Leanna.

Leroy, I am pretty sure we have the coordinates of the property you were seeking. From what we can determine, it belonged to a Franco Santiago. It has been abandoned for years, and we think that he and his wife got dysentery and died about forty-five years ago. I have tried to buy you some time, and the American Government is cooperating with us. I understand that an individual is expected to arrive in Managua tomorrow. Rest assured that this individual will receive our full cooperation. Please find attached the coordinates you requested. Yours truly, Leanna.

As I reflected on the information from Leanna, I was overcome with fatigue. I stared straight ahead as the last rays of the day's sun danced on the creek. Madonna had very little trouble getting me to the dinner table, and after dinner I soon headed to bed.

I awoke early the next morning and realized I had been given a good night's sleep. I felt like my old batteries had been recharged. I looked at my watch and figured Rye would be at the airport. I needed to call him before he was airborne. As I waited for him to answer, it dawned on me that I had forgotten something: transportation. How could I have been so stupid?

"I was fixing to call you, Dee. I'm about to board."

"I forgot about your transportation in Nicaragua. How will you get around once you get there?"

"The old Kawasaki KX 2-stroke is already in the belly of the airplane. I can get wherever I want faster than a speeding bullet," he said with a laugh.

His laugh was reassuring and a calmness came over me. "You be careful, boy. I'll talk to Manny this morning. He'll be expecting you this evening."

"By the way, Dee, I left you a little toy on your mantle yesterday. Plug it into the USB port on your computer, and you will be able to follow my every move, compliment of the U.S. Government. You will be able to talk to me when you see a blue light in the right corner of the screen. And when you do, please speak softly. The audio on this thing is very loud. It will enable you to follow me on the entire trip, so sit back, don't worry, and enjoy the ride."

I went to get a cup of coffee and decided to call Wango. After getting through his receptionist, I heard a familiar voice. "Leroy, I am in a meeting right now, and I am glad you called. I'm putting you on speaker. There are some important people in my office, and we are discussing the situation with Lela. A lot of thought has been put into securing her release, and we think the most effective course of action is to let Rye bring her home. He has been given some high-tech equipment, and we are monitoring the area where we think she is being held. Also, we have deployed additional Special Forces off the coast of Nicaragua for backup if needed. We fully expect her to be extracted in the next seventy-two hours. Now, what questions do you have for us?"

I was somewhat taken aback. I mumbled, "It will be the first time the government has ever done anything for me." I heard a burst of laughter, and I immediately apologized, "Wango, you know I didn't mean that. I thank you for your efforts. I thank all of you!"

"No apology necessary. I have told the people in this room all about you, and most of them know Lela and what a national treasure she truly is. We are also well-versed in what Rye is capable of, and that is why the decision was made to let him go it alone."

I jumped in, "What about the ransom? And what can you tell me about the bank?"

"A plan is in place for the money to be put in the account, and the CIA is involved in tracking all of this down. The bank is the First Global Bank of the West Indies at Cave Hill. The account is held by two British men who we believe are arms dealers."

I snapped, "I bet it's the two guys that supplied the weapons and ammo to the rebels when I was involved in that situation in Nicaragua many years ago."

"We know all about the part you played in saving Nicaragua from what would have been a terrible civil war, and you may never know how much the people of Nicaragua appreciate your service. America owes you a debt of gratitude as well. Leanna is keeping us up-to-date of the situation on the ground and has proven invaluable. Leroy, you relax and take it easy. This is all going to be okay. I will call you if anything develops that you need to know about."

"Thanks, Wango. I am grateful."

CHAPTER 31

It was almost noon, and it dawned on me that I had not checked for the toy Rye for left me. I scrambled to get to it. Well, shuffled was more like it. There it was, a little rectangular device that I was not familiar with at all. I scrutinized it, but it made no sense. The darn thing did not seem to have anything I could plug into anything. I toyed with it for about fifteen minutes before I finally figured out that the top cover flipped over at a ninety degree angle, and the USB male plug popped down.

I plugged it into the side of my laptop, and it started buzzing and humming like it was almost as ancient as I was. All of a sudden an image appeared on the screen. I realized that I was looking at the back of an airplane seat. I was confused and trying to figure out what was going on, when a blue light appeared in the top right corner. I remembered what Rye had told me, and I whispered, "Rye, is that you?"

A text box appeared on the screen and the following words popped up: "Copy that, Dee. I see you figured it out."

I was stunned. It was almost like I was on his shoulder, seeing what he was seeing. I scanned the plane, looking at people I did not know and even looking out the window at the ocean. As the plane banked to the right, I could almost hear every creak and noise that a plane makes as it banks into a turn. The pilot came over the intercom shortly after the seatbelt ding went off. "Ladies and gentlemen, we are beginning our descent into Managua. If you look out the window as we make our approach, you will still be able to see some of the tremendous damage that was left by Hurricane Isabelle. We hope you enjoyed your flight, and thank you for flying with us."

The damage was indeed catastrophic. Much of the forest was nothing but a mangled mess of twisted trees. Vast piles of what looked like garbage were everywhere. Soon we touched down, and Rye prepared to deplane. I saw the text screen with a message that said: "Welcome to Managua. I will get back in touch once I leave the airport."

I was amazed. It seemed I was going to be along for the ride. I went into the kitchen and gave Madonna a little pat on the rear to assure her I was still among the living.

"Leroy, what on earth is wrong with you?"

I still knew how to get that Cherokee in her fired up.

I laughed and said, "Boy is on the ground in Managua and headed towards Manny's house."

"How would you know he has arrived? You can sometimes just be a little bit cocky."

I laughed and said, "Take my word for it. This is going to work out." Her look told me she was worried sick, but if she didn't worry, I would be worried.

As I passed the television, I saw a very bright picture of Lela, and it stopped me dead in my tracks. The story of Lela's kidnapping was breaking on the national news. As I turned up the volume, the reporter was saying that the Nicaraguan Government was working in conjunction with the U.S. Government to secure her release. They had one of the high-profile philanthropists, one of the most significant contributors to Quality of Life, on TV, and he was saying how distraught the organization was and wanted everybody to know they were doing everything that they could to secure Lela's safe return.

I snapped it off. I had heard enough of that crap.

I went back to my laptop and turned it on, and I was soon looking at a highway with cars whizzing by like crazy. I realized that I was on board with Rye as he headed out of Managua toward Rivas. I glanced to see that the blue light was on, and I whispered, "You better speed up, boy."

This time, instead of a text box, I heard his voice. "Dee, this old thing motors pretty good. What do you think?"

I looked at the speedometer, and it was bumping eighty. No wonder those cars appeared to be whizzing by us. It was not them but Rye that was doing the flying. "Rye, it runs great, but the road is about to get real curvy, and you will take a sharp right and then a sharp left."

"Dede, are you having flashbacks to when you were teaching me how to drive one of these things on that old Xbox we had?"

"No, Rye, I am trying to tell you—" But it was too late. We were in the sharp S curve. The KX-2 felt like it was almost parallel to the ground before Rye managed to catch it.

The speed slowed quickly, and Rye said, "How in the world did you know about this road?"

"No time to explain. This road is going to be like that all the way to Rivas, so slow it down, okay?"

To Rye's credit, he did slow down some but not enough to suit me.

In almost no time at all, we approached Rivas. "Rye, you are coming up to the small town, so slow down. I want to look at it as you go through."

The old town looked just as it had those many years ago. The San Lupe was more weathered but still open, and the Café Teais was now named something else, but I couldn't catch the name. As we went out of town, we approached the curve where I had picked Petey up in the rain, and it gave me cold chills. "You are coming up to Manny's house. It will be on the right." And bam. There was the driveway. As we pulled in, I noticed the place still looked the same but older. Somehow it did not look as cheerful, and I guessed it was because of Melinda.

Before Rye could get parked, Manny was out the door. "My, my, my," said Manny as he grabbed Rye and hugged him. "Rye, you have grown so much. You are a man. You are huge, and, best of all, you make all of us Black Knights proud." I couldn't see Rye's face, but I would have bet he was blushing. "Come in, come in," said Manny.

Rye grabbed the big suitcase off of the back of the KX-2, and they went into the house. As they made their way in, I wondered how many bungee cords Rye had had to use to strap that big suitcase to the back of the bike. I noticed that Manny looked remarkably well considering his age, and he seemed to be moving around pretty good.

"Manny," Rye said, "do you want to say hello to Leroy? He is looking at you right now."

"What are you talking about?" Manny asked.

"Say hello, Dee. Manny thinks I'm pulling his leg."

I promptly replied, "Where did you get that ridiculous shirt, Manny?"

Manny's face dropped. "Laroy, is that really you?"

"You didn't think I was going to miss out on this deal, did you?"

He was almost speechless, but then he regained his composure and said, "How is your health? I've been worried about you."

"Don't worry about me. You just help Rye and get my baby back home."

"You know I will, you old scoundrel," Manny laughed.

"Rye, how much can I use this gizmo?" I inquired.

"You can leave it on all you want, compliments of Uncle Sam."

Manny said, "Rye you must be starving and tired. Let's get something to eat and turn in. We have a busy day tomorrow."

I said, "That's right, guys. You need food and rest. This old scoundrel is going to turn this thing off and hit the sack, but I will be waking you all up early in the morning."

Manny laughed and said, "Rye, I guess you know like I do that Laroy will wake us up before daylight."

"See you bright and early, boys!" And with that, I shut the old laptop down.

Up at 4:30 the next day, I made coffee and went out on the enclosed porch and waited for the break of day. I wondered how some people could make it without coffee; I knew I couldn't. Presently, I went in and got the laptop, pushed the button, and soon it was humming. A picture came into focus. It was Manny sitting at the kitchen table. I waited until he put his cup up to his lips and shouted, "Good morning!"

I thought Manny was going to jump out of his skin as he spat coffee all over the table. "Dang you, Laroy! I don't know if I like all this technology stuff! It is just too sneaky!"

About that time, the text screen appeared. "What are you two old farts doing? Can't a man get a little sleep?" With that, Rye came into view and said to Manny, "Dee has always been that way. Always waking people up."

Manny laughed, "He was never the same after he went into the Army."

Rye poured himself a cup of coffee and sat down at the table. After a few minutes of small talk, Manny went to cook breakfast. Soon Manny was back with what appeared to be fried eggs, bacon, and toast. As they began to eat, I said, "Manny, that sure smells good."

The look on Manny's face was something I would never forget as he replied, "Don't you even go there. I know darn well you can't smell through that darn contraption."

We all got a good laugh, and I noticed that the sun was beginning to rise at Bluff Shores.

"Okay, guys," Rye said. "I need to do a little equipment check." He came back from the bedroom with the big suitcase, and they went outside. He unzipped it and took out four black cones that appeared to be four or five inches high and about the same in circumference. He placed the cones on the ground in a small circle, reached into the bag, and removed a small box. From the box, he removed a small drone and said to Manny, "Let's get a look around."

The little bird was soon airborne. It circled the property at treetop height and zoomed in and out from a visual standpoint. A small screen was on the ground and Manny stared at it intently. On my screen, I had a split screen view, which showed the drone in the air on one side and the view from the drone on the other. I soon figured out that I could toggle between whichever view I wanted. I heard Rye say to Manny, "Let's give Leroy a little tour down memory lane."

Soon we were buzzing down the road, and, in the blink of an eye, we were at the lake. That beautiful lake that I had thought I would never see again except in my dreams. Then it zoomed in to give a cryptic view of the water's surface, and I could see what appeared to be thousands and thousands of fish. There also seemed to be a small boat on the bottom about forty yards offshore.

Manny was in awe. "I knew this lake had some good fishing, but I never dreamed it had so many." The cryptic view turned off, and Rye said, "Now let's take Dee up to his favorite cave."

I knew right then that Manny had told Rye all about my trip to Rivas. Sure enough, we crossed the road and began an ascent up the mountain. As we approached the plateau where the cave was, Rye slowed the little bird and dropped it down below treetop level. He guided it across the plateau at about nine feet off the ground, right up to the entrance of the cave, and he let it hover for a few seconds. Cold chills came over me as I flashed back to Comacho and Elvio coming out of that cave so many years ago.

Once back at the house, Rye took the drone on one last spin, and it went down to the exit from the tunnel where Manny had a viewpoint of the lake. He brought it back and said, "Manny, look up. Can you see or hear the drone?" Manny shook his head no. "Good. If you can't hear it or see it, neither can anyone else." He brought the bird down to a soft landing right in front of the black cones.

Rye returned the equipment to the suitcase and strapped it on KX-2. Then he looked at Manny and said, "I am going to get Lela. If I find her today and the opportunity presents itself, I will be back tonight, but I expect that it won't be until tomorrow or possibly even the next day. I appreciate your hospitality, and I want you to know that I appreciate your service to our country."

Manny seemed a little speechless. He looked at Rye and said, "Son, you be careful. I have told you everything I can about the environment you are going to encounter. If I was sitting where Lela is right now, I couldn't think of a better person to come to the rescue."

Rye shook Manny's hand, got on the dirt bike, and pulled out on the road, headed north towards Jinotega.

We went through Rivas without raising much notice, even though we were going pretty fast. The next couple of hours was one of the roughest rides I could have imagined. It was fast and rough, and I knew Rye was used to it, but I was glad I was seated in my house. Soon a little screen appeared that showed what looked to be a red line with a blinking green X at the top. We were getting close to the green X, and eventually we pulled off the road. Rye pushed the dirt bike into the woods, took the big suitcase off, laid the bike down, and concealed it with foliage.

He picked up the suitcase and proceeded west along the marked trail. I assumed the old shack would be at the end, the location being preprogrammed from the coordinates that Leanna had secured for us. I prayed we would find Lela there.

Presently we were in the water. It was a swamp that, although not very deep, was tough to negotiate. A little berm appeared on our left and Rye went over to it. He set the big suitcase down and pulled out a backpack. He took out the black cones, the drone, and a short case. Inside the case was a rifle, which he quickly assembled. It was a rifle like I had never seen before. He removed a few more items and pushed the big suitcase down behind the berm. "I'm sorry, Dede, but that is probably the end of the line for that piece of luggage." With that done, we proceeded to work our way towards the green X.

On the screen, we appeared to be getting close to our target. Rye stopped moving forward as soon as he began to see patches of dry ground. He found a spot that seemed to provide a lot of natural cover and set out his equipment. In a matter of minutes, the drone took off, and I was looking at a split screen again, so I toggled the split screen into the wide view. In no time flat, we were high above a shack. It appeared unoccupied at first glance. I had a sinking feeling. What if Lela was not there?

As he continued working the area, Rye zoomed in and out. He stopped the bird near the edge of some woods by the shack and zoomed in very close. There on the ground was a cigarette butt, and I could barely make out some foot tracks. The drone moved very slowly back towards the cabin, following those tracks until they became invisible. My spirits soared. At least we had a little hope. I guessed it was close to being noon when a young man appeared from within the shack. He looked nervous as he scanned the area around the hut, then he disappeared back inside.

The little text box appeared. "Sit tight, Dee. It may be a while."

Rye settled in between two rocks, and from what I could tell he blended into the earth perfectly. They would have to step on him to find him. I realized that boy was hiding in plain sight with the drone right up above. I just kept staring at that shack; I wanted to see inside so badly. Suddenly, a red light started blinking in the top left corner, and I felt a surge of apprehension flow through my body. We had company.

A man appeared behind Rye. I wanted to scream. He walked within four or five feet of the boy. As he approached the shack, two more men appeared and began talking. Soon there was some laughter and a third man appeared. I froze. It was Petey. He had aged and seemed like he had trouble standing. The conversation turned serious. They appeared to be arguing, and there were a lot of gestures. Soon the visitor turned and headed back towards Rye. As he got closer, I got a good look at him. It was without a doubt one of the young British men I had seen in Café Teais years ago. Although the hair was now somewhat gray, I had no doubt it was one of the arms dealers. That was the connection. The two British guys had hatched this whole plot to kidnap an American to hold for ransom, and Petey was just the one gullible enough to work for them. I was filled with rage. I wanted Rye to take that guy out right then and there. Those vermin only spread misery everywhere they went.

At almost 2:30, a man came out of the shack to scan the area again. About a minute later, two men came out with Lela. She was blindfolded and appeared to have her hands bound behind her back. They walked her to a thick clump of trees and removed the rope that bound her hands. One of the men went around to the other side of the trees and stood with his back to them. The other man also had his back turned to the trees.

My heart was in my throat as I wondered if Rye was going to spring into action. They were giving Lela a bathroom break. How sweet. I would have killed them both if I could have. Soon they retied Lela's hands and led her back into the shack and closed the door. She had appeared unhurt and looked to be in good shape. I didn't know what the plan was, but I fully expected Rye to get her out of there.

"We found her, Dee. When she comes out again, we're bringing her home."

I looked at the screen. The blue light was on. "It all makes sense now," I said quietly. "That was Petey. I saw him. And his connection too. They're a couple of small-time British arms dealers that I met a long time ago in Rivas."

"I know. Manny told me all about your trip to Rivas and what happened on that mountain. Dede, in case I never told you, you are one hell of a man."

"Boy, you keep your mind on your business."

I heard a slight chuckle. "Call Mom and Dad and tell them we found Lela and that we will be headed home tomorrow."

"Did I ever tell you that sometimes you are a little bit too cocky?"

"Get some rest. It's going to be a long night, and the little black box will wake you when you need to see something."

CHAPTER 32

I informed Madonna that Rye had found Lela and that she was okay. Tears of joy flowed freely down her cheeks.

"Leroy, I just can't stand to watch what you have obviously been watching. Can you imagine how much stress Penny and Jon are under? Call them. Call them now."

I nodded and took a deep breath as I prepared myself for what I had to do. Penny answered her phone, and, as calmly as possible, I explained to her what Rye had instructed me to say.

The silence on the other end of the line told me it was still sinking in. Then a scream followed as all the emotion came pouring out. All the love, all the feelings that a mother can have for her daughter was in that cry. After she settled down, she asked, "Does he have her?"

I told her that he had a plan and that he was going to have her soon.

"Are you sure everything will work out?"

"Penny, you have the best Black Knight in the world just a hundred and twenty feet from her, and the bad guys don't have a clue. You're darn right it will work out."

As I hung up, I realized that I may have been a little bit responsible for Rye being so cocky. I was already dead tired, sleepy, and emotionally drained. I decided to take Rye's advice and get some rest. I wasn't sure how long I had been asleep when I was awakened by an annoying beeping sound coming from my laptop. I sat up in bed and realized it was Rye.

"Dee, let's get a closer look at this shack." He brought the little bird down to the edge of the front porch, and my screen turned into an infrared look. He focused the camera on a crack in the door, and we could see inside. There before us was one of the men on a sleeping bag on the floor. To the right was a broken down old bed occupied by Petey. On the other side of the room was a cot which held the other man. In the far back left corner, in an old, rundown chair, was Lela. She seemed to be resting, but I was betting that her mind was working overtime.

As the little bird pulled out, Rye said, "We go in at 5:30. Don't worry. It's going to be okay."

I knew I would not be able to sleep, and my mind switched to scenario mode, even though I did not have a clue how this was going to go down. I watched as midnight approached, and the hands of time swung more slowly than at any time in my life.

It was about 4:30 when Rye chimed in, "Up and at 'em, Dee."

As it approached daylight and got close to 5:30, I saw the barrel of the rifle pointing towards the shack. I became very nervous as I waited. Suddenly, one of the young men appeared on the front porch and appeared to be taking a leak. A muffled sound and a small wisp of smoke came from the rifle. The young man glanced over his shoulder and instantly grabbed a long knife from the sheath on his leg and charged straight towards Rye. Rye did not move. He was almost on top of him when I saw the butt of Rye's rifle come crashing against the side of the young man's head. He collapsed with a thud and Rye charged the shack.

Once inside, Rye worked quickly. Lela, Petey, and the other young man appeared to be unconscious. He ripped the blindfold off Lela's face and unbound her hands. Next, he went to Petey, blindfolded him, bound his hands behind his back, and placed him in the middle of the floor. Then he approached the young man on the cot who was beginning to move slightly. Rye pounced on the guy and had him bound and blindfolded in a flash. Rye then placed that young man on the floor beside Petey.

Lela began to sit up, and as she looked around, she had a dazed look on her face. She cried out, "Rye? Rye, is that you?"

Rye walked over to her and said, "You ready to go home, sis?" She started to cry, and Rye said, "No time for that. We got to get out of here."

Petey was beginning to come around and so was the other man. Rye walked over to Petey and said, "You old buzzard, if you ever lay a hand on another American, I will personally come back here and cut your tongue out. Do you understand?" Petey mumbled something. Rye reached down and jerked his head back and said, "Have you got something to say?"

Petey's eye flashed in anger. "I don't know who you are, Yankee, but I could not have killed the woman. For some reason she reminded me of a Yankee I met a long time ago. Once I got my money, I was going to kill the British rat and return the young lady back to the mission in Jinotega."

Rye replaced the blindfold over Petey's eyes and slid the bed out into the middle of the floor. He bound the feet of both men and tied one on each end of the bed. Rye looked at Lela and said, "Let's go."

Once back outside, Rye stopped and bound the hands and feet of the still unconscious young man who had charged him, then he dragged him to a tree and secured him to it. He glanced at Lela and said, "I think he'll make it, sis. He only ran into the butt end of a rifle."

They approached the area where Rye had been hiding outside the shack. He gathered up his gear and instructed her to follow him. They worked their way back towards the berm and the old suitcase, and before long they were back to the dirt bike. As Rye uncovered it and pushed it towards the road, he suddenly stopped and turned to his sister. "Lela, aren't you going to say good morning to Dee?"

"Good morning, baby!" I shouted.

The look on her face was pure joy. "Poppa! Oh, Poppa, is that you? I love you!"

I laughed, and a wonderful feeling of relief sweeping over me. "Don't you two sit around there and gab! Get on those wheels and get back to Rivas. I will call Manny and tell him you're headed back. You can get a shower, some food, and then get ready to head home."

"Poppa, I can't believe it!" her voice soared. "I'm coming home!"

The ride back to Rivas was not quite as fast and rough as the ride the day before, but a lot of that had to do with Lela chewing on Rye's ear. "Slow down, Rye! You know I hate it when you go fast on this thing."

Rye was laughing as he always did when he could get Lela on a dirt bike with him.

I called Manny and told him what had transpired. Manny said, "I just caught some fish yesterday. I will fix them some of my famous fish tacos."

I tried not to laugh, but I couldn't help it. "I almost wish I was there to eat one of those famous tacos."

"Laroy, you won't ever change."

I hung up and called Penny. "Penny, your girl is on her way back to Rivas with Rye. All is well, my dear. All is well." As I hung up, I could not see the tears of joy, but I certainly felt them.

In about two hours, Lela and Rye passed by the beautiful lake, and Rye slowed down. I got one last look at all that beauty. As they pulled into Manny's house, his front door swung open, and he came out to greet them. There were hugs all around, and in Manny's eyes I could see a sparkle that probably had not been there since before Melinda's death. He found some old clothes of Melinda's that he gave to Lela. After her shower, she came out of the bathroom looking as beautiful as any woman could look, considering what she had just experienced. Rye seemed as relaxed as could be expected for a warrior.

They sat down to fish tacos and tea. I was surprised at how much food they consumed, and I reconsidered my judgment of Manny's cooking.

After eating, Rye looked at Manny and said, "We hate to go, but I have got to get sis home, and there's a bird in Managua that has our name written all over it."

Manny laughed and said, "I don't blame you guys at all. I bet nobody is pulling for you two to get on that bird more than Laroy."

I couldn't stand it any longer. "Manny," I said. "I want you to know that I love you like a brother. I worry that I may never see you again, but you will always be in my heart."

"Laroy, are you going soft on me? I will bet you a dollar I will see you again, but you are probably right. It may be in those hunting and fishing grounds in the sky," he said, managing a small chuckle.

I couldn't share his laughter. I just simply mumbled, "Goodbye, my friend."

As Rye and Lela left Manny's, they didn't get very far from Rivas before I said to them, "You kids be safe. I will see you when you get home. I have had enough excitement for one day."

They both laughed, and Rye said, "See you, Dee! Tell everyone we should be airborne in two or three hours."

Lela said, "You get your rest, Poppa, because you're expected to have us a big breakfast fixed by 9:00 in the morning."

I laughed and then suddenly choked. "What about Emanuel? I forgot Emanuel!"

Rye interrupted, "No, Dee. Emanuel was along for the ride, same as you. I just had his communication cut off. The last thing I needed was a nervous husband."

I breathed a sigh of relief. "You mean he could see everything happening, but that was it?"

"Don't worry. I explained all of my reasoning to him, and he agreed. He is a pretty smart guy, even though he is a lawyer."

I simply replied, "Okay, I get it." I was still feeling light-headed from all the excitement, and I decided I needed to go calm down. "Breakfast at 9:00 tomorrow, it is. See you then."

I went inside and ambled over to the coffee pot. I figured one last cup for the day and then a hot bath. As I turned, it felt as if something hit me hard in the chest. My knees buckled. I tried to catch myself, but I couldn't. I hit the floor and heard Madonna scream, and then there was nothing.

When I finally came to, my eyes would barely focus. I wondered where I was. Finally, I knew I was in ICU. Wires everywhere. The beep of those monitors that are designed for no other purpose than to scare you to death. I could barely turn my head, but I saw Madonna sitting in the corner.

I mumbled, and she jumped. "Oh, Leroy! Don't move. You have had a terrible heart attack. I couldn't revive you at home. I thought… I thought you were dead. When the paramedics arrived, they couldn't get a pulse. They shocked you, and they finally detected a pulse."

"How long have I been here?" I whispered.

"Almost twenty-four hours. Lela and Rye got home last night, and they are on their way over here now, but the doctor has said no visitors. Penny and Jon are in the waiting room. They've been here since early this morning. Oh, Leroy. I don't know how much time we have. The doctor says there is nothing more that they can do. I will always love you, Leroy. I will always love you."

"Now, dear," I managed to get out. "We have had a good run, and we have been lucky. You know I have always worshipped the ground you walk on. Don't worry. It will be okay. Madonna, for once in my life, I have no fear." I looked at my Indian Princess and said, "My love, when Rye and Lela get here, bring them in along with Penny and Jon. I don't have long. I don't know how I know, but I know."

It was only a few minutes before I felt their presence in the room. I knew I was dying. I was barely able to speak, but I knew what was going on around me. My Madonna was sitting on the end of the bed, crying softly. All the battles we had fought and all the tough times we had been through had brought us to this. It was indeed the circle of life. Penny was also crying, while Jon tried to console her.

There stood Lela. The tears in her eyes told me that she too knew my time was short. My Lela was the most stunning beauty I had ever seen in my life. That heart was bigger and more precious than the largest gold mine that existed on planet earth. I could feel the warmth from her heart even as I lay dying.

I began to feel a faint, floating feeling, as if I were beginning to ascend into the air. I looked at Rye. Such a big, strapping man he had become. It was apparent to me that no military uniform could hide those rock-solid muscles and that square jaw of steel. "Warrior" was written all over him, and I could not hide the love I had for that boy even if I tried. He was mumbling a prayer, and although I could not make out exactly what he was saying, I was very comforted by the fact that he knew God.

My eyes closed wearily, and so many things flashed through my mind. A time at the coast when Lela was thirteen, bright-eyed, and growing independently. It was a simple drop in the ocean and as impermanent as a sandcastle confronting the surf. After the tangible is washed away, the dreams continue on. I was in no pain.

Then, from the familiar scenes that played in my mind, a prism of light slowly appeared, and I was enveloped in it completely. I could clearly see I was on the back porch, staring at my old friend the Gray Heron. It suddenly took flight! As he headed down the creek, I knew he was going home to roost for the night. I could clearly see his westward flight into the setting sun. He was not the most graceful creature, but his beauty had enriched my life. As suddenly as the prism had opened, it closed.

The final sounds I heard as I drew my last breath and slipped into eternity was a soft "Dee?" and the rushing of feathered wings.

ACKNOWLEDGEMENTS

Where would any writer be without beta readers? I had three, and the encouragement and support I received from them were heartfelt. My sister Jackie, who taught me in the first-grade and instilled in me the belief that I could write my own book, my neighbor Jane, who was so very supportive, and my chief critic and friend, Scott, who gave me his highly valued opinion, to these three I owe many thanks. I thank you, and the Gray Heron lives because of you. To my editors, the talented Miss Sierra, whose help I will always cherish, and the venerable Mr. Lollar, whose advice and support was a blessing, I thank you both.

I also want to make a few notes about Leroy's involvement in Nicaragua for those who are curious. In trying to decide in which country Leroy's adventure would take place, it came down to Venezuela or Nicaragua. Once I decided on Nicaragua, it came down to which town. Managua I deemed too large and therefore settled on the small town of Rivas. I have never set foot in Nicaragua, but I have an attraction to its storied history. One of my favorite authors, O. Henry, is accredited with coining the phrase "banana republic." His book, *Cabbages and Kings*, is phenomenal. In my youth I was an avid sports fan, and baseball was an important part of my young life. Roberto Clemente was at the top of my list as one of the all-time greats. Tragically, he was killed in a plane crash in 1972 while delivering hurricane relief supplies to his home country of Nicaragua.

The history of the banana republic is filled with rebels and coups, and it occurred to me that it would only be natural for Leroy to try and prevent the next coup at the request of his friend. I make no judgment about the country of Nicaragua. In time, history will judge. I only know that I smell trouble brewing in this beautiful country, and, of course, coffee. I ran all of this by my silent confidante, the Gray Heron. The squawk seemed to indicate he agreed.

After writing the scene of Leroy's trip up the mountain in Rivas, I had a frightening thought. What if there were no mountains in Rivas? I looked on the internet for pictures and discovered that a beautiful mountain towers over the town of Rivas. A lot of luck is involved in writing a book, and a Gray Heron to bounce your thoughts off of helps as well. I hope you found *Gray Heron* a joy to read. It was a thrill to write.

ABOUT THE AUTHOR

John Wilde was born in 1950, and life was anything but
typical. As a boy, his world was filled with constant change.
His home served as a way-station for children waiting for
adoption, and twenty-seven foster kids filtered in and out
of his life as he grew up. With all their different struggles
and hardships, those kids molded him into who he is today
and helped him understand why love is the greatest healer.
During his forty-four years of working in sales, he developed a passion for writing. *Gray Heron* is his first published
work, and he has plans for more.

www.ingramcontent.com/pod-product-compliance
Lightning Source LLC
Chambersburg PA
CBHW030634020726
47493CB00006B/1715